MOON MAGIC
CLEARWATER WITCHES #4

Madeline Freeman

For information:

http://www.madelinefreeman.net

Moon Magic — Clearwater Witches, Book 4
ISBN: 1519614950
ISBN-13: 978-1519614957

DEDICATION

To Brian:
Thank you for believing in me, supporting me, and loving me.

And to the One who makes all things new.

ACKNOWLEDGMENTS

Thank you Steven Novak for the fabulous cover.

Thank you Arran at Editing 720 for your services.

Chapter One
Krissa

The first one died because I trusted the wrong person and cast the wrong spell. I killed the second to save my father's life—and to keep my town safe. But this is the only person I've wanted to kill out of pure hate.

It's not that I'm looking for her. After picking up some supplies at my aunt Jodi's shop, Tucker Ingram and I are headed up Main Street to his car when something catches my attention. I should've just kept walking. I should've ignored the flash in my peripheral vision as I passed Wide Awake Cafe.

But I didn't. I turned and saw something that causes what little lunch Tucker convinced me to eat threaten to rush back up and splatter the pavement. Sitting at a high-top table among a group of people I recognize only vaguely from the track team is Owen Marsh. He runs a casual hand through his blond hair as he laughs at something someone says. But he's not the one who draws my eye.

Her name is Laura or Lauren or Laurie. I've never had an occasion to find out anything about her. But now I wish I would have; I wish I knew everything there is to know about her. I study the way her dark blonde hair swishes around her shoulders in tight spiral curls, the soft line of her jaw, the way her lips curve when she looks at Owen. As her fingers trace lightly down his arm, it takes everything in me not to cast a spell to snap each one.

She's flirting with him. Of course she is—why wouldn't she? Owen is a great guy, a great catch. Any girl would be lucky to be with him.

I would know.

My body goes cold. Are they together now? I suddenly wish I paid more attention to the goings-on at school. How long have they been a couple? Or are things just beginning between them?

Tucker tugs at my elbow. He bends down to speak into my ear. Mere months ago such closeness would have made my skin crawl, but today I'm completely unaffected as his breath tickles my skin. "Come on, K. Griffin's expecting us. We've got to get going."

I know he knows why I stopped. I'm not sure if it's better or worse that he isn't drawing attention to it. I could ask him if he's privy to any more information than I am, but it's doubtful. As he's honed his psychic abilities, his attendance at school has become increasingly erratic. He often shows up only for tests or quizzes, and even then I'm sure he pulls answers from the minds of others. He spends so much time at Griffin Holloway's apartment I'm surprised Griffin hasn't started charging him for a portion of the rent.

When I don't leave immediately, Tucker sighs. "You want me to read them?"

I shake my head, panic flaring. If he reads them, I might have a better sense of what's going on—but what if my suspicions are confirmed? Will that make me feel better? I doubt it.

He crosses his arms over his chest, the paper bag from Jodi's shop crinkling in his hand. "Why don't you just go talk to him? You know you want to. And I bet he wants you to."

It's this more than anything that gets me moving. How many times in the last four months has Owen tried to get me to talk to him? I don't know if a number exists to accurately quantify it. And each time I pushed him away. Maybe I pushed him away one time too many. Maybe this is my punishment.

Not like I don't deserve it.

I'm about to leave, about to follow Tucker over to his car, when Owen's eyes flick up. Those beautiful, clear blue eyes land on my face, and for a moment the whole world melts away. It's like there's just the two of us. The way it's supposed to be. But then the feeling passes as hesitation flits across his face. I lift my hand to wave—it's the only thing I can think do to not feel so creepy about staring. But it takes him a second to smile back, and when he does it's just a brief upturn of the corners of his mouth. It's perfunctory. It's polite. He's not glad to see me—of course he's not. It's then that his companions notice his attention is on the window, but before they can all turn I dash after Tucker.

"I hate this."

Tucker blows out a breath. "If you hate it, then do something about it."

I shake my head. "You know I can't."

"No, I don't know, actually," he says, ducking into his car. "Every time the subject comes up, you suddenly get real interested in something else." He watches as I slide into the passenger seat. "I know I'm not great with touchy-feely stuff, but maybe it would help to tell me about it. Explain it to me."

I yank at the seatbelt and jam the latch into the buckle. "How are things going between you and Crystal?" I counter, my tone acidic.

Tucker's blue-gray eyes darken and narrow. "That's a low blow, and you know it." He glowers out the windshield as he pulls out onto Main.

He's right, but I don't apologize. Crystal hurt him twice—first when she broke up with him in front of the whole school, and then when she shut him out when he tried to reconnect with her four months ago. Things are different between Owen and me because I'm the one who did the shutting out. "Let's just agree not to talk about each other's love lives." I cross my arms over my chest, attempting to hide the emotions roiling inside me. I tamp down the unadulterated hate still coursing through my veins from seeing that girl so close to Owen. *My* Owen.

No. I can't keep thinking of him like that. Not now, not with the way things are. Maybe one day.

I just have to hope that one day doesn't come too late.

Chapter Two
Crystal

My hands clutch the sachet of herbs and stones. I breathe in through my nose and out through my mouth, doing everything I can to connect with the energy around me. This used to be so easy. Now, it takes every fiber of my being to convince myself I'm doing something right.

I hear Dana's breath beside me. Dana Crawford, a girl I had once written off as useless because of her lack of abilities. It's funny how quickly things can change.

Even though I'm not convinced I'm connected with nature, I begin reciting the incantation we've practiced. After a few times through, Dana joins me. Our voices are low—there's no need to yell, not if we're doing it right. I bring my hands together, rubbing the silken bag between them. There is energy in the things I hold. Jodi Barnette has explained to me several times at her shop that even if someone is not a witch, she can call on the energies present naturally in stones and herbs to bring about a desired result.

I just never thought I wouldn't be a witch.

We continue chanting. I keep expecting to feel something—anything—but nothing changes. It's so different from the way things used to be. When I used to work a spell, I'd feel energy surging inside me. But then everything changed.

Dana's voice drops off, leaving me to chant alone.

My eyes snap open. "What are you doing?"

Dana sighs, leaning back against her mattress and dropping her own bag of herbs and stones onto the cream-colored carpet of her bedroom. "It's not working."

"You don't know that," I insist.

"I've got a pretty good idea."

"You can't give up so easily." But I drop my bag to the floor, too. She's right, of course. It isn't working. I don't know why I'm surprised. Nothing ever works.

It's been four months since I lost my abilities. When I woke up after the exorcism, everything was a jumbled mess in my mind. I could remember only bits and pieces of the previous weeks. Much of it felt like a dream. It turns out I had another person's consciousness living in my head. Her name was Bess Taylor, and she was a relative who lived back when Seth Whitacre was alive—the first time, that is. In fact, she was his girlfriend—or whatever the equivalent of a girlfriend was back then. According to Krissa, she died in a fire back before the original elder council locked Seth away. The first time Krissa went up against Seth, he mentioned that he was trying to bring her back. It looks like he was trying to bring her back through me. When I learned all the things I had done as her, I felt guilty. I betrayed my friends. I fed information to our enemy. I started a fire that could have killed people. But my guilt was soon replaced by indignation—rage—when I realized all that had been taken from me. Somehow when Anya led the exorcism spell to remove Bess's consciousness from my body, my abilities went with her. And I have spent every waking moment since then trying to get them back.

Dana was new to abilities. She only had them as a result of the elder council spell. But since Seth died before the council could finish its work, she was left with memories of the council and of magic but no powers of her own. When we realized we were both after the same thing, we teamed up. We've been allies ever since.

Dana presses her lips together as she brings her eyes to mine. "Do you think maybe it's time to ask for some—"

"Don't say it," I snap. It comes out harsher than I mean it to, and I regret my tone when hurt flickers across her face. She's been the closest thing I've had to a friend these last four months, and I don't want to lose her. When I continue, I make an effort to speak more softly. "Anya basically told us back when it happened there was nothing she knew of that could get our abilities back."

"But Anya isn't a witch," Dana says. "Maybe if we asked—"

"We've already talked to Jodi," I mutter. We've been in Hannah's Herbs so many times in the last four months, I'm pretty sure we know the inventory better than the employees. We've asked Jodi countless questions, and she's patiently answered all of them. She's the one who suggested the particular blend of herbs and stones we're using today. She knows we're trying to use magic, and she's helped as much as possible. Although we haven't come out and said what our end goal is—to be able to use abilities without having to channel through stones or herbs—I have a feeling she knows. While I don't know Jodi very well, I have a feeling if she knew anything that could help us, she wouldn't hold back.

"Maybe Jodi's not the one we need to talk to," Dana offers tentatively, like it's an idea she's been mulling over for a while. "Maybe we need to bring this to your old circle."

My skin tingles at this reference to the other witches in town. My *old* circle. It never used to be that way.

I formed that circle. They didn't even know about who they were—*what* they were—before I told them. I was their leader. But now who am I? They still try to be friendly to me at school, but it's clear we were only connected because of the one thing we had in common—our magic. Even Lexie Taylor, my cousin, is distant—too wrapped up with her new boyfriend to care about me. "They know what happened to us and they haven't offered to help." I can't hide an edge of bitterness when I say it. In fact, they've barely mentioned what happened to me. I assume it's too uncomfortable a subject for them—after all, what do you say to someone in my position? Still, their lack of empathy leads me to only one conclusion: They don't care whether I get my abilities back. "We can do this ourselves."

Dana's eyebrows hitch upward. "How can you expect them to help when you won't even talk about it with them? When you won't let *me* talk about it with them?" She crosses her arms over her chest petulantly. "Do you know how hard it is keeping all this from Fox? He'd help us if we asked—I'm sure of it."

It's only with great effort I don't roll my eyes at the mention of Fox Holloway, member of my old circle and Dana's new boyfriend. The two have been cozy since the psychic abilities the elder council spell afforded her allowed her to read Krissa Barnette's mind and learn her—*our*—one big secret: We went back in time to find the crystal Seth had been locked in, and by doing so we altered history, coming back to a reality slightly different from our own. Dana told the truth to Fox—who had been Krissa's boyfriend when we found ourselves here—and since then the two have been close. It's true: I've asked her—quite firmly—not to discuss our plight and our progress with Fox. To my knowledge, he hasn't even asked. "And what? You think Fox just *happens* to know a spell that will give us back our abilities? Please. We're better off doing this alone."

An expression flickers across Dana's face, a mix of irritation and disbelief, but it's gone before I can remark on it. She blows out a breath. "Well, I'm gonna go out on a limb and say this spell's a dud. Have you got another for us to try?"

I shift and tug my phone from my back pocket. With a few taps and swipes of my thumb, I've pulled up a webpage. "Since this one didn't work, there's another one I was thinking might. It's actually two spells—one to kind of charge us up, and then one that's the *actual* spell."

"Sounds great," Dana says, her voice almost resigned.

I chafe at her tone. "Look, if you don't want to do this anymore, I can do it on my own. If you don't want your abilities back—"

"I do!" she insists immediately. "It's just... I really think we need help. And not just advice. I think we need someone who actually *has* magic to work these spells for us. I think you need to come to terms with the idea that maybe this isn't something we can do on our own."

I press my lips together. She has a point—I know it. It's not as if the thought hasn't crossed my mind on several occasions. As much as I try to convince myself I won't ask for help because my friends don't seem to care, I know there's something else holding me back: Fear. What if Fox or Lexie or one of the other witches *does* help us and nothing happens? What happens when their best efforts don't work? At that point, all hope will be lost, and I'm not ready to give up yet. "We'll need to get some more supplies."

Dana groans as she gets to her feet. "Of course we do. Looks like we're going to the shop again today after all."

Chapter Three
Sasha

I rest my hand on the door that leads inside Jodi Barnette's shop. I've never been in here before—and with good reason. *She's* in here. She nearly always is. I haven't seen her face to face since that day in the broken-down cabin in the woods, the day I tortured her. My own sister. What's more, I would do it again in a heartbeat if I thought it would help *him*.

Help him? He's beyond that now. He's gone. Seth is dead. Sometimes it's still difficult for me to believe that. I waited my whole life for his arrival, and he was here and gone in a flash. The blink of an eye.

It wasn't supposed to be this way.

The Devoted always believed that when Seth came back, he would usher in a new era—one where our abilities would be known and revered by all. But now he's gone, and I'm still in hiding.

Four months have passed since he died. As much as I want to leave Clearwater, I can't: Elliot won't go and I can't move on without him. He's the only one in the world I have left. All the other members of the Devoted are gone—dead. My entire way of life was wiped from existence. Part of me wishes I could start over, but where would I go? I never prepared for a life where I'd have to live among the ordinary. At least here in Clearwater, there are others with abilities. Even if I despise them all.

An idea has been buzzing in my head now for months. I haven't told Elliot. I don't think he would approve. Soon after Seth died, he started spending time with my sister Anya. The two were close when we were younger, before she left the Devoted. Like me, Elliot lost everything the night Seth died. I think it's because of that he's decided to hold on to Anya. As if she could be a new family to make up for the one he lost.

Except she's a traitor. The fact that Seth is dead is partially her fault. I know she was part of the plan. For that, I can never forgive her.

Yet here I am.

Anya made it clear from almost the moment Seth died that she wanted me back in her life. We haven't spoken face to face, but she's passed messages through Elliot. According to him, she holds no ill will toward me, despite the torture, because as far as she's concerned, I spent my whole life brainwashed by the Devoted. I almost punched Elliot when he told me that. He talked about us being brainwashed without so much as an eye roll—like he agreed with her. Just a couple weeks had passed since everything happened, and he was already talking as if he'd put our entire lives with the Devoted behind him. I asked him flat out if he believed Anya, and while he didn't say yes, he didn't say no either. He told me that as far as he's concerned, we need to focus on the future. That's all that matters to him.

When I didn't respond to Anya's initial invitation back into her life, she didn't press. Although I know Elliot sees her for dinner at least once a week, there have been no further messages, save a card at Christmas.

Today I'm finally going to take her up on her offer. I imagine she'll be pleased—over the moon, even. And I'll let her be. She can think whatever she wants. My plan will work better if she accepts me without question.

Because today is not the day I reunite with my long-lost sister. Today is the day I begin to avenge Seth's death.

My plan didn't come fully into focus until earlier this week when Elliot mentioned something I didn't know. Of course I knew Seth was dead. I knew that nearly the moment it happened—felt his presence in the world disappear. Since then I've pieced together that Krissa Barnette's circle was there, along with her father. I figured the whole group did some sort of spell to kill him.

But that's not the case after all. It wasn't magic that murdered him, it was a knife through the heart. And that knife was wielded by Krissa.

The fact that Seth's killer walks the same streets I do makes my blood boil. When I first found out, it took everything in me not to hunt her down and take her life. Now I'm glad I didn't let my temper get the best of me. A quick death would be too good for her. She deserves to suffer, and I need to figure out the best way to make that happen.

That's why I'm here.

I take in a breath before pulling open the door to Hannah's Herbs. Bells tinkle above my head, a cheerful noise. I allow the sound to fill my body and inform the smile that curls my lips.

The shop is long and narrow, with rows of shelves perpendicular to the walls giving the illusion of organization in a place full of natural elements. Jagged stones rest in a glass case up front, catching and scattering the sunlight streaming through the window. Cuttings of herbs spill out of aluminum planters in tangles. The whole place has a thick, earthy scent, and as I take a step in, I try to ignore how much it smells like the kitchen at my parents' house.

Anya stands behind the cash register, her dark hair swept up in a high ponytail. The style makes her look taller—even though the two of us were cursed with our mother's short stature. Standing across from her, completing a transaction, are two of Krissa's contemporaries. Crystal Jamison looks the same as ever, her wavy chestnut-brown hair perfectly styled, her outfit carefully selected to accentuate both her body and her family's wealth. Her posture is ramrod straight, but there's an air of unease around her. Maybe she's not exactly the same after all. At her side is Dana Crawford, a girl who draws Elliot's eye whenever she's near. I suppose I can't blame him. She's the kind of girl with curves in all the right places, and she seems to know exactly how to show them off.

"I'm sorry I can't be more help, girls," Anya is saying. "I'll be sure to pass your questions along to Jodi."

"We appreciate it," Crystal says.

I wonder what that's all about. I remember Anya seeming to

know everything when I was little. The idea that there's something magic-related that she doesn't know takes a second for me to process. While it's true she left when I was still young, so it's possible she didn't know quite as much as I thought she did, there's something about the pitying way she looks at the girls, the way their shoulders slump, that makes me think something interesting is happening.

Crystal takes the paper bag off the counter and starts toward the door, toward me. There's a slight hesitation in her step as she nears. My smile is still in place, but it doesn't seem to put her at ease. But I'm not here for her. I direct my gaze to my sister.

Anya's eyes widen as they land on me. The surprise is evident on her face. For a moment, I wonder if I'm doing the right thing. She's so pleased to see me. Is it right for me to lie to her?

I shake the thought from my head. Anya will get whatever she gets from me, and she'll deserve every bit of it. If she had stayed with the Devoted, it's possible Seth would still be here now. She's the one who left, who found Krissa's dad and took him away as part of her plan to defeat Seth. So what if I'm not here to give her a fairy tale ending? It's her own fault, and I refuse to feel guilty.

I take long, purposeful strides toward my sister, not even glancing at Crystal and Dana as I pass them. My eyes are trained on Anya. Her mouth twitches like she wants to say something but is doing her best to hold it back. She waits until I'm mere feet away before speaking.

"Can I help you find something?" she asks, as if I were any other customer. It's painfully clear she's trying not to get her hopes up.

I take in a breath. I've played the scene out over and over in my head. I want it to come out just right. I want to seem sincere, of course, but I don't want to oversell it. I don't want to give her any reason to doubt me or my motives. "I came here... I came to see you."

Anya's face breaks out in a smile of pure joy. She comes out from behind the register but doesn't close the distance between us. She obviously wants to, but she's afraid. She doesn't want to push too hard. "I'm glad you're here. Elliot tells me you're doing all right, but it's good to see it for myself."

I don't like the idea that she and Elliot have been talking about me, but I try not to let my expression show it. "I am doing all right," I agree. "I'm... I'm adjusting."

She nods like she understands exactly what I mean. "Life without the Devoted takes some adjusting. I'm glad to hear you're doing okay."

Despite the number of times I've played out scenarios in my head of what Anya and I would say to each other in this moment, it's still hard for me to get the words out. But I know what needs to be said. "I'm sorry it's taken so long," I begin. "After... After everything happened, I didn't know what to do. I didn't know what to think. I know Elliot's been spending time with you. He's invited me to come more than once. And I know you wanted me to. I just couldn't. But now... I don't know what changed, but I realize just how short life is. And I don't want to spend the rest of mine alone." I take a step toward her, a calculated move. I'm an arm's length away now. "I realize how much I need my family. I need my sister."

That's all it takes. Anya reaches for me, pulling me to her. I return her embrace. Her arms are so tight I can hardly breathe. I don't remember the last time I've been hugged this way. My eyes begin to prickle and burn, and I blink rapidly to rid them of the sensation.

It's nothing, I tell myself. Just trying to sell the bit.

When Anya finally pulls away, there are tears in her eyes. "Sasha, I've missed you so much."

I attempt to swallow, but it takes a few tries before I manage. For some reason, there's a lump in my throat. "I've missed you, too."

She wants to believe my words, so she does, even though they're not true.

They're *not*.

Chapter Four
Krissa

Tucker leads the way up the threadbare stairs to Griffin's apartment. The two of us have been spending most of our free time here in the months since Griffin Holloway moved out of his father's house. After the elder council spell failed to wipe the memories of its members, Griffin found it more and more difficult to live under his father's rule. Even though his dad had known about magic before because of his wife, he hadn't put down ground rules about using it until he found out his sons were both witches. Griffin managed to deal with the new rules through Christmas and the new year, but after one too many fights with his dad, he decided that moving out was his best course of action.

The apartment building is a few blocks away from Main on State Street—probably Clearwater's second most-used road. It's not much, but it's a safe space for Griffin to live by his own rules. It's also a place for Tucker and me to spend our time.

Since the night Seth died—the night I killed him—I haven't been the same. It's not like it was when Zane died. I was awash with guilt over his death, even though it hadn't really been my fault. Things are different now. Zane died because of the spell I worked. I hadn't meant anything bad to happen, yet it did. But with Seth, there was no magic involved. It was my hand that pushed the knife through his back. I looked into his eyes as the light faded from them, and I have yet to feel an ounce of remorse.

I'm a murderer, and I don't care.

Luckily, Tucker and Griffin don't care either.

Tucker bangs two times on Griffin's door before letting himself in. I follow. The small apartment is nothing to write home about, but it's away from the prying eyes of any adult. Since he moved in two months ago, Griffin has managed to acquire a handful of pieces of furniture—a sagging, dilapidated couch, a stained coffee table, a handful of milk crates shoved full of car magazines. The only relatively new piece in the entire place is a flat-screen TV. Although I've never asked, I'm fairly certain he used magic to procure it.

"Yeah, just come right in, why don't you?" Griffin mumbles from the kitchen. He sounds even more irritable than usual.

I rub the hemp bracelet woven with small chunks of Apache tears and snowflake obsidian—a charm I created months ago to keep my mind clear of other people's thoughts and emotions. Occasionally, I wish I could still use that part of my psychic abilities. It would be handy if I could sense why Griffin is so grumpy—then I'd know whether Tucker and I should venture forward or not.

Despite the fact that Tucker *can* use his abilities to figure out what's going on, he doesn't appear to take this opportunity to do so. Instead, he hands me the bag from the shop and strides toward the TV, probably to start up whatever video game he's been playing lately.

I head into the kitchen. Griffin is dabbing a broken piece of aloe plant onto the skin of his right hand. The flesh is angry and red—he must've burned it at work. It wouldn't be the first time. He works on cars, so scrapes and burns aren't abnormal, but this one looks worse than average.

"Aren't you glad I got that plant for you?" I ask, trying to keep my tone light.

Griffin sneers over his shoulder. "Yeah, I'm thrilled," he mutters sarcastically. "I'd like it even better if the thing did anything to help." He eyes the paper bag I'm holding. "You didn't happen to bring any calendula, did you?"

I shake my head, the corners of my mouth upturning. "What am I, psychic?"

He curls his lip, clearly not amused by my joke. "Unless you have something to help me, why don't you leave me alone? I'm not really in the mood to deal with you right now."

Instead of backing away, which I'm sure is what he wants me to do, I press in closer. It's true I have no calendula, but I might still be able to help. Without asking for his permission, I knock his left hand out of the way and cover his right with my own. I'm not a natural healer, not like Bria Tate, but for the last few months, I've been working on strengthening those abilities in myself. Since I'm not using my psychic abilities to sense emotions or thoughts, I've been refining other skills so they don't atrophy completely. There are so many other things I can do as a psychic, including healing.

Griffin attempts to pull away, but I hold his wrist. When he catches my gaze, I raise my eyebrows, daring him to yank away again. After a beat, he rolls his eyes. "Fine, do what you're going to do."

I suppress a smile as I inspect his injury more closely. The burn is shiny, red, and angry. I can tell it hurts even without being able to sense exactly how Griffin is feeling. I focus my energy on the burn. So far, I've only managed to heal small paper cuts I've sustained while pretending to do classwork, but the process is the same. I take in a breath and focus healing energy toward Griffin's blistered flesh. The warmth builds up in my chest and I imagine it flowing down into my arms, toward my fingers, like a sparkling golden light. Once the light reaches my fingertips, in my mind's eye I see it coating Griffin's injury. In my head, his skin is perfectly healed and whole. The reality is somewhat less impressive. While the burn is markedly better, appearing as if it's been healing for at least a week, the skin is still red, and it may scar.

I sigh in frustration. "Let me try again."

Griffin finally succeeds in pulling his arm from my grasp and inspects the skin. "I'm not your guinea pig." He offers one of his characteristic half-smiles and shoves my shoulder gently, affectionately. "Thanks. It doesn't hurt anymore."

I'm not satisfied with the job, despite Griffin's assurances. "If you let me, I might be able to get rid of some of the scarring." I reach for his arm again, but he pulls away.

"For real, K, it's fine. Besides, chicks dig scars, right?" There's a teasing glint in his eye, but there's also something behind it, something calculating. Although he's a witch and not a psychic, I feel like he's looking into my thoughts. "How many merit badges did you earn doing that just now, by the way?"

I shake my head in an attempt to dispel the heat creeping into my cheeks. "I don't know what you're talking about."

Griffin's eyes narrow. "Yes, you do. Don't pretend like you don't."

I do my best to ignore his insinuation, to pretend it's baseless. I'm actually surprised by the comment—it's not as if Griffin is well known for being observant of the emotions of others. That's part of the reason I've been spending time with him. He's not ordinarily the kind of person who wants to talk about hopes or dreams or feelings. I force a smile to brush away his comment. "If this is the kind of abuse I get for trying to help you out, next time I'll just let you suffer." I stick my tongue out at him as I turn and head out of the kitchen.

Tucker pauses the first-person shooter game he's playing as Griffin and I enter. "We would have been here sooner, but she saw someone in town."

I punch him in the arm as I go by, not stopping until I'm seated on the far end of the couch. My nose wrinkles involuntarily the way it always does at the lingering scent of cigarettes. Although Griffin doesn't smoke, the previous owners clearly did. I make a mental note to look through the Barnette grimoire for a spell that might help remove the stench.

Griffin leans against the wall separating the kitchen from the living room and crosses his arms over his chest. "Let me guess..."

"There's no need to guess," I say, an unintended edge to my tone. "Tucker needs to mind his own business."

"There's no need to guess, all right," Griffin mutters. He sighs as he follows my trajectory. "Look, I'm not usually one to pry into someone else's business—"

"And yet you're about to," I grumble under my breath.

Griffin arches an eyebrow. "How long are you gonna stay in hiding?"

My skin prickles and I roll my shoulders. "Hiding? You're

acting like I've gone to ground or something. What am I now, some kind of international spy?" I say it like it's a joke, like he must be messing around, even though I'm pretty sure that's not the direction this conversation is headed.

Tucker sets down his controller. He and Griffin exchange glances. I don't like their looks at all. "You ever going to talk to him?"

My eyes glide between Tucker's and Griffin's faces. "What is this, an intervention?"

"Why, do you need one?" Griffin's tone is serious, which concerns me, since his default setting is sarcastic.

I hold up my hands. "Look, I'm glad you guys care so much and all, but..." I let the sentence fall, unfinished, unsure how I would even complete it.

"I saw the way you looked at him through that window," Tucker says. "You can lie and say things are over between the two of you all you want, but I know the truth."

I study the looks of concern mirrored on each of their faces. This turn in the conversation couldn't be more surprising if they suddenly professed their undying love for me. "Where is this coming from? Since when do you to care about my feelings for Owen?"

A smile flashes across Tucker's face, like he's been vindicated. "I knew it. So you admit you've got feelings for him still?"

Panic surges in me. Is Owen putting him up to this line of questioning? Is he going to report back everything I say as soon as our conversation is over? I shake the concern from my mind before it's fully formed. Despite the fact that Tucker is a far more decent guy in this reality that he was in the one I came from, I can't see Owen suddenly deciding to pal around with him. "It doesn't really matter, does it? We're not together, and he's clearly moving on with his life."

Griffin exhales noisily as he lowers himself onto the coffee table. "I'm not gonna pry, and I don't mean to get all up in your business, but I think Tucker may have a point—and you know how painful it is for me to admit that." He offers a conspiratorial wink, which I don't return. "But you can't tell me you're not hiding from something. Don't take this the wrong way, but in all the years you and Fox were together, you and I were never really friends. I don't think your sudden interest in me has much to do with you missing my little brother."

I'm not sure how to respond. It's true that after I killed Seth I stopped spending so much time nurturing the friendships I began only weeks earlier. I've barely spoken to West, Bria, or Felix in months. It's not just Owen I've lost touch with. For weeks, all through the holiday season and into the new year, I barely spoke to anyone. And when I came out of my self-inflicted silence, Tucker was the one I started to connect with. He and Griffin had already formed an alliance, into which I was granted admittance. Although I'm sure I could come up with a suitable lie to explain why these are the two people I've chosen to open up to—as little as I've been required to—I know the truth. I simply can't expect the same kind of acceptance from anyone else. It's not like Griffin and Tucker are evil—not by any means—but they both have the air of a bad boy. No one would expect either of them to help an old lady across the street or chase down a purse-snatcher. Neither holds me to the kind of standards my other friends invariably would—standards I don't think I would meet now. Maybe I'll never meet them again. The night Seth died, I changed. I'll never be the girl I once was. All I can do now is move forward into the new life I've carved out for myself. And I just can't see Owen fitting into that world.

I throw my head back and sigh. "Look, guys, it's good to know you care and all, but let's drop this. I'm fine. Can we just order a pizza or something and get on with the night? You guys are kind of freaking me out with your concern right now."

Although the looks on their faces clearly show they're not pleased with me so quickly shutting down the conversation, neither presses the matter. Griffin pulls out his phone and starts giving different food options. Tucker picks up his controller and un-pauses his game. As our night falls into its usual casual rhythm, I take in a breath of relief. I'm thankful for these two, and I would hate for our easy relationship to morph into something serious and uncomfortable. At this point, Tucker and Griffin are the only friends I have, and I don't want to lose them.

Chapter Five
Sasha

I scrub the lonely, chipped plate of the melted cheese I didn't bother prying off at the end of my meal. Tonight's dinner looked far more promising on the picture on the front of the box than it was in reality. The water is hot, so hot it pinkens the skin on my fingers, but I don't add any from the cold tap. The searing heat feels good. It anchors me back to reality, my mission. Going to see Anya shook me more than I thought it would. I can't get over how nice she was to me, how excited to see me. If our roles were reversed, I don't think I would have reacted the same way.

A knock sounds at the apartment door as I turn off the water and set the plate on the drying rack. I cross the small space to the door, not bothering to glance through the tiny peephole to see who is standing outside before pulling the door open. Only one person ever comes to visit me.

Elliot's blue eyes are wide and sparkling. When his gaze meets mine, a broad smile stretches across his mouth. I can't recall the last time he was this happy to see me. I don't bother with a verbal invitation into the apartment, and he doesn't wait for one before crossing the threshold.

I've known Elliot my whole life—or as near to it as possible. Not every child born to the Devoted was accompanied by a vision from one of our psychics, but he and I both were. It was foretold that the two of us would be the most powerful witch and psychic in generations. Because of this, from the moment Elliot was born, almost a year to the day after me, the two of us have been thrown together. My earliest memories are laced with him. I can recall with perfect clarity what he looked like when he lost his two front teeth. I remember the exact location of his first pimple. I can still see the excited gleam in his eye when he told me about his first crush, along with the completely defeated look he got after the girl told him she wouldn't be his girlfriend because he and I were meant to be together.

There's never been even an ounce of romantic interest between the two of us, despite the fact that everyone in the Devoted wished there would be. It was their greatest hope that one day we would have children of our own, that those children would have abilities that rivaled ours. It's not that Elliot isn't good-looking—quite the contrary. He wears his dark hair close-cropped, and I thought on more than one occasion that he looks something like a European model might. His eyes are bright and kind, and the angles of his face are pleasing. But I've never been able to see Elliot as anything but a friend—almost a brother. The one time we tried our hand at kissing—for experimental purposes only—the two of us made a blood oath to never do it again because it felt so weird, so wrong.

Still, for all the years I've known him, I can't recall ever seeing him this excited.

"What's up?" I ask as I close the door behind him.

"I just heard." He moves deeper into the apartment. The place is nothing spectacular—a simple, dingy, one-bedroom place above the bookstore—but there's no place I'd rather be. This was the apartment Seth lived in briefly when he stayed in Clearwater. Being here makes me feel close to him. I've added some furniture, but besides that I've left the place largely untouched. The card table tucked against the wall is still scattered with papers he left. Eventually I should probably move them to keep them safe, but I haven't been able to bring myself to do it yet. "I think it's great," Elliot continues.

I take in a breath to calm my rising emotions. Of course he knows. It's not like I thought I could keep it a secret from him, but I anticipated being the one to tell him I made contact with Anya. I can't help the flare of jealousy at the idea that he sees her without me, despite the fact that I know the two of them are close. They always were, even when we were growing up. He hasn't kept it from me that he's reconnected with her, but it still stings to think about him just popping by the shop to chat with my sister. What's worse is I'm not sure he would have come to visit me at all if it wasn't for the fact that I saw Anya earlier. We still spend time together, of course, but not as frequently as we used to.

Right after Seth and the rest of the Devoted died, after Elliot convinced me to stay here in Clearwater, he tried to tell me that maybe things were better this way. He never liked the idea that the two of us would be forced to marry and procreate any more than I did, but it hurt when he was elated that now we wouldn't have to do that. He tried to tell me that now we could live the lives we always wanted to, and he couldn't understand when I said the only life I wanted to live was the one where Seth came back to fulfill the prophecy I spent my whole life believing in. I think we both spent the last few months waiting for the other person to come around. I hate that he thinks I'm the one who broke, and it's that fact alone that makes me consider telling him that my reconnection with Anya is not as straightforward as it seems. There was a time when I could have told him this without any reservation, but I know those days are past. If I tell him I only went to see Anya as the first step in getting intel on Krissa Barnette to hurt her, I run the risk of him disclosing my plan to my sister.

Instead, I hitch a smile onto my face and follow him to the living room. "It is great," I say, keeping my tone light. "I think it's... I think it's guilt that's kept me from going to her sooner." It's the line I prepared for this conversation. "I know you told me she wouldn't hold it against me, but I couldn't believe it. I couldn't believe she'd still want me to be her sister after everything I did to her."

We sink down onto the couch, our knees almost touching, and Elliot reaches over to squeeze my hand. "We can start over. Have a new life—a real life. I'm glad you're finally accepting that."

My body tenses, but I force the muscles to unclench. Elliot knows me better than anyone, and I can't let him think I'm anything but sincere in my desire to reconnect with my only family. "I'm glad I have you to help me accept it." As well as he knows me, I know him, and the surest way to take Elliot's attention off me is to put it on him. One of his few weaknesses is flattery.

"Have you already eaten? We could go out and grab a bite."

I offer a rueful smile. "I wish I hadn't, but you're about twenty minutes too late."

He snorts, probably imagining what nightmarish food I prepared for myself. He knows I've always been a disaster in the kitchen. "Have you got a minute? If I'm honest, I didn't come just because you saw Anya today. I mean, that's part of it. There's something I've wanted to ask you for help with for a while now, but I figured you'd shoot me down. But now... Maybe you'll be a little more open."

A pain shoots through my chest at the idea that Elliot thought he couldn't come to me for help about something, anything. For as intertwined as our lives have always been, it's hard to think there would be any reason for him to think I wouldn't help him. "Sure, anything."

The corners of his mouth quirk up in a smile before he continues. "You remember my mom's youngest brother?"

I cast my thoughts backward several years. The man in question was much younger than Elliot's mom, more like an older brother than an uncle. He got the two of us into plenty of trouble, but we also had some of our greatest adventures with him at our side. That is, until the Devoted cast him out of our ranks because he failed to develop any kind of ability. "Nate. Of course. What about him?"

Elliot cocks his head and gives me a look that tells me I should know exactly what about him. "I want to find him. Part of me always has, but I was afraid he wouldn't want to see me. If I'm honest, I was afraid what the Devoted would do to me if I did find him."

I swallow around the lump rapidly forming in my throat. "Find him?" Finding those who had been cast out is something that was only ever whispered about in the Devoted. To say it out loud put someone at risk of being cast out themselves. Those without abilities were not to be missed. We were not to spare a second thought for them once they were gone. We were told over and over again that keeping around family members who did not manifest abilities would simply dilute our already languishing bloodlines. "How can I help? I don't know where they sent castaways."

His eyebrows pull together in the center. "I never thought you did. What I need help with is some kind of spell. According to Anya, the Devoted used magic to keep the castaways from being detected by anyone who might try to find them. It was just a precaution, in case someone lost a child they couldn't bear parting with. I guess they figured if people didn't know where the castaways ended up, there wouldn't be the temptation to go join them." He closes his eyes and shakes his head, as if it's the most barbaric thing he can think of. I do my best to keep my face neutral, as if I could agree with him. And even though Elliot promised me a long time ago he wouldn't invade my thoughts with his psychic abilities, I also try to push down my silent agreement with what our leaders did. I don't even see why a spell would be necessary—it's not like castaways are worth finding.

He looks at me expectantly, and I know he's waiting for an answer. I'm just not sure I can give him the one he wants. "I don't know, Elliot. What makes you think I can break a spell like that?"

He shrugs. "I don't know, maybe the fact that you're the strongest witch the Devoted have seen in generations." He rolls his eyes for effect as he quotes the line the two of us have heard countless times in our lives. "Anya seems to think that since the Devoted are all gone now, it might be easier to break the spell."

I roll my shoulders, uncomfortable. Not once since his uncle was sent away has Elliot mentioned his desire to have Nate back. Why now? But I already know the answer. Besides me and Anya, Elliot has no one left in the world. He's always been more of a people person than I, so I guess it makes sense that he wants to cobble together some kind of family. But that doesn't make it a good idea. "I'm not sure you thought this through. It's been what—ten years? A lot can happen in a decade. What if he doesn't want to see you?"

Elliot holds out his hands. "I was nine when they kicked him out. Do you think he's going to hold me accountable?"

"I don't know. Maybe he doesn't want anything to do with the Devoted. Maybe he's got a whole new life now and he doesn't want to be reminded of the past. Or maybe something's happened to him. What if we find he died in a car accident five years ago? Would you still want to know?" I cover his hand with mine. I'm not trying to burst his bubble, and I hope he understands that. But one of us has to be the realist. "Don't you think it's better to start over fresh now than to live in the past?"

For the first time since his arrival, Elliot's face falls. It's a quality he's always possessed, the ability to go from sunshine to thunderstorm in the blink of an eye. His expression clouds as he meets my eyes again. "What about us? Are we better left in the past too?"

I shake my head. "Don't be dramatic. You know that's not what I mean."

"How do I know that? Our lives are drastically different than they were even six months ago. I know you and I have been on opposite sides when it comes to how we feel about those changes. Maybe it's best if we both just go our separate ways from here. You didn't want to stay here in Clearwater. You only did because I asked you to. Maybe it's time for you to move on."

I huff. Elliot's penchant for melodrama grates my nerves. I have no intention of leaving Clearwater, at least not until I have my revenge. There was a time when I would bring Elliot in on my plan, but now is not it. The fact is, I can't trust him to be in lockstep with me anymore. It's an odd situation to be in, considering we've always been there for each other in the past. I could take him up on his offer right now, pull away, keep to myself. I could break off our friendship. It might make things easier, not having to keep my plans from him to be sure Anya doesn't catch wind of them. But can I really do that? Can I really cut Elliot out so completely? Before the questions are even fully formed in my mind, I already know the answer. No. Despite our differences, I can't let go. I scoot closer to him on the couch and sling my arm over his shoulder. "Don't think you can get away from me so easily. Elliot, no matter what, you're still my best friend."

Elliot's stormy expression clears, and he offers a small smile. "You sure?"

I ball my hand into a fist and thump him on the shoulder. "Keep it up, jerk. See if I help you."

This elicits a grin. "So you'll do it? You'll help?"

I sigh. As much as I think it's a bad idea, I know if I deny him assistance, he'll question my loyalty to him, and that will only lead to him questioning my purposes in rejoining Anya's life. "I think that's what I just said. Keep up, will you?"

He slides his arm around my waist and gives me a side hug. "This means a lot to me. Thank you."

I allow him to squeeze me for a beat longer before shoving him away playfully. "Let's not get all sappy," I warn, but I can't help smiling. "You want something to drink?" Without waiting for his response, I stand and move toward the kitchen.

"Sure," he says, not bothering to ask for options. I know his preferences as well as I know my own. "I'm sure you'll be able to break whatever enchantment is keeping the castaways hidden. I've got a good feeling about this. You'll find them. I have no doubt."

I raise an eyebrow as I pull open the refrigerator door. "What, you expect me to find all of them?" The thought is frankly alarming. Although I never tried to count how many people were cast out of our community as I was growing up, the number has to reach into the dozens—and those are just the ones I paid attention to. Does he really want me to locate everyone? That seems like a bad idea on many levels. Sure, Nate might be happy to see him, but what about the people to whom we have little or no connection? Would they be happy to have a reminder of the life they could've had if only they hadn't been born lacking? I feel like it might cause some people more pain than it's worth.

"Not everyone," Elliot says with a laugh. "Just Nate and Misha."

I freeze as my hand touches the half-full carton of milk. Misha. That name hasn't crossed my mind in thirteen years.

Misha, my other sister.

I fight against the flood of memories that crash over me. She was older, the middle child. Although she was much closer in age to Anya, she never missed an opportunity to play some silly make-believe game with me, and she never complained when I wanted to tag along with her. I always looked up to Anya, but I loved Misha desperately. The hardest thing when she was cast out was being told by my parents that I needed to forget about her. They claimed she wasn't worthy of my love, and I believed them. I put her out of my mind—something made easier by Anya's disappearance soon after Misha was put out. I was encouraged to miss my eldest sister because she had manifested abilities. Her loss was a blow to the community. I was able to redirect all my feelings about Misha's loss into Anya's, and as time passed, I came to agree with what my parents told me.

But now all those feelings flood me. Elliot and Anya want to find Misha. Even if they can, will I want to see her? Will she want to see me? What happens if they do find her and I realize I still love her? It's been drilled into me not to waste my emotions on someone inferior. What if I can't help caring for my sister even though she's ordinary? What does that say about me?

Chapter Six
Crystal

I blink and press the heels of my hands against my closed eyelids. It feels like I've been staring at the computer screen for my entire life. The colors on this particular website are garish and clash horribly. I have half a mind to email the webmaster and ask if they were tripping on acid or something when they put together this particular combination but decide it's probably not worth my time. If the overall look of the site is any indication, it probably hasn't been updated in ten years or so. Attempting to email the webmaster would be an exercise in futility—as it seems my search is becoming.

I'm getting desperate. I know Dana senses it, even if she won't say it. And I certainly won't tell her that. If I say it out loud, it will be too true—too unchangeable.

"Crystal, it's time for dinner," my mom calls.

I lock my computer before closing it. Mom came in the other day to pick up laundry and bumped my desk hard enough to wake the computer up. I happened to walk by at just the right moment—and nothing incriminating was up on the web browser—but it was a close call. Though we've never spoken about it, I'm positive my mom knows—or at least has an inkling—that her baby sister, my once-again dead aunt Crystal, dabbled in witchcraft. I'm not sure what her thoughts on the matter would be if she found out I was practicing it as well, and I'm not interested in finding out.

Not waiting to be called a second time, I leave my room. Dad is already sitting at the dining room table, and mom is bringing a drink from the kitchen. I swing by the refrigerator, pouring myself a glass of lemonade before joining them.

"Wow, Mom, dinner looks amazing," I say. It's kind of an unwritten family rule that someone has to compliment my mother at every meal. She's made it abundantly clear throughout my lifetime that she hates planning and cooking meals, and left to her own devices she would subsist solely on sandwiches, so Dad and I take turns making sure she knows we appreciate the work that goes into each dinner. Tonight, she's made what appear to be enchiladas. While she usually sticks to old standbys, every once in a while she will branch out and try a recipe one of her friends shared on social media. There's actually even money that tonight's meal will suck.

Mom smiles. I'm sure she knows about the unspoken pact Dad and I have, but she accepts my praise anyway. As we take turns spooning globs of tortilla, meat, and cheese onto our plates, my parents engage in a kind of silent conversation spoken with their eyes. I've seen them look at each other this way before, and I'm pretty sure when they do start talking it won't be good for me.

Once our plates are full, my dad shifts in his seat just slightly—just enough to draw my attention. He has a quiet, gentle manner about him, one that always puts me at ease. But now it's clear he is not at ease with whatever it is he's about to say. Dad skewers a piece of chicken that's escaped its tortilla and lifts it as though he's about to take a bite, but it hovers halfway between the table and his mouth as he locks eyes with me. "So, honey, how's school going?"

It's a trick question and I know it. Our district gives students and parents online access to grades, and while I know my parents don't check daily, they do check regularly. My grades aren't abysmal, but they aren't to the standard I've set over the years, either. I don't want to lie, but I'm not sure exactly how to respond. I give a noncommittal shrug as I take a bite of my food to buy time.

Dad lets out of breath and looks at Mom, sighing as if I'm being difficult. He brings his forkful the remaining distance to his mouth, a cue for my mom to take over the questioning.

"We're a little concerned about your math grade." When it comes to questioning procedures, Mom is much more to the point.

I swallow my bite and contemplate taking a second to give me more time to formulate a response but decide against it. "I'm having a little trouble with this chapter." It's not a lie—not entirely, anyway. I am having trouble with this chapter, but mostly because I'm not paying any attention in class and not making an effort on the homework.

"According to the grade book, you're missing several assignments." Mom eyes me shrewdly. I get my wavy chestnut hair from her, along with my slight build. It's times like this that I wonder if I'll look like her when I'm a mom. Will I be this concerned about things that won't matter in my child's life in ten or twenty years? Sometimes I wish I could tell her how so many things she worries about for me really have no bearing on my life. It's the things she doesn't know about—my magic, or lack thereof—that will really influence the person I become.

I debate exactly what to tell her. She's told me before I'm not a very good liar, so I don't make it a practice. Although, to be honest, the last time I tried lying to her about something was back in early middle school, and she may have told me I was bad at it just to keep me from trying again. It might be worth it to try my luck. "I think maybe Mrs. Hill lost some of those assignments. I heard someone else in class complaining about that the other day. I figured he was making a stink because he hadn't actually done them, but if you're saying things are missing in the grade book for me, maybe there's something to his story."

I take another bite as Mom and Dad go back to their wordless conversation. I wonder if I'll ever have that with someone—the ability to gauge what they're thinking with little more than an eyebrow raise or a quirk of the lip.

A nagging voice in the back of my mind starts up with the familiar refrain, but I shove it back. Now is not the time to think of what would be different if I hadn't pushed Tucker away again. Now is not the time to think about distractions.

Dad swallows his mouthful and leans toward me over the table. "Saying your teacher is losing your assignments is quite an accusation. I want you to go and check in with her tomorrow. See if maybe the assignment is in a different pile, or maybe sitting in a stack at home. Your aunt used to complain that students would accuse her of losing things that they turned in late that simply hadn't been graded yet." His mouth twitches and his eyes dart to my mom the way they do every time he mentions his sister-in-law. Before she was the principal of Clearwater High, she was a teacher there. I assume, anyway. That particular part of her history is mostly a mystery to me, since I didn't live it. In my reality—the one I lived in before Krissa and I went back in time—my aunt had been dead for nearly two decades.

I give myself a little shake, not willing to give too much thought to the aunt I barely got to know. Every time I start thinking that way, I can't help getting angry that I lost the one person I desperately wanted in my life, yet Krissa has gotten everyone she loves back. In our reality, her mother died—that's why she moved here in the first place. But in this timeline, her mom is alive and well. Even her father, who had been out of her life for years, has returned. And when we went up against Seth, she lost nothing. I've lost everything.

"Honey, is there something wrong?" Dad asks, his face pinched with concern.

I can't imagine what expressions have been playing out across my face the last few seconds. I fight to relax my features into a neutral position before forcing a small smile. "I'm fine. I'll talk to my teacher tomorrow."

But Dad is still looking at me like I'm fragile. His shoulders sag as he releases a breath. "I know you miss her. I know how much you loved your aunt. But the last thing she would want is for you to let your studies slip because of her. You know how important education was to her. Now, if you need to talk to someone..."

Mom stands abruptly, her thighs bumping against the table. "I need to get something," she mutters, leaving the room.

I curse myself that the conversation has gone in this direction. It's not like talking about my aunt is off-limits, but it always seems to strike a chord in my mom. I promise myself to start pretending to care in math, if even just to keep a conversation like this from repeating.

"I'll do better. If the teacher really doesn't have my assignments, I'll make them up."

Dad looks relieved by my words and applies himself to his dinner with much more gusto than before. I can't blame him—despite looking like a sloppy mess, this meal definitely falls in the fifty percent that turn out really well. It's not until he reaches for a salt shaker that I pause in my own eating. I eye him carefully as he sprinkles on a little, and then a little more and a little more.

"Dad," I say, a hint of warning in my voice. At his last checkup, the doctor told him he needs to cut sodium from his diet. I insisted we remove the salt shaker from the table entirely after that, but he declared it wouldn't be an issue, that he wouldn't be tempted. It must only be in his distraction that he's reached for it now, as evidenced by the sheepish look he gives.

"Oh, come on. A little bit won't hurt."

"It's not a little bit I'm worried about," I say, not managing to hide the smile that upturns the corners of my mouth. "You, sir, have a bit of an obsession when it comes to salt."

His eyes go wide as he gestures to himself innocently. "Moi?"

"Yeah, like you don't know what I'm talking about," I say, rolling my eyes.

He shakes his head as he cuts off another strip of enchilada. "You don't need to give me such a hard time, you know. I am a grown man, after all."

"Of course you are. And I want you to continue growing. I want you to keep growing until you're a shriveled old man. I want you to be around forever."

He smiles, stretching his hand across the table. "I'll do my best, honey."

I reach for his hand and squeeze it. "You better."

Less than a minute later, Mom returns. The barest hint of pink around her eyes suggests her reaction to the mention of her sister. I keep having to remind myself how new this is for her. As far as she's concerned, her sister was part of her life until a few months ago.

After dinner, I head back to my room. I unlock my computer and brace my eyes for the hideous website. Some links toward the bottom boast spells to enhance magical abilities, and I open up the notebook I keep hidden with my school supplies and start scanning the pages for similarities to the spells described on the site. Who knows? Maybe there's something here I haven't already tried.

I hope there is. I'm starting to think there's nothing that will help. If that's the case, where does it leave me? It doesn't matter what my grade in math is or how much my parents care—without my magic, I'm not me.

Chapter Seven
Krissa

When Tucker drops me off in front of my house, it's late—way past my curfew. Once upon a time, in a different life, I didn't even have a curfew, and now I might as well not have one for as much attention as I pay to it.

I turned off my phone hours ago when the constant barrage of text messages started to irritate me. It's par for the course at this point.

Although the April air is getting warmer during the day, it's still cold enough to make me shiver at night. As I approach the wraparound porch, I wish I had thought to grab a sweatshirt earlier today.

The light is on, but I know it wasn't done as a kindness. Its light cuts through the darkness like a beacon, its purpose to remind me of the hour.

Once upon a time, in a different life, this would have caused me guilt. But this isn't that life.

The front door is unlocked—it always is—and I ease it open and step over the threshold. I kick off my shoes and head for the stairs, but before I can get there, someone shifts in the living room. Even without the benefit of that part of my psychic abilities, I know exactly who it is before I turn. "Hey, Dad."

"You have any idea what time it is?" His voice is low, but not out of consideration for my mom and Jodi, who are no doubt asleep upstairs. It trembles with the barest hint of anger. I know he's working to control it, as he has countless times in the last few months.

"I'm not actually sure," I say, leaning against the archway between the hallway and living room. "I had to turn off my phone because it kept getting blown up with text messages."

He sputters, his anger flaring. I'm baiting him, but I can't help it. "You turned it off?" he asks incredulously. "What if there was an emergency?"

I cross my arms over my chest. "Was there? An emergency?"

His mouth tightens. "No, there wasn't. But you already knew that. Just like I know you were out with Griffin and Tucker again." He cocks his head, narrowing his eyes. "What, you're not going to deny it?"

I shrug. "What's the point?"

He stands, crossing to me in three long strides. "Have you been drinking again?"

I groan. Of course he would bring that up. He pulls it out every few weeks or so in an attempt to get a rise from me. It happened once—only once. Tucker and Griffin offered me some beer, and I took them up on it. I figured it might help me escape my new normal. But drinking didn't give me the distance from the unpleasant realities I would've liked. Instead of making me forget, it was like the alcohol was a laser pointer that highlighted all the reasons I had to be displeased with the current state of things. "No, Dad. I'm not drunk."

"That's not what I asked."

I roll my eyes, not bothering to dignify his question with a response. I decided after that one night that drinking wasn't for me. But even if I hadn't, I could make it so no one knew I had done it. I found a spell in the family grimoire for "the abatement of drunkenness" that I've used on Tucker two or three times so he'd be sober enough to drive home.

"I don't trust those boys," Dad says.

It's not the first time he's made this pronouncement either. "You trusted them enough when you needed them. What? Now that we don't have some big bad guy to take down, they're not good enough for you anymore?"

Dad runs a hand through his graying hair, exasperated. "But

you weren't exactly best friends with either of them back then either, were you?"

I can't hold his gaze. "A lot can change."

"Don't I know it," he mutters. He lets out a breath and his entire posture softens. "I don't want to fight."

"Finally, something we can agree on."

He catches my eye, and the concern there threatens to break me. "Sweetie, I think you should talk to someone about what you're going through. I've done some research on some counselors and psychologists who might be able to help you process everything."

I take a step back, the walls that had started to gently crumble redoubling. "Talk to someone? Who do you expect me to talk to? Better yet—what you expect me to say? I can't tell anyone the truth. Dad, I killed a man. I stabbed him in the heart. I watched the life drain from his face. Who can I tell that to? They'll either believe me and lock me up for murder, or they won't believe me and they'll lock me up for being crazy." I shake my head, backing toward the stairs. "No. I can't tell anyone what really happened. You just have to let me deal with things on my own." The next words that escape my mouth are sharp like a dagger. "After all, you're good at that."

The stairs behind me creak under someone's weight. Mom's voice is tired when she speaks. "Give it a rest, you two. If you're not careful, you'll wake Jodi." A large yawn indicates we've already woken her.

A prickle of embarrassment crawls up my neck and into my cheeks, and I'm glad it's dark enough that no one can see it. Without waiting for my dad to formulate some new accusation or complaint, I head up the stairs, giving my mom's shoulder a brief squeeze as I brush past her. Dad has made it to the top of the flight by the time I reach the stairs that will lead me to the third floor. The two exchange a brief, murmured conversation before Mom leads the way to their bedroom.

It should make me happy that the two of them are getting their relationship back to where it was before Dad left, but I can't dredge up the appropriate emotion. It's not even that I'm being selfish. It's just too hard for me to feel anything anymore.

I know Dad is only trying to help, but life would be so much easier if he'd just stop. Mom and Jodi are both giving me space and I wish he'd do the same. Then again, Mom and Jodi don't know what I've done. Dad made the decision to keep it from them, to tell them that we defeated Seth in broad strokes only, and I'm glad he did. At least there are two people I care about who don't see me as a killer. I don't know how I'd deal if I saw in them the same repulsion I detect just beneath the surface of everyone who knows.

Chapter Eight
Sasha

When Elliot and I first came to Clearwater, we shared a beat-up Honda Civic. Since we lived together and spent most of our time with each other, it made sense to just have the one. But once we decided to relocate here permanently and get our separate places, Elliot insisted I should keep the car. It wasn't exactly in stellar condition when we got it, and as I pull into the parking lot of Allegro Bread Company, the roar as I accelerate indicates I'm in need of a new muffler—possibly an entire new exhaust system. I ease the vehicle into the empty spot beside a sleek dark orange Chevy SS—Elliot's car—and curse myself, not for the first time, for taking him up on his offer. It could be me in the nice car. It may have taken me more effort to acquire it, unlike the ease with which Elliot likely used his psychic abilities to persuade someone to give it to him, but it would have been worth it. The first time I saw it, I berated him for not doing the chivalrous thing and giving me the nicer ride, but all he did was stick out his tongue. With Elliot in my life, I've never had to wonder what it would be like to have a brother.

Besides the spot I pulled into, there isn't another empty one in sight. I suppose I shouldn't be surprised—after all, it is lunchtime and this is a popular place. It's not typically the kind of restaurant I would choose to eat at, but when I insisted Anya and I meet for lunch instead of dinner, this was the location she chose.

A man in his forties with an ample stomach and a broad smile holds the door open for me and I force a polite nod. It's taken months to extend simple courtesies like this to the ordinary. The Devoted did their best to avoid them, but on the off chance we interacted with someone without abilities, we never went out of our way to be pleasant. People without abilities are below people like me. It kills me that I have to pretend otherwise.

Anya waves from a booth near the door when I enter. Her smile is broad and genuine. She already has a tray of food in front of her, along with another in the empty space to her right. Elliot is nowhere in sight. Although I'm not really hungry, I join the long line of patrons waiting to place their order at the counter. I hope by the time I make it to the table, Elliot will be back from wherever he's gone. I scan the menu board hanging behind the counter without much interest and select the first thing that looks relatively appealing. As I wait for my turn with the cashier, I survey the restaurant. The walls are painted cheery colors—oranges and yellows with a richness added that keeps them from being too bright. The walls are lined with mass-produced paintings that are supposed to look unique. The effect is supposed to be cozy, but it misses the mark, instead feeling clinical and sterile—too perfectly designed by some corporation to be real.

I place my order and move down to the end of the counter to wait for it. A quick glance in my sister's direction tells me Elliot still has not made his way back to the table. By the time my order is ready, Anya is still alone. I steel myself as I walk toward her.

"Isn't this place great?" Anya asks as I sit. "The food here is so good."

I nod noncommittally and heft a spoonful of soup to my mouth. It's far too hot and my eyes tear as I attempt to swallow it. "Yeah, great," I manage, reaching for my drink. "Where's Elliot?"

"He said he had to make a phone call. He should be back any second."

This news piques my interest. Who could Elliot be calling? Everyone he knows is sitting at this table. Anya didn't volunteer the information and I wonder if she even knows. I could ask, but something makes me hesitate. What if she knows something about Elliot that I don't? The two have been spending time together in the last few months—probably more time than Elliot and I have spent together. Part of me is afraid that somehow she knows him better than I do now.

Anya watches as I sip my drink. I cast around for something to say, but nothing comes to mind. What on earth could the two of us possibly talk about? Before she disappeared from the Devoted, we talked all the time. Even the gap in our ages didn't keep us from being close. But now, she's like a stranger. I guess thirteen years apart will do that.

Movement by the restaurant's side door catches my eye, and I smile with relief as Elliot approaches the table. He offers a grin as he slides into the booth beside Anya. "Sorry about that," he says, picking up his sandwich.

I raise an eyebrow. "Phone call?"

Elliot rolls his eyes as he takes a bite of his meal. "Yeah, nosy," he says around a mouthful of food.

I know I'm prying, but I can't help it. There was a time not too long ago that I knew everything about Elliot. Being faced with the fact that's no longer the case hits me harder than I'd like to admit. I could ask directly, but it won't mean as much if he tells me because he feels he has to. I want him to want to.

I shake my head as I scoop another spoonful of soup, careful this time to blow on it. Probably it's nothing. Maybe he's calling about his car or something to do with his apartment. If it's important, he'll tell me.

At least I want to believe he will.

Anya starts talking, telling anecdotes about customers at the shop. I nod at appropriate intervals, but I'm not really paying attention. I need to make an effort; I know that. I just didn't think it would be this hard to pretend like I really care about her life. I wish there was a way for my plan to work without having to go through these pleasantries. But I know I can't. There's no way I can just reappear in my sister's life and immediately start grilling her about Krissa and her weaknesses. I have to be patient. Luckily, patience is a virtue I possess.

Although several people have walked into the restaurant since Elliot joined us, my eyes are drawn to a particular couple as they enter. It's the guy's tall frame that catches my eye, his smooth, almost catlike movements. Fox Holloway is hard to miss. Dana Crawford walks behind him, a broad smile on her face as she clutches Fox's arm. Neither of them notices me, and I'm not sure if that's good or bad. It would help me sell the bit if the right people see me spending time with my sister. Then again, I'm not sure how close she and her ex-boyfriend are anymore.

Anya clucks her tongue. When I glance at her, her eyes are fixed on Fox and Dana. Anger swells without my consent. Is that sad look on her face related to the fact that Krissa is no longer in a relationship with this guy? Why should she care? I know she worked with Krissa's dad for years, but why should that mean she cares about Krissa's relationships?

Elliot picks up on Anya's diverted attention and mentions what I refuse to. "That's Krissa's ex-boyfriend, right?"

Anya nods vaguely. "And Dana Crawford." She pulls her gaze from the two of them to look at Elliot and me. "I feel so bad for her. She was a member of the elder council. But something went wrong with the spell."

I can't help noticing what she doesn't say: The elder council spell was designed to break after they locked Seth away. Of course, something went wrong with it because that's not how things ended.

Anya's eyes drift back to Dana as she continues. "She was supposed to be left without any memory of the existence of abilities. But she remembers, and she wants hers back."

I file away this new information. I haven't spent much time cataloging the comings and goings of the former council members. I figured since Seth was gone, they all just went back to their normal lives. This is the first I've heard that things didn't go exactly to plan for them.

"But really, it's Crystal Jamison I'm more concerned for," Anya continues. But instead of explaining what she means, she takes a bite of her sandwich.

I raise an eyebrow at Elliot, wondering if he's as lost as I am. Since Anya's mouth is full, he picks up where she left off. "Crystal lost her abilities too."

I struggle to process this information. It doesn't surprise me that Dana no longer has abilities: She wasn't born with them. It was a spell that gave them to her to begin with. But Crystal Jamison is a natural-born witch. I've never heard of anything that could make someone like her ordinary. Although I couldn't care less about Crystal, her plight chills me. If it could happen to her, could it happen to me? Before I can ask about it, Anya is speaking again.

"Those two are in the shop almost every day. They're trying everything they can to get their abilities back." A pitying look washes over my sister's face.

"Is that even possible?" I ask.

Anya shrugs. "Not by any spell I've ever heard of."

"What about the elder council spell?" I press. "That gave abilities to people who didn't have them."

She sighs and it's obvious this is ground she's covered before. "You know as well as I do there's no spell to create a witch or psychic. The council spell was crafted carefully and took generations to collect the abilities that would have naturally manifested in those families. And it was never designed to provide them with powers long-term. Once their task was complete, the abilities were absorbed back into nature. There's no way to get them back."

Something tugs at the back of my memory, so indistinct I'm sure it's part of a dream. Murmurs and whispers about a spell to allow an ordinary person to wield magic. But Anya just said there's no such thing, so maybe this idea was simply something conjured by my imagination, although I'm not sure under what circumstances I'd pretend something like that were real. I voice the question on the tip of my tongue: "How did Crystal manage to lose her abilities?"

Anya's mouth presses into a tight line, as if she's debating telling me. Before I can be sure that is what's going on in her mind, she's speaking. "Four months ago, Crystal was inhabited by a spirit."

I glance at Elliot to make sure I heard her right. He gives a slight nod. "You mean she was possessed?"

Anya nods. "The spirit was also a witch—Bess Taylor. And when we cast her out, Crystal woke up with no abilities. Somehow Bess took Crystal's magic with her."

The fact that a possessing spirit could take away someone's powers is eclipsed in my mind by another piece of information. "Wait—Bess Taylor? Like... Seth's Bess?"

"The very same." An expression flickers across Anya's features, too quick for me to make out.

My brain fights to make sense of this. Bess Taylor's story is well known among the Devoted. Her fate is part of the reason we're told to fear the ordinary: Despite their lack of abilities, they can still harm us and those we love. But I've never heard any prophecy about her returning along with Seth. In fact, besides knowing she was Seth's beloved and how she died at the hands of the ordinary overrunning Clearwater, she was never talked about much—by the Devoted, at least.

Something clicks in my mind. I remember when a recruitment team came back to town once. Dad brought a couple of the single guys to our house to be treated to a home-cooked meal made by my mom. Although I'm not terribly domestic, Mom asked for my help in the kitchen. As I peeled potatoes, one of the guys told the others a story about some people he met—a group outside our own who knew about Seth. But instead of waiting for him to return, they were fascinated with Bess. He said they believed she knew a secret, something they would stop at nothing to learn. He described them as ruthless in their pursuit. When he attempted to recruit a couple of their stronger witches to the Devoted, they threatened his life and left him so shaken he was considering leaving the team to avoid ever crossing paths with one of their number again.

Elliot and Anya's conversation drifts from Crystal's plight, but I barely hear them. My mind is spinning with possibilities. If this group is looking for contact with Bess Taylor, perhaps I can point them in Crystal's direction. If they're as dangerous as the man feared, their presence could assist me in my pursuit. Maybe one way I can strike out at Krissa is through one of her friends.

Chapter Nine
Crystal

My eyes glaze over as I stare at the incomprehensible jumble of numbers and letters on the page before me. I've struggled through more than a dozen problems from one of my many missing math assignments, and at this point my brain is basically mush. At least when I had magic, listening to the teacher work through the sample assignments on the board was usually enough for me to work a spell to complete the homework almost automatically. It's been far too long since I've attempted to stumble through equations like this on my own. With a sigh, I scribble in a few numbers followed by x, hoping the teacher doesn't check this far.

Usually, Dana and I meet up at her place right after school to try out new ways to get our abilities back. Since her dad died, she's been living with her mom's sister, who works until late in the evening. Basically, so long as Dana doesn't leave a mess for her aunt to clean up, she can do whatever she wants. But after my parents expressed their concern over my academics, I decided it would be to my benefit to at least attempt to bring up my grade. This way, I can show them my progress at the dinner table so they'll lighten up and not feel the need to check on a daily basis.

I slam the math book closed and shove it into my backpack. I select the notebook with the record of all the spells Dana and I have tried and take it with me as I leave the room. I check the time on my phone before dropping it into the purse I left on the table by the front door and mutter a curse. A text message notification flashes across the screen. It's Dana: She's wondering where I am since I assured her I'd be to her place by now. It's only a five-minute drive, so I don't bother sending a response. Slipping into a pair of flats, I pick up my purse and move to open the front door. Before I can twist the knob, a knock sounds.

Surprised, I pull my hand away. Who on earth could it be? Probably some solicitor. I keep telling my mom we need one of those signs to alert people to the fact we don't want whatever it is they're selling, and although she keeps promising to pick one up, she has yet to. If Dad or I answer the door, there's no problem: Dad has zero qualms saying thanks but no thanks, and I'm a minor, so they can't sell to me. But if Mom answers, she feels it's only polite to listen to their spiel, and nine times out of ten she ends up purchasing something.

"I don't have time for this," I murmur, pulling open the door. I'm about to announce to the person on the porch that I'm not interested in whatever she's peddling, but I stop short when I catch a glimpse of wavy red hair. "Lexie?"

Through the upper glass of the screen door, my cousin offers a smile so faint I wonder if I'm imagining it. In fact, I wonder if I'm imagining her presence altogether. When I cast my mind back, I can't recall the last time I saw her at my house—in this reality or my own.

"Can I come in?" she asks, her voice slightly muffled by the door still between us.

As if on cue, my purse vibrates slightly as my phone receives another text. I don't have to check to know it's from Dana. I open the storm door, but only a few inches. "Actually, I'm on my way out." The opening isn't large enough for me to pass through, but I'm afraid to make it any wider in case Lexie takes it as an invitation despite my words. Although I should head for my car, I stay inside the house. I feel safer with something between us.

Lexie doesn't make a move to enter, but she doesn't back away either. "I'm sorry. I should've called first. But I won't stay long, I promise." She places her hand on the metal handle but doesn't tug at it. She doesn't want to force her way into my presence, but she already has. If she really intended to respect me and my plans, she'd leave. The fact that she hasn't speaks volumes.

There was a time I could've knocked her out of the way with a single spell, but now isn't that time. I'm powerless. As that thought overwhelms me, I push open the screen to allow her entrance.

Lexie walks in as if she owns the place, heading straight for the living room and taking a seat in my usual spot on the couch. I don't join her. I stand, leaning against the entryway table. Disappointment flickers over Lexie's peaches-and-cream complexion, like she's actually upset I haven't taken a spot beside her.

"You wanted to talk," I say, crossing my arms over my chest. "So talk."

Lexie shifts against the cushions, as if she has to be in just the right position to speak. "Okay. So." She glances down at her cuticles as if the words she wants to say are inscribed there. When she finds nothing, her gaze drifts upward again. "I know neither of us has ever been the best with the mushy family fuzzies. And I'm aware we've never exactly been besties, but... I miss you."

It takes a few moments to process her words. "You... miss me?"

She nods, the crease between her eyebrows suggesting she's as mystified by the confession as I am. "We've had our ups and downs—lots and lots of downs. And I know you've needed your space these last few months, but I don't think you realize just how scary it was when we had to get that spirit out of you. I thought I'd lost you—and while I was waiting for you to wake up, waiting to see if you were okay, I realized a lot of the things that kept us from being close were so trivial. And I get that things have been hard for you. I get you're in a state of adjustment. But don't you think it's time to move on?"

I study her face. It's more open and honest than I can remember ever having seen it, but that doesn't keep her words from cutting through me. "Move on? What exactly do you think I should be moving on from?"

Lexie heaves a sigh. "Look, I knew it would come out wrong. Don't get all offended. What I mean is, I think it's time for you to get back to your life. Stop shutting everyone out. I don't know if you think we don't care about you anymore or what, but whatever's keeping you from us is in your head. We all miss you.

The circle misses you."

"The circle misses me?" I sneer. "There wouldn't be a circle if it wasn't for me."

"I know. It's not like we've forgotten."

"So, what? Should I just show up at the Holloways' house one night? Sit around while you guys practice spells? Thanks, but no thanks."

Lexie shakes her head, visibly flustered. "Come on, Crystal, that's not all we do—"

"Oh really? Since when? Because I don't ever remember going to the beach and having a picnic with you guys, or hanging out at Bridget's house with everyone to watch a movie."

Lexie releases an exasperated groan, balling her fists as she stands. "Why are you being so difficult?"

"Why are you being so naïve?" I counter.

She throws up her hands. "I know what you're trying to do. You and Dana. Fox says she spends all of her free time with you."

Anger bubbles up in me. "And what exactly are you accusing me of?"

Lexie sputters. "I'm not accusing you of anything. I just..." She shakes her head. "I'm just worried."

I narrow my eyes. "You're worried? Well, don't bother troubling yourself over me."

"Don't be like that," Lexie grumbles, rolling her eyes. She takes in a breath, closing her eyes for a beat before releasing it. "I think it's time for you to come to terms with what happened to you."

"That's easy for you to say," I snap.

Her shoulders sag as the fight goes out of her. "What if you never get your magic back? What if this is just the way you are now? When will you finally accept it?"

The anger that's been simmering just under the surface boils over. Digging my nails into the flesh of my palms, I stalk across the room until my face is inches from hers. "I will never stop," I growl, my voice low. "Sure, it's easy for you to suggest, standing there with your magic intact. You can't even imagine what it's like to be me right now. Part of who I am is gone. You wonder why I haven't gotten back to my real life yet? Maybe because I'm not the same person. If I'm not a witch, I'm not me. So forgive me if I'm not adjusting like you want me to. There's no adjustment to this. So, no, I will not stop. I'll find a way. If you don't want to support me, fine. I don't need your help—I don't need anyone. And when I get my abilities back, you and the others will see I was right all along. I'll be stronger than ever, and you'll regret ever doubting me."

Lexie's eyes widen in shock, but I don't linger to enjoy the expression. Pivoting on my heel, I cross to the front door. I yank it open and call over my shoulder, "You can show yourself out."

I don't look back as I stalk across the lawn to my car. She'll see. Everyone will see. Dana and I are going to get our abilities back.

We have to.

Chapter Ten
Krissa

I enter the last number on the final page of inventory I've been working on for two shifts now. Although I usually enjoy the mindless, repetitive task of counting items in the store, I haven't been able to lose myself in the monotony as well as usual today. For once, being done with this particular assignment is a relief.

Jodi is at the register, cashing out a customer. She smiles as she converses with the older woman. There is an easiness in the way they banter back and forth that I envy. How long has it been since I was able to talk with someone like that? Even with Tucker and Griffin, I don't feel I'm that free, and they're really the only people I talk to anymore.

The customer waves at Jodi before crossing to the door. The bells tinkle as she steps out onto the sidewalk. For the moment, Jodi and I are alone.

My head down, I cross to my aunt and set the clipboard onto the counter. "I'm all done. What would you like me to work on next?"

Jodi doesn't respond right away, and against my better judgment I glance up at her. She's studying me, the way she has countless times before. If she were a psychic, I would be worried she were trying to read my thoughts. In a way, I suppose that's exactly what she's attempting, except she's reading my body language. After a beat, she sighs. "You're so industrious when you're here that I don't know if there's anything left to do. I never thought I'd say this, but maybe you need to not work quite so hard."

"If you don't want to pay me for doing nothing, I could leave early," I offer.

Jodi raises an eyebrow. "Why, you got plans tonight?"

I shake my head. Typically, on nights I work I just go home after my shift. Occasionally, I'll go to Griffin's, but he's working late tonight. Even though Tucker will probably be at his apartment, I won't go if Griffin isn't there.

"Your dad mentioned you were home after curfew again last night." There's no edge of accusation to Jodi's voice. She's simply relaying a fact.

I nod. "I didn't even have a curfew until he got back." I'm not telling her anything she doesn't already know. In fact, I overheard her talking with my dad after he instituted the new policy. She tried to convince him that I'd gone this long without a specific time to be home and everything had worked out fine. For his part, Dad had been polite, but he gently reminded his sister that I was his daughter, not hers.

Jodi's face goes thoughtful, like she's considering her next words carefully. "Until recently, a curfew was never necessary. You always came home at a decent hour on your own."

I bite back a groan. Did Dad put her up to this? He's not getting anywhere with me, so he sends in a replacement? I'm ready with my practiced defense. "How many times have I been late to school? Are my grades slipping?"

The questions are rhetorical, and Jodi doesn't bother answering them. "I'm just saying things have been different since you've been spending so much time with Griffin and Tucker."

I know she has a point, but I refuse to concede it. "It's not like hanging out with Griffin is anything new. Need I remind you, he's been a member of my circle as long as I have."

"Your circle?" Jodi's eyebrows arch. "Does your circle even exist anymore? I didn't think the witches had been meeting up since the binding spell was broken. And I haven't heard you talking about any of the psychics besides Tucker."

"If you have something to say, say it." I'm not in the mood to dance around the subject. If Jodi wants to know something, I wish she would just come out with it.

Jodi's face softens. I bristle at her expression. It's much too close to pity for my liking. When she talks, her gaze doesn't quite meet mine. "Look, I don't know all that happened that night. Your dad seems to think it's easier for everyone that way. All I know for sure is that something changed in you the night Seth died."

I do my best not to flinch at his name. She knows he's gone, of course. She may even assume the truth. But, so far as she's concerned, it was my dad's responsibility to get rid of him. He spent five years away from us so he could learn how to take on the combined powers of the psychics and witches in my circle. It was his plan to take Seth off guard by him being the one to cast the spell to trap him in a crystal once more. But things went sideways when Bess Taylor, who was inhabiting Crystal Jamison's body, told him our plan, ruining the element of surprise. Dad fought as hard as he could, but in the end, Seth was stronger. He was about to kill my father, and without the use of my abilities, I did the only thing I could. And I haven't regretted it for a second. That fact is the one that's so difficult to deal with. What kind of person kills someone without any remorse?

I know the answer: An evil person. That darkness lives inside me. Of course I haven't been able to go back to the girl I was before that moment. She's gone, and I don't know if I can ever get her back.

I realize I haven't responded. "What do you want me to say?" There's no use denying it. She's right. Telling her what I've done won't change anything. I'm not sure what she wants from me.

Jodi comes out from behind the register, moving until she stands in front of me. She reaches forward, brushing my upper arm with her fingertips. I can tell by the look in her eyes that she would like to do more—pull me into her arms, hold me, hug me—but she knows I won't let her. "I know you have your reasons for spending so much time with Griffin and Tucker. You don't do anything without a reason. But maybe it's time for you to reconnect with some of your other friends. I know Crystal already has a lot to deal with, and it might be awkward to talk with Fox, but may be you could spend some time with Lexie or Bridget."

I snort. I've never been particularly close with Bridget Burke or this reality's version of Lexie. I can't imagine going to either of them for any reason.

Seeming to realize this, Jodi presses her lips together. "How about Felix? The two of you seemed to be getting closer before everything went down. Or maybe Owen—"

I shake my head at this suggestion almost before it leaves her lips. I can't go to him the way I am. Since the day we met, he's been an unwavering light of goodness in my life. I can't inflict myself on him, not with the darkness that's festering inside me. And Felix, with his happy-go-lucky demeanor—how can I talk with him after what I've done?

Jodi opens her mouth to say something else, but before she can, the bells above the front door tinkle as a new customer walks in. The forty-something man is barely two steps into the shop before he's calling out a question in Jodi's direction. She holds my gaze for a beat longer before crossing to him, her hand indicating the direction they should go to find what he's looking for.

Although Jodi didn't officially say I could leave early, I take her distraction as an opportunity to do just that. I have no desire to continue this conversation once this man leaves.

What she doesn't realize is I've had this conversation numerous times in my own mind, and each time I've come to the same conclusion: My friends are better off without me in their lives. I'll hang around Griffin and Tucker for the companionship they provide, confident I won't negatively impact either one of them. Neither one possesses the purest of hearts, so I can expect them to accept me. Honestly, they are the only ones I can expect that from.

Chapter Eleven
Sasha

I scan the posts in yet another sub-forum, looking for any indication that someone in the thread actually knows what they're talking about. The laptop perched across my thighs is growing warm, creating a sheen of sweat between me and the machine. I should open the window overlooking the street, but the April air has a bite to it today that I'd rather not deal with.

I've lost track of how many discussion boards I've read in the last few days, each one more obscure than the last. After my lunch date with Anya and Elliot, I spent the evening piecing together memories of what I'd heard about the group with an interest in Bess Taylor. It took some creative online research, but eventually I came up with a name and a purpose. The group call themselves the Amaranthine Coven, and their driving desire is immortality.

Immortality. I actually didn't believe it when I first strung the pieces together. I figured I had something wrong. But then I saw something in a post from several years ago that got me thinking maybe I was right after all. There was a reference to Bess Taylor. The poster didn't mention her by name, but I knew the story well enough to know that's who he meant. She was referenced alongside Seth—although, again, he wasn't mentioned by name—and to my surprise, he wasn't the focus of the story. Instead, it was Bess who took center stage. According to this person, she was researching ways to prolong life, even to the point of living forever.

It wasn't until after I found this that I remembered a cautionary tale my mom told me once when I was little. I had been in town with Sasha and Misha when I met a little ordinary girl. She and I got to talking while my sisters weren't paying attention. When they saw me, they pulled me out of the store so fast I didn't get a chance to say goodbye to the girl. They yelled at me on the way home, but I didn't understand why. The girl had seemed nice. Maybe all my family's talk of the ordinary being so bad wasn't right. When I got home, Anya reported what happened to my mom. Instead of yelling, she simply sat me down and told me stories. I remember one only vaguely. It was about how questioning what we knew to be true could be dangerous. There was a time, generations ago, when a sect rose up within the Devoted. This group insisted that Seth was not the one we should be waiting for. They claimed that Bess Taylor was more important, that she had information that could benefit our group more than Seth ever could. They were cast out for their heresy.

But now that I'm researching, it seems that group may have become the modern Amaranthine Coven. And it seems that group is still waiting for Bess to return.

What they don't know is she already has. Even though she is no longer possessing Crystal Jamison, there's a chance Crystal may know the information they seek.

I tried to find the person who posted the story several years ago, but the trail quickly grew cold. That's why I'm searching through new forums, hoping to come across something more recent.

I'm about to close down this particular thread when something catches my eye. The reference is obscure, so vague I barely recognize it, but it's worth a shot. I click on the username and type out a direct message. I keep my inquiry brief and veiled, just in case this person is not what I think he is.

No sooner do I hit send than the doorknob to my apartment begins to twist. My muscles tense, ready for action, but then the door opens to reveal Elliot. My posture relaxes and I immediately feel foolish. Who else would be at my door? All this thinking about the Amaranthine has me on edge.

Elliot grins, holding up a brown paper takeout bag. "I hope

you're hungry." He closes the door behind him, heading to my kitchen before I even have a chance to respond.

I shove the laptop's screen down toward the keyboard and set it on the floor, edging it under the dinged end table. I spring to my feet and cross to Elliot, but his eyes look past me.

"What are you up to?" he asks, not quite hiding a note of suspicion.

I roll my eyes, forcing what I hope looks like a good-natured grin. As much as I don't want to lie to him, I'm not ready to tell him the truth. "Maybe I'm shopping for your birthday."

He pokes his tongue between his lips as he pulls down two plates from the nearly empty cupboard. "Yeah, I buy that," he mutters sarcastically.

"What's the occasion?" I ask, hoping the subject change takes. I've never been good at lying to him.

"No occasion. Can't I just come and have dinner with my best friend?"

I shove his shoulder playfully before opening up the brown bag. Chinese food. I pull out the cartons and open each one. Elliot never orders the same combination twice, so I have to inspect all his selections before spooning portions out onto my plate. I finally settle on some kind of beef dish in a brown sauce. Elliot mixes some of the beef with a chicken dish over a bed of white rice. Once our plates are made, he starts for the small card table. I don't know where he intends to sit, as it's still covered with a variety of books and papers. Wordlessly, I lead him over to the couch.

He follows without questioning my seating choice. We spend a few minutes in companionable silence as we apply ourselves to our meals. Half the food on his plate is gone before he speaks. "Lunch went well, I think. Don't you?"

I take my time finishing my mouthful of food before swallowing. "Yeah. It was nice."

Elliot nods thoughtfully. "I'm sure I don't have to tell you how happy Anya is that you finally came around."

I do my best not to shift at his words. It's not so much that Anya is happy that makes me uncomfortable, it's that I know this change in me is also making Elliot happy. In truth, I'm surprised he can't tell my interest in reconnecting with my sister isn't genuine. Maybe he wants it so badly he refuses to see what's right in front of him.

The laptop dings. The sound is probably signaling a response from the forum poster. My fingers itch to grab the computer to see what he said. But I can't do that, not now, not in front of Elliot. His posture tells me he's already curious about the sound. If I jump to check the message, there's no way he'll let me get away with not telling him what's up.

I want to tell him. I want to tell him badly. But I can't. If I'm going to have my revenge, Elliot can't know—at least not yet. I have to be sure he won't try to stop me. And as much as it pains me, I'm not right now.

To stall for time, I take a bite of beef and rice and roll my eyes. "I'll never understand why so many websites have sounds embedded in them," I say after swallowing.

He cocks his head. "What kind of site are you on that's making noises?"

"A naughty one, clearly." I offer my best salacious grin. As anticipated, Elliot's cheeks pinken. For as unsqueamish as he is in general, he's never failed to express discomfort if ever I mention anything even remotely having to do with sex. Certain words are even off-limits if I don't want to upset his delicate sensibilities: naughty, spank, lick, moist. Even in the most innocent of situations—as in, "This cake is so moist!"—Elliot shifts in his seat and averts his eyes until enough words are spoken or time has passed to sufficiently distance him from the offending syllable.

Attempting to prove I haven't affected him, he lifts another forkful of food to his mouth, but he can't make himself follow through. He lowers the fork to his plate again, pursing his lips. "You're just cruel," he grumbles.

"Hey, you asked," I say innocently, feigning ignorance as to the source of his irritation. Goodness, I've missed him. These last months when our contact was limited and our interactions stilted was more difficult than I let myself admit. I'm so glad to have him back. I'm itching to tell him what I have planned, but now's not the time. First, I have to get him to realize that he wants this as much as I do. He's so busy trying to forget about the life we've lived up until now that he's ignoring the fact that we have a duty to destroy those responsible for obliterating our hopes, for killing our families.

He's not there yet. I understand. Elliot's always been more the sensitive type. He barely spoke for weeks after his uncle Nate was cast out of the community. I didn't have that reaction when they sent Misha away. He even took the news of Anya's death—false as it turned out to be—harder than I did.

But eventually he always came around. I have to believe he will this time, too.

After finally managing a few more mouthfuls, Elliot excuses himself to my tiny bathroom. As soon as the door clicks behind him, I snatch my laptop off the floor and tilt it on my lap so I can read the screen without moving it. Elliot is annoyingly observant, and while I'm relatively certain I can put the computer back in its previous position, I doubt I could get the exact angle of the screen right. Instead, I hunch and squint to make sense of the glowing words and glide my fingertip over the touchpad to direct the cursor to the envelope icon. Seconds after my quick tap, a new page loads and I scan the message. A smile curls my lips by the time I get to the end. From the poster's response, I'm pretty sure I've found what I'm looking for. My fingers itch to send a quick reply, but a flush from down the hall alerts me to the fact my time is, for the moment, at an end. I hurriedly replace to computer in its former location on the floor and am working on a mouthful of food by the time Elliot returns.

He eyes me curiously as he reclaims his seat. "What's up? Why are you smiling?"

I had hoped my expression would remain neutral, but, again, Elliot notices things. Besides, he's a complete expert on my face, so any change must be obvious to him. I swallow my food and offer a small shrug. "I'm just glad you're here." While it's not the reason I'm smiling, it's also not a lie.

Elliot stretches his hand across the space dividing us and squeezes my knee. "I'm glad, too."

After our meals are finished, Elliot takes the liberty of washing our dishes and stowing the leftovers in my nearly bare fridge. He insists we watch a movie. I can't think of a logical reason to decline, so the two of us crowd around the screen of his phone since I don't have a TV.

I should be enjoying this time, but the message awaiting my reply tugs at the back of my mind. With a quick reply, I'll set in motion a plan that has the potential to put one of Krissa's friends in danger. And if there's anything I learned about her in the time Seth had us watching over her, it's that Krissa will stop at nothing to protect those she cares about.

That flaw will be her undoing. I'll make sure of it.

Chapter Twelve
Crystal

Although my mother raises an eyebrow at the book-shaped package that arrives for me in the mail, she doesn't ask what it is. For my sixteenth birthday, my parents gave me a debit card linked to the account they put my weekly allowance in. Since then, it hasn't been unheard of for me to receive things I've ordered in the mail. So long as I don't overdraw, they've never had a problem with it.

As much as I want to take the package back into my room and scour the contents as soon as Mom hands it to me, I know better than to appear too eager. That's a sure invitation for questions. Instead, I feign interest at small talk as Mom prepares dinner. I chat at the dining room table when the family sits down to eat. I even stick around through two sitcoms after the meal before finally excusing myself to my room.

The package sits atop my desk exactly where I left it. I know I should spend some time working on additional missing math assignments, but the lure of what has arrived for me is too strong. Shoving the math book out of the way, I exploit every available inch of desktop. I rip open the brown paper packaging and slide the leather-bound volume into the empty space.

It's not the first grimoire I've purchased, but it's the first that has the same feel as the one passed through the Taylor line. One had appeared to be nearly brand-new, simply distressed to look aged, and another was literally a store-bought journal with fluffy kitties on the front. Needless to say, neither of them had been particularly helpful. Another seemed more legitimate, but it had not provided any useful information. However, as I run my fingers over the cracked leather, a thrum of anticipation courses through me. This one will help me, I know it. It has to.

I crack the spine gently, not wanting to dislodge any of the yellowing pages. Some are so thin and brittle I worry I might cause them to crumble as I turn them. Some of the spells are in languages I can't decipher, and others are so worn with age they're impossible to read. But the majority of the book is mercifully intact.

I pore over each page, reading through commentaries of people who are long since dead, hoping one of them has the solution to my plight. Many of the spells are similar to ones I know already from my family's grimoire. Others are so obscure as to be irrelevant for my life. And still others make my skin crawl to read. One claims to provide the caster with the life essence of another person. Another promises to inflict horrific pain on a person who has done the caster wrong.

Just what kind of grimoire did I buy? Are there really people who cast spells like these? While it's true that I don't have the purest track record when it comes to my own use of magic, I never actually hurt someone with a spell. Scared them, sure, but that's entirely different.

It's long after my parents call good night through the door and after my eyes have already gone scratchy with the need to sleep that one spell in particular catches my attention. It's a siphoning spell. According to the commentary, the purpose is to allow one person to draw abilities from another. As I read the incantation silently, a shiver goes through my body. This is the kind of spell Seth used on the Devoted. After I woke up from my possession, I was filled in on many aspects of that night—one of which included how Krissa's dad fought Seth, and how he couldn't get the upper hand due to the fact that Seth was drawing energy from the members of the Devoted. Lexie described what it was like to watch person after person collapse to the ground, dead, after he drained everything from them.

I could never use a spell like that. I could never kill someone so that I could have abilities.

But the only reason the Devoted died was because Seth was battling with Krissa's dad. At the time, I asked why the Devoted would allow Seth such unrestricted use of their abilities. Anya explained that in addition to the Devoted being prepared to do anything for Seth, the siphoning spell wasn't inherently dangerous. If Seth hadn't needed to heal himself over and over again during the battle, he wouldn't have had to draw such a mass of energy.

So really, the siphoning spell—in its purest form—would work more like the anchoring spell the witches used on Seth's crystal or the binding spell Jodi's circle performed on us: It would allow a person to draw extra energy from a source outside herself. Technically, I suppose it's really not that bad.

I skim the spell again. It's just an incantation—no herbs or stones to charge beforehand, no complicated potion. Just words. Just simple words that would allow a person to access the abilities of others.

I'm reciting the words before I've made the conscious decision to try the spell. I stumble through the unfamiliar vocabulary a few times before the incantation smooths on my tongue. I murmur it quietly so as not to disturb my parents, but as I say it, excitement builds in me. If I could just borrow the abilities of the other witches in town, I could get back to being myself. If I just draw a little bit from each one, it's possible no one will even notice.

I repeat the word again and again, waiting for something to happen, for some tingle or flash to alert me that the spell has worked. But this time, as every time before, nothing changes.

I close the book with more force than is strictly necessary, and the pages crinkle their discontent. I almost don't care. Part of me wants to light the useless grimoire on fire. But I know it's not the book's fault. It's me. Of course the spell won't work for me: I'm not a witch.

Maybe it's a good thing. Am I really to the point where I would be okay stealing magic from my friends without their consent? What does that say about me?

Lexie's words echo through my head. What if I never get my

abilities back? What will it take for me to accept that new reality?

Maybe I should stop now, give up before I get too desperate. But even as the thought crosses my mind, I know I won't—I can't. There has to be something I haven't tried yet. There has to be a way.

Chapter Thirteen
Krissa

If dread is how I usually approach the school day, today I'm experiencing a double dose.

As much as I try to ignore it, the conversation Jodi and I had continues to echo through my mind. I've fought against it for months now, but maybe she has a point. Maybe it is time to reconnect with my friends—expand my circle to include more than just Griffin and Tucker. Perhaps I'm not giving them enough credit. I've never really considered Felix, Bria, or West to be weak.

Although West is in my first hour, I chicken out and don't approach him. Lexie is also in that class, but she and I were never close in this reality, so it doesn't even cross my mind to try with her. Owen is in second hour, but I have no intention of talking to him. As much as I'm willing to try to reconnect with my friends, he is off-limits. At least for now. I don't know how I'll react if I find out for sure he's with that girl I saw him with the other day. Until I know more, I should leave well enough alone.

Both West and Felix are in my Spanish class, yet I opt to sit in back with Tucker like I have for months. Halfway through class, Tucker taps my arm with the eraser end of his pencil.

I cock an eyebrow. "Yeah?" My voice comes out more irritated than I would have liked.

An expression flits over his face, as if my behavior has confirmed his suspicion. "If you keep watching them like that, they're gonna start thinking you're stalking them or something."

I try to arrange my face into a politely confused expression, but

I can tell by the glint in Tucker's eyes he doesn't buy it. Unsure of exactly what to tell him, I turn my full attention to the Spanish book in front of me. It's still closed on my desk, so my illusion of going back to work fails.

"What's up? You finally going to talk to them?"

It's definitely a question. He hasn't read me—not like he could anyway, thanks to the charm I'm wearing. He's genuinely curious. The crease around his eyes shows his concern. A pang of guilt stabs through my core. Just months ago, my perception of Tucker was that he was violent, dangerous, and cared little for anyone but himself. And while it may be true he doesn't expand his bubble of caring much beyond himself, I'm surprised to learn it extends to me. How have I not noticed this before? When did it happen? All this time, I've been hanging around him largely for an escape. I figured someone like him wouldn't be bothered by someone like me. How did I not notice him beginning to regard me as a friend?

I chew on my lower lip before hazarding a glance at him. "Do you think it's a bad idea?"

He regards me for a moment before responding. "I think it might be a step in the right direction."

Before I can ask him what he considers to be the right direction, the bell rings to dismiss class. I stand quickly, my eyes following Felix and West's progress out the door. At once I feel silly: It's not like I don't know where they're going.

If I'm going to do this, I may as well get it over in one fell swoop. West, Bria, and Felix all sit at the same lunch table. After getting his memories from my old timeline, Owen spent about a month sitting with them. But after I stopped sitting there and it was clear I wasn't coming back, he drifted away. Now he sits with his friends from the track team. Not for the first time, I wish I'd been paying more attention to him. Does that Laurie girl sit at his table? I have no idea because I've been content to hunker down at a table in back with Tucker, keeping my head down and not paying much attention to what was happening around me.

I still haven't made my way up the aisle. Tearing my eyes from West and Felix, I turn my attention to my desk. The day's assignment sits there, completely unfinished. I'm fairly certain we were supposed to turn it in at the end of class. With a sigh, I touch my pen to the paper, reciting a well-practiced spell that uses the information in my mind to fill in the answers. I haven't been paying as much attention as I should lately, so I know some of the answers will be gibberish. Still, it's better than nothing.

Tucker is at my elbow as I start toward the teacher's desk. "Pretty sure I'm gonna cut out now," he says, keeping his voice low.

I place my assignment in the turn-in tray before glancing at him. "Yeah? I thought you had a test next hour?"

He shrugs as the two of us exit the classroom and join in the stream of bodies heading down the hall. "I'll be back for that. I just won't be in the lunchroom today. So, you know, there's no need to keep me company."

I roll my eyes at the obviousness of his words. He doesn't want to give me an excuse not to go sit with my old friends. Again, I'm surprised at how well he knows me. Although for the moment I'm resolved to go sit with them, it's entirely possible that by the time I get down to the lunchroom that resolve will have cracked and I'll find myself back in my comfort zone, away from everyone. Of course, I would tell myself it was so as not to abandon Tucker. So instead, he's abandoning me. Before I can respond, he bumps my shoulder with his and takes off toward the nearest stairwell.

I take more time at my locker than is strictly necessary. By the time I've traded my Spanish supplies for my paper-bag lunch, the bell to indicate I should already be at my next destination has already rung.

As I walk toward the lunchroom, I play the scene out in my mind. However, my brain can't seem to get past the point where I sit down at the table. For a moment, I consider slipping off my well-crafted bracelet charm so I can reach out and brush the minds of my former friends. However, in addition to the fact that allowing myself to feel their thoughts and emotions would likely open a floodgate I'm ill-prepared to handle, the three of them are psychics and would no doubt sense my intrusion. It's not worth the gamble. I can't imagine they'd be pleased if my first contact with them in months was a brain scan. No, I'll just have to do this the old-fashioned way.

My pace is so slow as I emerge from the hall into the commons that connects to the cafeteria that one of the room monitors warns me to hurry along or she'll be forced to give me a detention. While I don't think she really has that power, I do pick up my pace. If I allow myself to dawdle any longer, it's likely the period will be over by the time I reach the tables.

When I round the lunch line, the table I seek comes into view. Felix and Bria are both laughing, presumably at something West said. I've missed seeing them smile like that. The only time I really see any of them anymore is in class, and that seldom affords them the opportunity to laugh with abandon.

I stop so abruptly that someone behind me collides with my back. He grumbles profanities as he steadies himself and walks around me, but I barely hear him. I take in a deep, steadying breath before hitching a smile onto my face and starting purposefully toward the table. This will work. After all, these people are my friends. They'll probably be happy to see me. Happy I'm finally coming back to myself. I'll smile and I'll laugh, and I'll keep the darkness that lurks in the corners of my mind at bay. I won't taint them.

West says something else when I'm still too far away to catch it, but it results in Felix and Bria hooting with laughter. Felix bangs his fist on the table, and Bria wipes beneath her eyes. For a moment, I can imagine this is any other day, that I'm just joining them like I did yesterday and the day before. The smile on my face softens, becoming more natural, as I stride closer before claiming the empty spot to Bria's right.

I open my mouth, ready to ask what's so funny, but before I can, the laughter dies from their faces. Instead, I'm greeted by looks of shock. Felix's expression seems tinged with anger. My insides go cold as the smile freezes and cracks on my face. Whatever reaction I was expecting, this certainly is not it. Have I done something to offend them? Should I have asked before I took a seat? I try to swallow, but my throat is dry. It takes three tries before I manage. In all that time, not one of them has spoken. I don't even think they blinked.

I release a shaky breath. "So," I begin, my voice thin, "what's so funny?"

I wait for a response, my gaze drifting from one face to another, but their shock seems so complete it has stilled their tongues. I gulp. Apparently this is all on me. I wish my brain had been able to come up with a plausible chain of events once I sat down at this table. Now, it's all I can do to find something to say. I turn to Bria. "Are you ready for the test in math?" It's a ridiculously lame topic, but it's all I can think of.

She doesn't take the bait. She swivels her gaze to Felix, as if waiting for his permission before speaking. Which doesn't make sense. It's not as if Felix is the leader of the group.

It takes a second before my brain comprehends what's happening. Felix and I were the closest. Bria is gauging his reaction to my appearance. In fact, I realize with a jolt, the three of them may be engaged in mental conversation right now. It's possible they're processing my appearance together, just beyond my level of awareness. Not for the first time today, I question the wisdom of having cut off the part of my abilities that allows me to sense other people. If I only knew how they were feeling right now, it might ease the tight knot of tension tying itself around my insides. But letting them in runs the risk of letting everything in, so I choose not to break the dam.

I turn to West. "How do you think you did on the essay?" I ask, referring to the assignment we turned in earlier this week. I wish my questions weren't so impersonal, but beyond schoolwork, I have no idea what's been going on in their lives. Guilt floods me. I should've been paying more attention. Even in my self-imposed isolation, I could have watched them more closely to see what was going on with them.

Like Bria, West doesn't respond, although his mouth twitches like he wants to. Again I get the sense he's holding back, waiting for Felix.

With effort, I turn to look at him. He and I were so close. Once I found myself in this reality, he was the first person I really connected with. He was the first one who accepted me for being me, not for being who everyone thought I was. He's the only one I told my secret to, that I wasn't from this timeline. After what happened with Seth, I shut him out completely. For the first time, I wonder what that did to him. With everything going on in my head—my lack of guilt over cold-blooded murder—I figured it was best for everyone if they didn't have to deal with me. But what if I made the wrong choice? What if I hurt Felix by shutting him out? What if he doesn't understand it was for his own good?

I swallow, catching his gaze with mine. His hazel eyes are clouded over, and I'm pretty sure I'm glad I don't know what he's thinking. "Is it okay that I'm sitting here?" I figure there's no use trying for small talk with him. I might as well cut to the chase.

Felix's jaw works like he's chewing on possible responses. He's quiet for so long I'm convinced he's not going to say anything. The muscles in my legs tighten, readying my body to stand, when he finally speaks. "You think it's that easy?"

I'm not sure what he means. Am I supposed to do something before I can sit here? Do I have to give them an apology? I don't know what he expects.

Before I can formulate a question, he's talking again. "What, you thought you could just come and sit down and pretend like it's a normal day? It's been months, Krissa. You haven't spoken to us in months."

In the silence following his words, I know I'm expected to mount a defense. They want me to explain what's been going on, but I can't find the words. What explanation can I possibly give that would be good enough to cover over the pain in his eyes? "I needed time," I begin lamely.

At this, West snorts. "From us. You needed time from us, but you run to be friends with Griffin and Tucker?"

I press my lips together. "You don't understand—"

He doesn't let me finish. "Damn right I don't understand. Did you forget that during the binding spell I was linked to Griffin? I know what kind of person he is, Krissa. He's a dick. He only cares about himself. Barely cares about his own brother. But you decided he was the person you needed after everything that happened? What made you think he could care about you more than we could?" He snorts. "And don't get me started on Tucker

Ingram."

I rankle at his words. Although it's true that just months ago I would have agreed with his assessment, I don't like the way he's talking about them. Griffin and Tucker, the two who accepted me into their circle without hesitation or expectations. I know what kind of people they are, but they were there when I needed them. Is West really going to hold that against them? "If you'll just let me explain..."

The three of them watch me with eyebrows raised. When I don't continue, Bria cocks her head to the side. "Please, go ahead. I'd love to hear this."

What can I tell them? What can I say to make them understand, to erase the hurt from their eyes? If I had been a complete recluse and closed everyone out, would they be reacting like this? Is it the fact that I chose people who are not them that's making them angry right now? I don't know if I can give them a satisfactory answer, so I dodge the question. "Can we just start over? Just forget the last four months happened?"

At this suggestion, Felix surprises me by smiling. "Just forget it?" he asks, his tone light. "Yeah, that seems easy. Just forget how you ignored us for the last four months. Just forget how any time we reached out, you shut us down. Forget that while we wanted to be your friends, you chose Tucker and Griffin over us again and again. Sounds simple." He shrugs, and while his tone remains light, his eyes are cold as ice. "Then again, of course you'd think it's easy. After all, it was easy for you to forget us, to completely disregard what we all meant to each other."

I'm struck by the pain in his voice. How can he think this is been easy for me? I haven't been keeping my distance because I wanted to; I've been doing it to keep them safe. I wish I could just push that knowledge into his mind, but I know I can't. Especially not now—I don't want to open myself up to feel what he's feeling. It might break me.

I stand on shaky legs. "This was a mistake. I'm sorry." Without waiting for response, I start away. I'm not entirely sure where I'm going to go, but anywhere has to be better than staying here.

The usual deafening roar of the cafeteria ebbs in my ears,

replaced by a rushing sound. I clench my fists, my nails biting into my palms. I've experienced this sensation before. Back before I knew what I was, sometimes my abilities would boil up inside me until I could no longer contain them. When they erupted, invariably something would break. That hasn't happened since just after I moved here, since Jodi told me the truth about what I am. And I don't want anything to happen now. If I can just get away, clear my head, things will be okay. I'm halfway through the cafeteria when a hand lands on my arm. I jerk back instinctively, prepared to run away, to find somewhere to hide, but the owner of the arm jumps in front of me before I can. Bria's face is tight, worried. Her lower lip trembles for a second before her mouth opens. "You forgot your lunch." She holds out the brown paper bag, but she doesn't extend her arm fully. She keeps it close to her body, as if unsure what my reaction will be.

I reach forward tentatively. When I take it from her, I'm careful not to touch her fingers, although whether it's for her benefit or mine, I'm not sure. "Thanks." I won't eat it. There's no way I could keep food down at this point, and she has to know that.

Once relieved of the bag, she doesn't immediately leave. She rocks on the balls of her feet, tugging at the hem of her short skirt as if she can command the fabric to stretch and cover her ample thighs more fully. "Give him time." Her voice is so low I'm almost convinced I imagined it. "I'm sorry about how Felix reacted, but it was stupid just sitting down like that. I get that you needed time, and I don't hold your choice in friends against you, but Felix... I'll talk to him. I can't promise anything, but I'll talk to him."

Without waiting for a response, she pivots and scurries back to the table.

It takes several seconds before I can convince my body to take another step. It's slow going at first, but eventually I'm moving at a normal pace. I drop my lunch into a garbage bin on the way out.

She's right. It was stupid of me to think I could just slide back into their lives. But is she right about the other part? Will Felix ever accept me again? The fact that she came after me suggests she'd be willing to let me back into her life, and West may be of similar mind, but I'm not convinced Felix will ever forgive me. He and I were too close when everything went down.

And if he can't forgive me, is there any hope that Owen and I can ever reconnect? Maybe what I feared has already come to pass—I've waited too long. Some wounds don't heal, and it's possible I've already inflicted them.

***

When I first came to Clearwater, Owen offered to bring me to Jodi's shop after school. After I messed with the timeline, it was Felix who took on that job. But things have changed again. For Christmas, my parents got me a car. It's a decade old, but it's in good condition. Sometimes I wonder if they did it less for the convenience and more in an attempt to make me happy. Or there's the alternative—neither of them wanted to be bothered trying to make polite conversation with me in the car.

I pull into my usual space in the parking lot behind the shop. I was on complete autopilot the second half of the day. If it wasn't for magic, I'm sure I would've failed the math test I asked Bria about. Even with it, I'll be lucky to pass with even a D-.

I'm not sure if I'm glad to have the distraction of the shop today or not. If I didn't have to work, I know for certain I wouldn't be headed home. Instead, I'd probably be on my way to Griffin's house now. But would that really be the best thing? After a failed attempt to reconnect with my old friends, is it wise to run straight to one of the people I left them for?

No, it's best that I'm here today. The shop has been the one constant in my life. I pull open the back door and am greeted by the familiar aromas of the different herbs mingling in the air. I can still remember the first time I entered the store. Jodi had just told me that the shop would be mine one day, if I wanted it, and I was overwhelmed by the strange names of the herbs, stones, and homeopathic aids. I couldn't have known then what a comfort this place would become.

I stop in the employees-only area to swipe my timecard and grab my name badge. Before I'm able to head out onto the floor, Jodi emerges from the row of high shelves, a box balanced in her hands. She offers a grin. "Perfect. I was hoping you'd get here so I wouldn't have to restock the shelves." A measure of her jovial demeanor evaporates when she glimpses my face. I watch an internal struggle play out across her features. I've seen it so many times in the last few months that I almost feel I can hear her thoughts. She's unsure whether she should ask me what's going on. So often her questions are met with a noncommittal noise and a shrug from me, it's barely worth the effort to form the words, but still she feels duty-bound as my aunt to not give up.

I plan to do what I always do—give a vague answer and get to work. There's no sense in troubling her. But even before she speaks, my resolve begins to crack.

Jodi approaches me slowly, the way a person would draw near a frightened animal. She hands over the box of homeopathic pellets gingerly. "You okay? How was your day?"

I open my mouth, ready to tell her everything's fine, but somehow the syllables get mixed up on my tongue. "It was a disaster." The words tumble out of my mouth before I can stop them. "I did what you suggested—I tried to talk with Felix and West and Bria. They didn't want anything to do with me."

Jodi gently tugs the box from my hands and sets it on the low coffee table in front of the worn couch I've spent so many breaks on. She lifts her arms like she intends to pull me into a hug but thinks better of it. Instead she allows her hands to land gently on my shoulders. "Oh, honey. I'm sorry it didn't work out."

The embarrassment and frustration that's been bubbling just beneath the surface for the last few hours boils over and morphs into blazing anger. I take a step back, far enough away so she can't touch me anymore. "You should be sorry. This is all your fault. You let me believe they still cared. Well, you're wrong, they don't. So I'll thank you to stay out of my life from now on."

Jodi shrinks back from my words, but her face hardens. "I get that you're upset, but don't turn this on me. You spent four months shutting those kids out. The least you can do is give them some time."

Her words take the fight out of me. I release a shaky breath and move on unsteady legs toward the couch. I collapse onto it, joined moments later by Jodi. "It's hopeless," I murmur. "Maybe it's for the best. It's not like I deserve their friendship anyway."

Jodi flinches as if I've just insulted her. She reaches toward me but doesn't make contact. She leaves her hand on the cushion in the void that separates us. "I still don't know why you feel that way, but I promise you if you want their friendship, you deserve it. Maybe you just have to prove it."

I snort. "Yeah, easier said than done. How do I prove something like that?"

"Through action." Hesitation flickers across her features. "I think Crystal needs help. She's in here all the time. It's obvious she hasn't given up on the idea of getting her magic back, and I'm really afraid of what it's doing to her. The longer she holds out hope, the harder it's going to be to accept the inevitable." She closes her eyes and releases a breath. "I would say something, but I don't think it's my place. Besides, I don't think Crystal would listen to me anyway."

"What does this have to do with me?"

The ghost of a smile flickers across Jodi's face. "Maybe you could talk with her. You could try to help her come to terms with who she is now. Who knows? Maybe helping her will help you come to terms, too."

The tinkle of bells announces the arrival of a new customer. Jodi reaches forward quickly to squeeze my hand before she stands to head out onto the floor. Instead of Jodi's suggestion giving me hope, it only makes me feel worse. Of course I knew Crystal lost her abilities, but I had no idea she was still desperate to reclaim them. What kind of a friend am I that I didn't know that?

The answer is obvious: A bad one. I've been a terrible friend to everyone who has meant anything to me. Maybe Jodi's right. Maybe the way to prove myself is through actions. I'll talk to Crystal. I'll do whatever I can to help her adjust—even if I have no idea what to say.

Chapter Fourteen

Sasha

I pull into the parking lot of an Allegro Bread two towns over from Clearwater. I can't help wondering, if this guy is really who he says he is, why he would choose such an overcrowded, common place as this for our meeting. But as it's the only lead I have, I climb out the car and make my way inside.

I scan the place for him as I walk in, even though he said he'd find me. I'm not sure how he will, since he didn't ask me for any distinguishing information about myself, but I suppose if he is able to find me it'll go toward proving he really is Amaranthine. Bypassing the line, I search for an empty table, finally finding one tucked in the front corner. The two-person table is cozy, and I imagine a casual onlooker might suspect I'm meeting a date. But he's not, not even close. I'm only interested in him so far as he can wreak havoc in Krissa's life.

The restaurant is buzzing with activity, just as the one I met Elliot and Anya in had been. There are mothers with babies and toddlers, retired folks chatting loudly and laughing, businesspeople clearly on lunch break. Maybe the benefit of meeting at a place like this is the anonymity of a crowd. We won't stick out here.

I can't help scanning each new arrival as the doors open. The person I traded messages with seemed very interested in the information I was promising, but he may not be the one I'm meeting today. If I've really made contact with the Amaranthine, I could be meeting someone high up in the coven.

A harried-looking twenty-something mother walks in, bouncing an infant on her hip. Her glazed eyes sweep the room until they land on a familiar form. She waves her tired hand and is greeted by one in return. Clearly she's not the one I'm waiting for. A man in his late thirties comes in next, dressed all in black and giving off a beatnik vibe. I straighten. It's possible he's the one. But when he joins the line of patrons waiting to order without so much as a glance around the room, it becomes clear he's not.

My foot taps impatiently. Maybe I'm wrong. Surely if I had really made contact with members of the clan obsessed with the information Bess Taylor possessed, whoever they sent to learn what I know would be punctual—early, even. I check the time on my phone and resolve to leave if no one approaches within the next five minutes.

"Anyone sitting here?"

The voice makes me start. In the few seconds it took for me to check the time, a man in his mid-twenties appeared before me. He's tall, with broad shoulders, dressed in expensive-looking jeans and a charcoal button-down shirt. His chocolate-brown eyes glitter. It takes a moment to find my voice. "Actually, I'm waiting for someone."

Instead of moving away, the stranger pulls out the seat opposite me and sits, resting his elbows on the table and lacing his fingers. "I know."

My brain struggles to catch up. Is this him? Or does he think I'm someone else? I've heard of blind dates before. Could this guy think I'm someone he met on some dating site? What if the person I'm really waiting for is here now and doesn't realize I am who he's looking for because this guy is sitting with me? I said I'd be alone. What if I blow my chance at a meeting because this guy is trying to pick me up? "No, really. I have a very important meeting, so I'd appreciate it if you'd find somewhere else to sit."

The man cocks his head, studying me. I do my best not to blink under the intensity of his dark gaze. "I told you I'd find you, didn't I?"

His words press in on me. "Wait, you're him?" I appraise him once more. Would a group like this really send someone so young, so inexperienced, to meet about the information I have? I assumed I'd be meeting someone with more seniority. Maybe I was wrong after all. Maybe this guy isn't who I think he is.

He studies me in a way that makes me feel like he can read my thoughts. His gaze makes me uncomfortable, which is really saying something, considering I grew up with psychics who could do just that. He extends a hand across the table. "Brody Ford."

I stare at his upturned palm, but I don't place my hand in his. "Why do I have the feeling I'm not being taken very seriously?"

Brody's brow knits. "Why is that?"

I gesture to him. "Why else would they send a rookie?"

Brody flashes a smile and ducks his head as if I've given him a compliment. "I'm older than I look." He retracts his hand and casts a glance at the buzzing semi-chaos surrounding us. "It's amazing, isn't it? All these people, going about their small lives, never knowing how insignificant they are. Never knowing all that life could hold. But you know all about that, don't you, Sasha?"

I shiver at his use of my name. We didn't exchange them in our messages. I lean across the table. "You're psychic?"

His half-smile gives away nothing. "You think I wouldn't do some research before coming to this meeting? I had to know I wasn't going to be wasting my time." He leans back in his chair, relaxing an arm across the back and bringing his right ankle up to rest on his left knee. "Are you ready to prove to me I'm right? Prove I haven't wasted my time?"

Although his posture suggests relaxation, there's something in his demeanor that makes it clear he's not one to be trifled with. And despite the fact that he still doesn't look a day above twenty-five, he somehow gives off the aura of someone much older. I'm not sure how I didn't notice before. "I come from the Devoted. I heard a story once about how you and your people were looking for information Bess Taylor had before she died."

He nods. "I knew all this before I got here." Although nothing about his casual posture has changed, the air around him seems to charge with irritation. "You said you have some information we're looking for. I'd really like to know it." There's the barest hint of threat in his tone.

I swallow, hating that his gaze flicks down to my lips, my throat. I don't know the last time I felt so exposed, so weak. Although nothing in his behavior is threatening, I can't help feeling he could easily put me in danger. "I don't actually have the information myself," I say quickly.

Brody shifts, planting both feet on the ground as if ready to get up and leave. "I'm not in the habit of playing games."

I stretch a hand toward him, pulling back before actually making contact with his skin. "Neither am I. I don't have the information, but I know someone who does."

Brody relaxes, but just slightly. It's clear I have his attention for another few moments.

"I know you've been searching. I know you think Bess had information she wasn't able to pass on before she died."

He makes a circular motion with his hand, urging me to hurry up.

I draw back my shoulders and straighten my spine, trying to make it clear I'm not accustomed to being rushed. I fight the part of me urging to slow down just because he's treating me like I'm playing games. "What if I told you there was a way to access Bess's memories? To find out what it is she took to the grave?"

Brody's dark eyes narrow and he licks his lips. I'm not sure if he's even conscious of doing it, but the tell is obvious. I've got his full attention now. "If that were the case, I'd tell you I'm very interested. This is something my brethren and I have been searching for for generations. I'd like to know why you're so confident you can accomplish this when we haven't been able to."

The next part is tricky. This group split away from the Devoted because they didn't believe what we did about Seth and his return. What I'm about to share will only underscore that his group wasn't entirely wrong in breaking off. I try to swallow, but my throat has gone dry. I wish I'd bought an overpriced coffee drink before I sat down. "I assume you know Seth returned," I begin tentatively.

He nods slowly, only once. I wait for him to say something—some snide remark about how he didn't make it long, or how the world doesn't seem changed, but nothing comes. The lump in my throat begins to dissolve. "He met a girl, a relative of

Bess Taylor, and he somehow implanted her consciousness into this girl's mind."

Brody shifts in his seat, straightening as he leans toward me. "Are you saying she's back? Are you saying I can go talk to this girl, the one who knows what Bess knew?"

"Not exactly."

Brody's demeanor changes at once. Everything about him darkens, as if he'd be willing to snap my neck in an instant. "I'm not fond of riddles," he murmurs, his voice low and dangerous.

I fight to keep my eyes from scanning the vicinity. Surely he wouldn't hurt me here in front of all these witnesses. Then again, he's an unknown quantity. I assumed he was a psychic, but he hasn't confirmed that. If he's not, it's possible he brought others with him, despite our mutual assurances we'd be alone. How much would it take for a strong psychic or two to block Brody and me from the minds of the nearby patrons? "It's not a riddle," I say, pleased when my voice doesn't quaver. "When the girl's circle found out what happened, they did an exorcism. Bess's consciousness isn't in her anymore."

Brody presses his palms into the table and makes to stand. "I don't know what you're playing at, but—"

I cover one of his hands with my own. "I'm not playing at anything, I promise. I want to help you. I want you to find what you looking for." I squeeze my eyes closed. This is the part I was hoping I wouldn't have to say, the part that twists my stomach and presses heavily on my soul. "Seth is gone. Everything I waited for my whole life... It's all gone. There's no way I can bring him back. But if there's a way I can help you, I want to do it." I hold my breath, waiting as his eyes bore into me. If he's psychic, he'll be scanning me now, trying to determine whether I'm telling the truth. I've learned enough from Elliot over the years to know that on a surface pass, a person is just looking for obvious signs of deception. It's in my favor that I do want to help these people find what they're looking for. It suits my goals. It's that feeling that I hold on to, hoping if he is indeed searching me, that's the truth he stumbles on.

After a tense moment, Brody relaxes back into his chair. "So, who's this girl?"

Chapter Fifteen
Krissa

At school the next day, my stomach clenches unpleasantly as the bell rings to release me from third hour. Tucker didn't show up today, and Felix and West have been no friendlier than any day before, so I'm already a ball of nerves. I'm still licking my wounds after my failed attempt to reconnect with the psychics, but I try my best to tamp down the memory. I promised Jodi I'd talk to Crystal today, and I'm doing my best to convince myself things will go differently with her.

At least I hope they will.

In the hallway, I stuff my backpack in my locker before slamming the grated metal door and heading down the hall. I'm not going down to the cafeteria; I haven't seen Crystal there in months. It seems she, like me, has been lying low, although I'm not entirely sure why. Sure, she did things while possessed that she wouldn't ordinarily have done, but she didn't cause any lasting damage. We all understand she wasn't herself, and I know I don't hold anything against her. It wasn't she who betrayed us, it was Bess Taylor.

I understand needing space from people, but the fact that Crystal doesn't eat in the cafeteria complicates my mission. If I remove my charm, I could use my psychic abilities to do a quick sweep of the school, but I'm beyond hesitant to open myself up that way. A typical locater spell requires something connected to the person in question, but I saw a spell in the Barnette grimoire that might work. The handwritten notes that accompanied the incantation warned that the person needs to be relatively close for it to work at all, and it's not particularly precise, but I'm willing to try.

I round the corner, away from the chatter of people still making their way to the lunchroom. This hall is nearly deserted, with just a small knot of freshmen at the end, thoroughly caught up in themselves. I take a chance they won't notice me leaning against the cool cinder-block wall, murmuring to myself.

The spell requires a charged talisman that will warm when I'm close to my target. I slip the ring I wear off my finger. The setting is heavy and the stone is a smoky quartz. It's been passed down in my family for generations. I'm not sure if it's exactly the kind of item the spell calls for, but I don't really have anything else—besides the turkey sandwich Mom handed me on my way out the door this morning.

Closing my eyes, I center myself and connect with the elements surrounding me. Magic surges in me immediately, as easily as drawing a breath. On an exhale, I murmur the memorized incantation through three times, just as the grimoire instructed. When I open my eyes, nothing has changed. I glance at the ring but it sits still, looking every bit the same as always. I curl my fingers around it, but it even feels the same—the stone cool to the touch. I sigh. It didn't work. I shuffle toward the nearest stairwell with half a mind to aimlessly wander around the halls in search of Crystal, but as I go, the ring begins to warm in my hand.

Maybe the spell worked after all.

I take the shallow stairs two at a time on my way up to the third floor. With every step, the metal heats in my palm. This part of the building is mostly deserted, remnants of a time when the high school population in the area was higher than it is now. I don't have any classes up here, but I know there are a few that meet on this level.

The stairwell is in the corner between two hallways, and when I start down the one on the right, the ring cools. I pivot on my heel and retrace my steps to the other hallway.

The door to the second-to-last room is open, and I edge toward it carefully. When a quick peek reveals Crystal sitting alone in a desk, her lunch spread around a spiral notebook, the tension in my shoulders drains. It worked.

I tap on the door to announce my presence before entering. Crystal doesn't look up immediately, instead beckoning me closer with a curl of her finger. "Hey, come check this—" Her words die in her throat when her eyes finally snap up to greet me.

The forced smile that cracks my face feels thin as I cross to the desk beside her. "Hi."

She closes the notebook without looking at it, her eyebrows knitting as she scrutinizes me. "What are you doing here? How did you even find me?"

"I, um..." The answer to the second question is so easy, yet I stumble over it.

She seems to sense what I'm reluctant to say. Her eyes narrow and her lips purse. "Oh. You used magic. Of course." She leans back in her chair, pressing her palms against the attached desk. "Of *course* you did."

I study her, not sure what to say. I'm saved having to construct a reply by the arrival of someone else. Dana Crawford enters, the casual look on her face turning pinched when she catches sight of me. It's not the first time I've seen this expression—it's the same one I see whenever I catch a glimpse of her walking down the hall clutching Fox's arm possessively. It's a far cry from the haughty looks she gave after learning Crystal and my secret about changing the timeline and telling Fox the reason that I seemed closer to Owen than I should. I guess losing her psychic abilities with Seth's death took her down a peg or two. Not that I care. She can feel free to think she hurt me in some way. My only regret is that she hurt Fox in the process. Although it's hard to tell due to my self-imposed isolation, I get the sense Fox has been avoiding me. He does his best not to make eye contact, and I get the feeling he doesn't trust me. But I don't hold that against him because it's possible he shouldn't.

Dana recovers a beat too late, arranging her features into a mask bordering on accusation. "What's she doing here?"

Crystal doesn't seem surprised by Dana's tone. Her eyes barely flick in her friend's direction before returning to regard me coolly.

"I'm not sure yet."

I take in a breath and release it slowly. I'm not sure what their response will be to me, but I promised Jodi I would do this, so I'm going to see it through. "Jodi wanted me to talk to you."

Before I can get another word out, Crystal stands, rolling her eyes. "I should've known that's what you're here for. What, she too chicken to say something to us herself?"

I'm not entirely sure why Crystal thinks Jodi would be afraid to talk to her, since it's not as if she can retaliate with magic, but I keep that thought to myself. "She thought you might be more willing to listen to me. We're friends, after all." My eyes flick between Crystal and Dana and I chew on my lower lip. "Well, kind of."

Crystal isn't pacified. "I knew it. I knew she didn't approve of what we're doing. She acts all nice, but I could tell every time we went in she was judging us."

I snort at her paranoia. "Jodi *is* nice. That's why she wanted me to talk to you. She's afraid you guys aren't able to accept your new limitations."

Dana makes a scathing noise in the back of her throat, but Crystal waves a hand at her. "And why does she care?" Crystal asks.

I shrug. "I don't know. Maybe because she knows you better in this reality than you realize. Remember, you and I are supposed to have been friends for years. She's just worried."

Crystal cocks her head. "And what about you? Are you worried about me?" Her tone holds a hint of challenge.

I press my lips together, considering carefully my next words. "I want to help you. I can't imagine what you're going through. But I did some research and I found some spells you two might still be able to use, even without a direct link to abilities. If you want, I can go over them with you, help you master them. It won't be the same as really having magic or really being psychic, but it's something. A starting point. I know you don't want to hear this, but you might not ever get full abilities back. I want to help you find your new normal."

Dana crosses her arms over her chest. "Yeah, like we want help from you," she starts, her tone acerbic.

Crystal shushes her. "We'll think about it."

The surprise on Dana's face is obvious. A surge of pleasure rises in me at Crystal's complete disregard for Dana's opinion, but I push it down. Trying to keep my face as neutral as possible, I nod. "Let me know when you want to get together to try."

I don't stick around to wait for the discussion that is inevitably going to occur between Crystal and Dana. They're best left to sort their thoughts out by themselves. But as I walk out of the room, I feel lighter than I have in weeks—months. Although Crystal hasn't agreed to let me help her, the fact that she didn't completely shut me down is good enough. If I can help her get to a place where she can accept who she is now, maybe something inside me will change. Maybe I can reclaim a bit of the girl I used to be. And if I can do that, maybe the other things I want aren't as far away as I convinced myself they are.

The lunch bell rings as I start down the steps to the second floor. I'll need to stop by my locker to pick up my supplies for math. I dig into the brown paper bag still clutched in my hand and pull out my turkey sandwich. For the first time in I don't know how long, I actually feel hungry.

It's with a full mouth that I step into the second-floor hallway. I cycle through the week's plans in my head. There is work at the shop, of course, but I'm sure I could get off if I told Jodi I was going to help Crystal. I also have plans to hang out with Griffin and Tucker, but those can always be shifted. Things with those two are casual enough that they won't mind if I don't show up for the next night of pizza and random television.

I'm taking another bite of turkey and bread when my shoulder bumps against someone in the hall. Typically, I would murmur an apology, keeping my eyes down, but there's no talking now with my mouth full of food. Instead, I glance at the person beside me, ready to give a nonverbal sorry, but I stop short when I recognize who it is. Felix. He's eyeing me with veiled curiosity, which is more interest than he's shown in months, including yesterday when I sat down at his lunch table.

I chew quickly and swallow my bite. "Sorry about that," I say, surprised at how easy my tone is. Given his reaction to me yesterday, I probably shouldn't say anything to him, but I can't help myself. For the first time in a long time, I feel like me.

Felix nods, his eyebrows cinching as he studies me. "No worries." His tone is guarded, but it's far warmer than yesterday. I wonder how Bria's conversation with him went. "You seem to be in a good mood."

I consider this. When is the last time that's been true for me? So long ago, I can't even remember. "You know what? I think I am."

A smile tugs at the corners of his mouth. "Well, that's good, then."

"It is," I say. The skin on my face stretches in a way that so unfamiliar it takes me a moment to realize what's happening: I'm smiling. Not one of my forced smiles, or even the kind that happen when I'm with Tucker and Griffin, but a real smile.

Felix's face grows serious and he brushes the crook of my arm with his fingers. "Look, I'm sorry about yesterday—"

I shake my head, cutting him off. I can't tell him his behavior was all right, because it wasn't, but I don't want him to feel bad about it. He had a right to treat me that way, especially considering I've treated him recently. "Just promise next time I sit down by you, we can chat. Just like this."

"Okay. I think I can do that."

My math class is just ahead, and I'm about to say my goodbyes and head toward the room when Felix hooks his hand around my arm, tugging me gently to a stop. When I face him, his features are tight. "Felix, what—"

But when I hazard a glance back toward the math room, I know why he wanted me to stop. Owen stands just beyond the door, his face alight as he chats with Laurie or Lauren or whatever her name is. The bubble of happiness that's been building in my chest bursts as if pricked with a pin. Every possibility that's started swimming in my head since bumping into Felix dissolves back into darkness. What was I thinking? Even if I could turn back into the girl I was before that night in the warehouse, the fact is the world has moved on without me. Felix opens his mouth to say something, but I tug away from him, keeping my head down as I dart toward my classroom, using every bit of resolve within me to keep from looking up at Owen again.

Chapter Sixteen
Crystal

Dana's leg jiggles anxiously as she perches on the couch in my living room after school. She checks the time on her phone for about the tenth time in the last minute.

I roll my eyes and focus my attention back out the front window. "I don't know why you're acting so nervous. Krissa said she wants to help us."

"Maybe she wants to help *you*," she mutters.

I fight off another eye roll. I spent the second half of the school day considering Krissa's offer. By sixth hour, I figured the worst that could happen is she'd come armed only with things we've tried before. But maybe, just maybe, she'll have put her hands on *the* spell, the one that will help me and Dana get to a point where we can get our abilities back. I know that's not her intention—Krissa said she wanted to help us accept our limitations. But maybe she'll do more than that.

We decided to meet at my house, since today's the day both my parents work late. Dana's house is also an option, as her aunt is rarely at home, but I figured Dana wouldn't want Krissa there. I've only asked enough to satisfy my curiosity about why when I came back to myself after being possessed Dana was suddenly with Fox. Last thing I knew, Fox was still lamenting his breakup with Krissa. But I guess once he knew she wasn't the girl he thought he was, he was more than happy to give up on her and move on. To his credit, he hasn't told anyone else our secret. Besides one or two offhanded comments, he hasn't even talked about the timeline shift to me.

"When did she say she'd be here?" Dana asks, not for the first time. "Fox is supposed to pick me up, and—"

"I don't think the world will implode if Krissa and Fox are both here at the same time. I don't think she'll hex you, and I doubt she'll punch you. So just get over yourself already, okay?"

Dana makes a face, a tell that I've hit one of her insecurities. I'm surprised how well I've gotten to know her. I get where she's coming from, though. Hanging out with your boyfriend's ex has got to be strange in the best of circumstances. The fact that Dana is the reason Fox now completely ignores Krissa is a complicating factor.

A car I don't recognize pulls up into the driveway, and after a few seconds Krissa climbs out. When did she get a car? How much has happened while I've been so busy worrying about getting my magic back that I haven't paid attention to the world around me? She grabs a drawstring backpack before closing the door and heading to my porch. I meet her at the front door and open it before she has a chance to knock. Her face is more closed than it was when she left the classroom at lunchtime—more like it was when I approached her about coming here at the end of sixth hour. I wonder what happened in that span of time to make her retreat back into herself again. Although I've been distracted with my own endeavors, it hasn't been lost on me that Krissa has spent most of her school hours alone. The only person I've seen her with with any frequency is Tucker.

After the exorcism, he was so sweet, even better to me than he had been in the brief time we were together once I arrived in this timeline—nicer than he should be after the way I ended things with him. It was clear he wanted to get back together, but I couldn't. He was just starting to get a handle on the psychic abilities he manifested when the binding spell was cast. It was too hard for me to be around him after all I lost. Somehow the idea that the two of them are friends is comforting.

Krissa offers the briefest twitch of the corners of her mouth as she crosses the threshold. She shrugs the backpack on her shoulder. "Sorry I'm late. I had to pick up some supplies."

I don't bother telling her that whatever she has I've probably got stored in my bedroom already. With as many things as Dana and I have picked up from Hannah's herbs in the last few months, I'm pretty sure we can rival the store's inventory. Still, I take it as a good sign that she's come so prepared. Maybe she really can accomplish something Dana and I haven't been able to yet.

Dana visibly tenses as Krissa enters the living room, but Krissa doesn't seem to notice. She zeros in on the coffee table and kneels beside it, tipping the contents of her bag out on the smooth glass top. I do my best to identify elements as she arranges them. A variety of quartz, a handful of different herbs, and a heavy leather-bound tome that looks similar to my family's grimoire. Keeping her head down, she opens the book and flips through a few pages until she finds the one she's looking for. "Okay, I found something that might allow the two of you to cast some simple spells. It seems to have some roots in the vessel spell my dad used."

It sounds like she wants to go on explaining what the spell was used for, but she holds back. Since I don't remember much about the night the circle and Krissa's dad confronted Seth in his warehouse, I'm not entirely sure what went into the vessel spell, but I don't need a history lesson. I don't care about the origin of this particular bit of magic or who crafted it, I just want it to work. I'm about to ask what needs to happen before we can see if it does when a knock sounds at the front door. I glance at Dana. "Is Fox here already?"

Dana watches Krissa, looking for some reaction to the mention of Fox's name, but Krissa's eyes remain on the grimoire as if she didn't hear me. "No, he's not supposed to be here for another hour," Dana says after a beat, glaring like she's considering committing an act of violence against me.

A knock sounds again and I press my lips together. Who could it be? Neither of my parents are home, so it's probably not one of their friends. Could it be Lexie again? I hope not. "I'll be back."

Krissa barely nods as I jog toward the front door. I open it, prepared to tell whoever is on my porch to shove off, but the words die in my throat. There's something striking about the man who greets my eyes, something about the way he holds himself. He looks like he could be a grad student—young, dressed like a casual professional in a crisp black button-down and expensive jeans. But there's something about him that oozes authority. His dark chocolate eyes pin me in place and it takes a moment to find my voice. "Can I help you?"

He smiles, flashing dazzling white teeth. "I certainly hope so," he says, his tone easy and smooth. "Are you Crystal Jamison?"

I'm too surprised to respond. Why would someone be looking for me? Could this be some kind of college recruitment thing? No—that doesn't make any sense. Universities don't routinely send people unannounced to a high school junior's house. Especially not one like me, with my not-so-stellar GPA and decided lack of sports abilities. Could he be from the high school? An intervention about my grades? Again, no—not only would I probably recognize anyone from the school, it's not as if they'd send a guy over when my parents weren't home. But I can't think of any other logical reason for him to be here.

His head tips gently to the side and I realize I haven't responded yet. "Um—yes. I'm Crystal." What could he want? "Look," I begin, trying to make my voice as adult as possible, "I'm not sure what you're here for, but now's really not a good time."

The man's smile returns, but this time there's almost a predatory edge in the flash of his teeth. As if my words had been an invitation instead of the exact opposite of one, he steps over the threshold, his body passing so close I can feel the heat radiating off him.

When I turn, Krissa and Dana are both staring at me, eyes wide more with concern than curiosity. The fact that I'm not alone in the house right now provides little comfort. Part of me thinks maybe I'm safe because they're here, but another part is concerned that their presence only puts us all in danger.

He walks purposefully into the living room, taking a seat at the end of the couch Dana is perched on. She visibly blanches but doesn't move. Eyes never leaving my face, he unbuttons the sleeves of his dress shirt and takes his time rolling them up to expose his forearms. I'm surprised as he bares the skin of his right arm: There's a tattoo there. From the rest of his appearance, I wouldn't have taken him for a body art kind of guy. The ink is bright red, but I can't make out its shape. "You have company, so I'll be brief," he says once he's adjusted the sleeves to his liking. He looks comfortable, as if he's sat in that very spot on my couch every day of his life, as if we're in his house instead of mine. "You have information that I need."

In my periphery, Krissa turns her attention in my direction. I don't meet her eyes. I have no answers for her. At this point, I know what she knows. "Information?" I cringe as my voice creaks. I swallow before trying again. "What information could I have? I don't even know you."

He motions to the ottoman in its place below the window opposite him. An icy chunk of dread settles in my stomach as I cross to it, sliding it over the plush carpet so I'm even with Krissa at the coffee table. "My name is Brody, and I represent a group with a singular interest."

Krissa's fingers, which have been knotting and unknotting themselves over her grimoire, still. "Wait—*you* represent a group?" When Dana's eyes go wide, a clear warning not to anger the possibly dangerous stranger, Krissa presses on. "It's just... you don't look very old."

Although I wish she hadn't brought it up, she does have a point. What kind of group could he represent?

Brody doesn't appear offended or even flustered by Krissa's observation. "I'm older than I look." As he says it, the fingers of his left hand absently stroke the tattoo on his right forearm. From my new angle, I make out the shape. It's a flower with broad red petals and black veins running through it. But it's not the shape of the mark that transfixes me, it's the colors. They seem to glow faintly and undulate on his skin, the hues vibrant against his dark flesh.

I blink heavily and fix my gaze on his face. "Okay, so you're here for some group. I don't know why you think I have any information."

The corner of his mouth quirks upward. "Bess Taylor."

The air rushes from my lungs. How does he know? It's not as if we exactly broadcast the fact that I was possessed. When Anya sat down to try to explain everything I missed in the weeks I wasn't myself, she described how the Devoted sensed Seth's return once he was able to get some of his power back. Is the same true for this guy? I dismiss the idea immediately. If that were the case, why has it taken him so long to show up? Besides, Anya never mentioned a group who revered Bess the way the Devoted did Seth.

Maybe he doesn't know anything. Maybe he's just here because I'm a distant relative and he thinks something of hers was passed down to me. With that thought, my heartbeat slows down again. My throat is dry as I try to swallow. "I'm not sure what you mean."

He narrows his gaze. "I think you know more than you're letting on. I'll cut to the chase: I know her consciousness shared your body for a period. It's the most contact that anyone's had with her since she died. We have reason to believe she knew something—information my people have been in search of for lifetimes. And now you're going to give me that information."

Krissa tenses like a coil ready to spring, but she says nothing. For the first time since Brody's arrival, I'm glad for her presence. If he tries something, I have no doubt she would try to protect me. Although he's done nothing to suggest he's got powers, the fact that he's talking about Bess is enough for me to infer he's probably a witch. Dana and I are simply no match for him, a thought that turns my muscles to jelly. All this time I've been trying to get my magic back it's been so I could get back to being myself, so I could use my abilities in everyday life like I've grown accustomed to doing. I've never considered having them as providing a measure of safety I'm currently without.

Having Krissa beside me affords a measure of boldness I know I wouldn't have without her. "Whatever information you think I have, you're mistaken. Bess is gone and I don't remember anything from the time she was here. Sorry to disappoint." I stand, sweeping a hand toward the door. "Can I show you out?"

Brody stands, too, and for a second I'm convinced that's going to be it, that he'll just walk out. But instead of striding to the door, he approaches me, standing so close I can see the strands of honey and amber weaving around the dark brown pools of his irises and can feel the warmth of his breath tickling my face. Krissa is on her feet in a second, and while she does nothing more, her proximity is the only thing keeping me from flinching.

"I want to make something as clear as possible: We have been waiting too long for an opportunity like this." Brody's eyes bore into mine. "You will give me the information I want. She's not with you anymore, but you have a connection to Bess. I don't care what you have to do, but you're going to tell me what I need to know."

It takes everything in me not to shrink back under the intensity of his gaze. My fingers tremble and I fist my hands to keep the traitorous weakness from showing. "I don't even know what you want me to tell you."

He trails a finger down my cheek and I hold my breath. The sharp taste of fear stabs the back of my throat. "Her greatest desire is ours. That should give you all you need to go on." He scrapes his nail across my chin before removing his touch. After a beat, he starts toward the door. "Do whatever you have to, but get that information—and get it fast. We've been searching for generations and our great patience is beginning to wear thin."

I try twice to speak before the words make it past the lump in my throat. "What if I can't?"

Brody stops, turning slowly to face me again. "Then I guarantee you'll watch everyone you care about suffer before we kill you."

Krissa steps between us so quickly I almost jump. "You're not going to do a thing to hurt her. And if you even think about hurting any of her family or friends, I will end you."

Brody surveys her for the first time. He tilts his head like he's not sure what to make of her before a smile slowly creeps across his face. "Oh. So you're the one who killed Seth. I bet that's making you feel all tough and dangerous right now. But I can see in your eyes you're no threat." That predatory smile crosses his face again, and I'm thankful it's not directed at me. "I know evil, and you're not it."

Moments later, he's let himself out of the house and I take in my first deep breath in what feels like minutes. On the couch, Dana is clutching her chest like she's afraid her heart's going to burst out of it. Krissa's body remains rigid, her eyes on the door. Seconds tick by before she relaxes and turns to face me.

"Do you know what he's talking about—what information he wants?"

I shake my head. "No. No idea. I wasn't lying."

She blows out a breath. "Okay, then. Looks like my mission's changed a bit." She runs her hands over her pale blonde hair, gathering it at the base of her neck before releasing it. "I'm going to do whatever it takes to help you get that information. He's not going to hurt anyone. I promise."

Without waiting for a response, Krissa steps to the coffee table and drops down in front of her grimoire again. I have no reason to doubt her words, and I'm thankful for her help. But as she gingerly turns a few pages in the ancient book, I can't help the shiver that courses through me. What exactly does she intend to do if Brody does try to hurt me? He said she killed Seth, and the way he said it makes me question my assumptions about that night. Of course I know he's dead, but I figured the circle enacted whatever spell Anya and Mr. Barnette had planned. Is it possible I've had the wrong impression all these months? Did Krissa kill Seth on her own? And if so, is she really capable of doing something like that again?

Chapter Seventeen
Krissa

I stand outside the apartment building, but I don't alert anyone to my presence. The warm spring day is turning cooler now that the sun is going down, but the chill on my skin isn't enough to make me bring my finger up to the button. This is closer than I've ever been to the place where she lives. I only know it's the right building because I was in the car once when my dad dropped her off. I never really thought I'd have occasion to come here, but after what happened at Crystal's house this afternoon, things have changed.

Not allowing myself to hesitate any longer, I press my fingertip to the off-white button, cringing at the buzz it creates. It's only with effort that I don't turn around and head back to my car. I don't want to be here. I don't want to talk to her. But I promised Crystal I would help, and understanding who we're up against is a step in the right direction.

Seconds tick by and there's no response through the intercom. Maybe she's not here. Maybe I can put off this conversation until another day. I rock back on my heels, ready to step off the small landing, but just before I do a voice crackles through the speaker.

"Hello?" The voice is garbled, but I can still tell it's her.

I swallow. "Anya? It's Krissa. Can I come in?"

I expect her to ask what I'm doing here. In the last four months, I've done my best to not have to interact with her at all. But another buzz, this one lower than before, sounds from the door to my left. Anya's immediate, unquestioning response burns in a way

I can't quite identify.

I open the door and walk down the hall. This place looks much nicer than the building Griffin lives in, but it's still obvious it hasn't been updated in several years. The wallpaper is decked with sprawling, garish roses that appear to have a coating of dust over them. I walk until I find the door that matches the number beside Anya's name on the intercom. I raise my fist to knock, but before I can, the door opens. Anya's smile is broad, but I can see a measure of concern in her eyes. She's not stupid. She knows the only reason I would be here is if something's wrong.

"Come in," she says, stepping out of the doorway to allow me entry. I can't remember the last time I saw her up close. I sometimes catch a glimpse of her on her days at the shop—shifts I refuse to work. If Griffin or Tucker need something while she's there, I'll hang outside, occasionally glancing through the window. She's about my height, with dark hair and a slight build. She looks a lot like her sister, but physical traits seem to be the beginning and the end of their similarities. Her apartment is light on furniture, but she has several decorative touches that make the place feel homey. A half dozen small mirrors adorn one wall, catching the light and winking it back at us. Two large vases filled with feathers and paper flowers flank a long black table. The only pictures on the walls are of scenery. No people. For the first time, I wonder if she has anything to remind her of the family she left behind when she walked away from the Devoted.

"How can I help you?" Anya asks as she closes the door behind me. "I assume this isn't a social call."

I don't bother confirming her suspicion. I know she's aware I don't much care for her. When she first arrived in Clearwater, I didn't know what to make of her. She's the one who convinced my dad he had to leave my mom and me. He was with her for five years, and their familiarity with each other made me wonder exactly how close they became in that time. My parents are back together now, attempting to make up for the time apart. If anything happened between the two of them while Dad was away, Mom has decided to keep it in the past. It's no longer her relationship with my dad that makes me stay away from Anya. She took him away because she saw in a vision of the future that Seth would be defeated and that Dad had a role to play in it. But she didn't see everything. She didn't see that the vessel spell wouldn't be enough for Dad to trap Seth once more. She didn't see my hand in his eventual defeat. If only she'd been able to see the vessel spell wouldn't work, maybe we could've done something else. Maybe things wouldn't have ended up the way they are now.

I push away all those thoughts. No use having them swirl around in my mind. That's not why I'm here. "I was just at Crystal Jamison's house."

Anya nods. "How's she doing? I've tried to talk to her a couple of times, but I think after I told her I didn't know a way to get her magic back, she kind of wrote me off."

"That's why I was there. Jodi wanted me to talk to her, to help her come to terms with the way things are now. But she had a visitor." From the moment Brody started talking about what he wanted, I knew Anya would be the one to ask about him. She knows more about Seth's history, more about magic than anyone I know—including my dad and Jodi.

Before I can describe what happened, movement from down the hall catches my attention. I suck in a breath as Elliot emerges from the hallway. Did Anya have him hide when I showed up? Or was he just in the bathroom? Either way, I don't continue. Elliot and Sasha came to Clearwater to spy on me and the rest of the circle for Seth. They were loyal members of the Devoted, and even though Seth and the rest of their clan is dead, I don't trust either of them.

Elliot offers a tight smile and a nod. "Krissa. You're looking well."

I back toward the door. "This was a bad idea."

Anya reaches toward me. "Don't go. Clearly you need something—and you're probably pretty desperate, since you're here. Let me help you."

I shake my head. "I don't want to say anything in front of him."

Anya tsks. "I know your history with Elliot is... Well, it's even more complicated than your history with me. And I'll ask him to leave if you really want me to. Maybe this won't mean much to you, but I trust him. If you're here, it's because you think I can help in a way that other people can't. Elliot might be able to help, too."

I open my mouth, ready to tell her to make Elliot leave, but something she said gives me pause. Is she right? Could Elliot know something that could help? I'm here because I know Anya has information about magic that reaches outside of Clearwater. It's possible Elliot may, too. I blow out a breath. "He can stay. But it doesn't mean I trust him."

"You say the sweetest things," Elliot says, complete with eye roll.

I don't bother responding. It doesn't really matter what he thinks, and I have no interest in stroking his ego.

"Shall we sit?" Anya asks, leading the way to her couch.

I sit at the far end, hoping Elliot takes my lead. When he settles on the other end, I'm only slightly more at ease. "Something happened at Crystal's house. I'm worried, and I thought you might have information that could help." I quickly describe Brody and the things he said. As I speak, a line of worry etches itself between Anya's eyebrows. This is the first time she's ever seemed old to me. I know she has to be in her thirties, and by the time I'm done speaking, every one of those years is evident on her face. "Do you know who this guy is or what he could want?"

Anya shakes her head. "And that's what scares me. As far as I know, the only ones who knew about Seth—about anything that happened in Clearwater—were the Devoted who left town before the elder council wiped everyone's memories of magic. This is the first I've heard that there was another group who escaped. And as for what their interest in Bess might be, I've got no idea."

The bubble of hope I've been clinging to pops. Anya was my best chance at figuring out who this guy is and who he represents. Since she doesn't know, I'll have to split my time between researching a way to help Crystal get whatever information they want and figuring out who this group is and just how dangerous they are. "Well, it was worth a try." I stand. "If you can think of anything, let me—"

"Wait," Elliot says.

I pause, but he doesn't continue. I glance at Anya, who in turn looks at Elliot.

"Do you know something?" Anya asks.

Elliot presses his lips together in a tight line. The angles of his face seem to sharpen with concentration. "I'm not sure." He looks up at me. "Describe this Brody guy to me. Was there anything strange about him?"

"Besides the obvious?" I ask, slightly irritated. Does he actually know something? Or does he want this information for another reason? Part of me wants to ignore his question, but Anya is encouraging me with her eyes to go on. Sighing, I replay the scene in Crystal's living room over in my head. I already told them almost word for word what he said. But there was one other thing that I noticed about him, something I haven't mentioned yet. "He had a tattoo. Only it wasn't like a normal tattoo. It almost... It kind of seemed to glisten, like maybe it was new? Like maybe he kept ointment on it or something." I'm doing my best to describe it, but even that explanation doesn't exactly cover what it looked like.

Elliot straightens. "What was it a tattoo of?"

"Something red. A flower, maybe?"

Anya scrutinizes Elliot's face. "Does this mean something to you?"

"Maybe. I wasn't sure, but if you're right about the tattoo..." He shakes his head. "If you're dealing with who I think you're dealing with, it's not good."

My muscles tighten. I already had that sense, but there's something in the way Elliot says it that makes me even less at ease. The Devoted were a group committed to doing anything—including torture—to get what they wanted. Is the look on his face is any indication, this guy and the people he represents are even worse. "Who are they?"

He shakes his head, seeming to doubt himself. "I kind of figured they were just a story—something parents made up to keep their kids in line. They're called the Amaranthine. They didn't want to wait around for Seth, and I think I remember hearing that they thought someone else was more important. I always figured they meant someone with more power than Seth, which I always thought was impossible. So I guess it makes sense that it's information that they're after, not magic."

"What do they want?" Anya asks.

"Immortality," he says, his tone indicating he doesn't quite believe it. "My guess is they think Bess Taylor knew something about it." He looks at me. "Does Crystal know anything?"

I shake my head. "Not according to her. But I get the feeling they're not going to take no for an answer."

"I think you're right about that. If the stories are true, the Amaranthine are ruthless." He offers a grim smile. "My uncle Nate was a few years older than me, and when he'd watch me when my parents were out, I'd beg him to tell me stories about them. I figured he was making them all up, but maybe there was a grain of truth to them after all. He told me how they'd suck the life force out of people who crossed them. He said they had an assassin who did their dirty work, who'd kill people as a warning to others."

"If what you're saying is even a little true, there's no way they're going to leave Crystal alone until they get what they want." Anya turns to me, reaching out like she's going to place her hand on mine. At the last moment, she retracts it and rubs the back of her neck instead.

"I already figured that," I murmur. I had no reason to doubt Brody's resolve at Crystal's house, and despite my bravado when I threatened to end him, I'm afraid. Learning what Elliot knows doesn't ease that fear in the least.

Anya's face tightens. "I'll help any way I can."

"Thanks," I say too quickly. Although I can't imagine what she might get from offering assistance, I assume she's not being entirely altruistic. Or maybe she is. The idea that Anya might honestly be that kindhearted makes my stomach twist. How can she be so nice to me after how I've treated her since her arrival? "I'll let you know if I need anything." I pull my phone from my back pocket and pretend to check the time. "I have to get going."

Without waiting for a formal goodbye, I walk to the door, waving as I let myself out. Anya stands like she wants to say something more, but I close the door before she can.

As much as this new insight into the Amaranthine frightens me, it also lights a fire in the pit of my stomach. These people really are as dangerous as I assumed. I went to Crystal's house today hoping simply to help her and Dana come to terms with their lives as they are now, without full use of the abilities they'd come to rely on. But now my mission is more than that—more important and more dangerous.

If I can keep Crystal safe from the Amaranthine, maybe that act can in some way wash off some of the blood on my hands. If I can do some good, maybe there's still hope for me.

Chapter Eighteen
Sasha

I hear the impatient chirping of my cell phone as soon as I cut the water off in the shower. I sigh as I reach for the towel. Without looking, I know who the message is from. It's Elliot. It's always from Elliot.

By the time I towel my hair to the point that it's no longer dripping, my phone has chirped twice more. I hastily wrap the sodden cloth around my body. Elliot is not often the kind of guy who sends multiple texts. He understands I'll get to them when I have time. The fact that he's sending several messages can only mean something is wrong. I suppose there's an off chance some of the messages are from Anya, but I don't think we're at texting level in our relationship yet.

I scoop the phone off the edge of the sink and unlock the screen. Four texts from Elliot.

Are you home?

I'm coming over.

Are you ignoring me?

If you're not home when I get there, I'll just wait until you get back.

It's the last message that puts a little hurry in my step. According to the timestamp, he sent it three minutes ago. Depending on where he's coming from, he may already be parked and on his way up the stairs. Elliot doesn't have a key, but that won't stop him from entering. One of the first tasks he mastered when his abilities manifested was manipulating the tumblers in a lock with telekinesis. Although we're close, I have no interest in him walking in on me in my state of undress.

I ease out of the cramped bathroom and start for my slightly less cramped bedroom. There was little more than a mattress on the floor when I moved in. I wanted to keep the bed, of course—after all, Seth had slept here when this was his place. But it immediately became clear it was secondhand, probably something he found on the side of the road. He hadn't had the full measure of his abilities when he first arrived in Clearwater, so it wasn't exactly as if he could have used magic or psychic abilities to procure something better. So, the bed that's in here now is new, but I was sure to put it in the same position Seth's had been. I've also added a small nightstand. My clothes hang in the small closet. There's not much room, but anything is better than living out of a duffel bag, which is exactly what Elliot and I had been doing since we arrived in Clearwater.

I grab a T-shirt and a pair of jeans and pull them on, all the while straining my ears to detect an intrusion. It strikes me only as I'm pulling on a pair of socks that I haven't sent Elliot a response. Maybe an in-person visit isn't necessary. I've just opened the message app when a staccato knock sounds on the apartment door. Too late.

By the time I've made it into the living room, Elliot's already got the door open. His face is tight, the way it is when he's angry. What's happened? Why does he look so mad? I open my mouth to ask, but he's speaking before I can get the words out.

"I just came from your sister's place."

I haven't spoken to Anya in a few days, so I can't have done something to offend her. Unless it's the not talking to her that's the offense. But would Elliot really be so mad about such a slight? Would my lack of communication with my sister etch such angry lines into his face? "Yeah, I was going to call her later tonight."

He shakes his head. So that's not why he's so upset. He presses his lips together and inhales, nostrils flaring. "Krissa Barnette showed up. Do you have any idea why?" He tilts his head, squinting at me. Something in the way he does it tells me he thinks I should know. And I do have an inkling, but I'm not willing to give anything away. When I don't say anything, he continues. "Seems she was at Crystal Jamison's house when a guy showed up. He was asking questions about Bess Taylor. Had a red flower tattoo."

I do my best not to shrink under the intensity of his stare. "Oh?" I ask, trying to keep my voice innocent.

Elliot fists his hand as he stalks toward me. "Dammit, Sasha. Don't pretend like you don't know exactly what I'm talking about. The Amaranthine, Sasha? Are you serious? How can you be so stupid?"

I've dealt with Elliot's temper too many times in the past to be afraid he'll do anything with that fist, but that doesn't stop me from tensing as he comes closer. "Elliot..."

He shakes his head, holding his hand up to cut me off. "Don't even try to lie. What, you think I'm stupid enough to believe it's a coincidence that days after you find out about Crystal's possession the Amaranthine show up? Newsflash, I'm not. What are you thinking? What are you hoping to accomplish? You've heard the same stories I have. The Amaranthine are not the kind of people you mess with. I don't know what your angle is here, but you're going to end up getting yourself hurt."

I shake my head. "They won't hurt me. I'm the one who told him where to find the information they've been looking for."

Elliot curses under his breath. His expression clouds and I wonder if he wasn't secretly hoping I'd disagree with his assertions. "You can't trust them. What if Crystal can't give them the information they want? Have you thought about that? They could hurt her or her family—probably both. That's what you get for crossing the Amaranthine."

I roll my eyes, pivoting on my heel and crossing to the couch. "Well, then, I hope she doesn't let them down," I say, flopping onto the cushions.

Elliot stalks after me and sits at my side. "Do you think they'll stop at her? You're the one who contacted them. If they think you're just wasting their time, they could come after you. You and me and Anya. Have you thought about that?"

Indeed, I've considered this. It's a risk, sure, but a calculated one. I reached out in good faith. That has to count for something. If I can keep Brody's trust, it's possible that if things go south I can convince him Crystal is holding out. If I can stay in his good graces, with all likelihood he won't come after me. "They won't hurt us. And if they hurt Crystal, who cares?"

Elliot throws up his hands. "Do you hear yourself right now? What could you possibly be getting out of this? Why on earth would you bring these people here? Have you thought about the other consequences? What if they don't stop with Crystal? What if they're able to sense how much magic is here and they try to do something in the town?"

I snort. "Then I guess Krissa and her friends will have to save Clearwater again."

"And they might die in the process." Elliot's eyebrows draw together. "But you've already thought about that, haven't you?" He scrutinizes my face, and for a moment I wonder if he's probing me. There was a time a few years back that I tried to have him teach me to recognize a psychic intrusion, but no matter how many times we practiced, I never could. After a few seconds, Elliot shakes his head. "That's what this is all about, isn't it? You're hoping the Amaranthine don't get what they want and rain down fire on Krissa and the circle, don't you?"

The way he says it makes me feel like a foolish child. I don't like that he has that power over me. I cross my arms over my chest and narrow my eyes. "And what if I do?"

He rubs a hand over his face. "Sasha..."

"What?" I can't stand the way he's looking at me. Like he pities me.

A muscle in his jaw works, like he's carefully considering just which words to use. He's quiet for several seconds before deciding on the right ones. "I thought you'd moved on." His voice is quiet, like we're sharing secrets. "When Anya told me you'd made contact, I really hoped it was because you were ready to start a new life. I wouldn't even let myself consider that you might have some ulterior motives." He closes his eyes and shakes his head. "But you did, didn't you?"

The pity in his tone makes my blood boil. Where does he get off feeling sorry for me? I'm not the one in the wrong here. But of course, that's exactly what Elliot wants to make me think. He's always been great at that—twisting a situation to make someone else feel guilty. I think since he's psychic he knows exactly what buttons to push. But I refuse to let him. "You sit there like you're all disappointed in me, but let me clue you in on something—I'm the one who's disappointed in you. How can you give up so easily? Our parents died for their devotion. It would've been worth it if Seth had lived, but he didn't. It's because of those people he's dead. So, yes. I don't care if the Amaranthine hurt Crystal Jamison or the precious Krissa Barnette. In fact, I hope they do."

Elliot springs up from the couch as if he's been electrified and begins pacing. "It's over, Sasha. We lost the war. It's time to get used to the new world order. Yes, our parents are dead. Why do you think I reconnected with Anya so quickly? Why do you think I was so happy when I thought you were doing the same?" He lifts a hand and rubs the back of his neck. "You know she's responsible for it, too, right? She had a vision that Seth wasn't all we thought, and she also saw that he would be defeated. Instead of ignoring that, she left. She found Ben Barnette. She sided with Krissa's circle. So if the Amaranthine decide to take revenge on the people connected with Crystal, has it occurred to you your sister might be among the casualties?"

I clench my jaw, grinding my teeth together. Of course that's crossed my mind. And, if I'm honest, if something happens to Anya, I won't cry over it. I'd feel bad because she clearly means something to Elliot still, but that would be the end of it. But I can't tell him that. "They won't hurt us."

He glares at me. "Do you have their word on that? A contract? Or is it just a warm, fuzzy feeling?"

I throw up my hands. "I don't know what to tell you. I'm not sorry for what I've done. At least I *am* doing something. I'm trying to avenge Seth's death. Why can't you see that? I thought you of all people would get it. But I guess I was wrong." I stand, cutting into his path as he paces. I clutch his shoulders and narrow my eyes. "You can't tell anyone I'm involved."

"I have to. I don't think you understand the danger we're all in."

"So, what? Let me guess: You're going to run to Anya. And what do you think she'll do exactly? Even if she's able to find my contact in the Amaranthine, do you really think he's just going to leave because she asks him to? You know what I promised them. And if the stories we've heard are any indication, he's not going to leave just because we ask nicely."

Elliot's lips work and I can tell he's trying to fault my logic. After a beat, he shakes his head. "Well, I guess you're just going to have to find a way to help Crystal, then."

I shake my head. "No way."

"Do you know why Bess's consciousness was in Crystal to begin with? She must have reminded Seth of his beloved. If you're really trying to avenge him, why would you go out of your way to hurt her? Clearly she meant something to him."

I huff. This has crossed my mind, but I haven't seen it as reason enough not to follow through with my plan. "It has to be done."

"No, it doesn't. I get where you're coming from—believe me, I do. I know why you want this revenge so badly. Suddenly, nothing in our lives makes sense anymore. Everything changed that night. But that just means we have to change, too." He blows out of breath and places a hand on each of my shoulders. He bites his lower lip—a tell. He's about to say something he doesn't really want to say. "Have you ever thought this is the way things are supposed to be? Anya always did have the gift of precognition. Maybe she saw what she did so she'd leave, so we'd end up exactly where we are. Maybe... Maybe the Devoted were wrong."

I can't believe what I'm hearing. I can't believe Elliot—someone I know as well as myself—could ever say something like this. He grew up the same way I did, believed the things I did. How can his attitude have changed so completely in so short a time? It's like he's a stranger to me. White-hot anger bubbles up inside me. But I know better than to let him see it. If this is really what Elliot believes now, he's beyond logic. This is the way he's coping. Our world has been destroyed, so all he can think to do is turn his back on it. I can't trust him anymore, which means there's only one thing left to do. Lie. "It's just so hard for me to believe that," I say, injecting as much sadness into my tone as possible. "I've just been so mad. I thought—I thought that if I could make Krissa hurt, it would make me feel better. But you're right. The Amaranthine are far too dangerous. I wasn't thinking." I watch his face closely, trying to get a read on whether he believes me. When his eyebrow doesn't arc questioningly, I continue. "Just don't tell Anya. She'll be disappointed in me, and I don't want that. I'll find a way to help Crystal. I promise."

Elliot's brow pulls together as he studies me. I try to keep my face arranged in a mask of apology. I can only hope he keeps his promise and doesn't read me too deeply with his abilities. After a beat, he nods. "Okay. We'll figure this out." He rubs the back of his neck again. "I should get going. Let me know if you need any help."

I walk him to the door and we exchange our goodbyes. When I'm alone in the apartment once more, the wheels in my mind begin to spin. I know that Elliot will be checking in on me. I can't simply allow Crystal to fail. But I also know that if I approach her with an offer to help, she'll shoot me down immediately. I have a feeling Elliot won't take that as sufficient trying. No, I have to find a way to help her and still make Krissa suffer.

I think I have a way. I'll need to do some research, but if the thought taking form in my head is what I think it is, this might be even better than my original plan.

One way or another, Krissa Barnette is going to pay.

Chapter Nineteen
Krissa

Tucker spins around in the desk chair in my room, tipping his head back as he goes. I've already warned him several times that he's going to make himself sick, but, just like a young child, he doesn't heed my warnings. I'm ignoring him now, getting all my notes in order before my visitors arrive. It's been days since I met with Dana and Crystal, since Brody showed up at Crystal's house. After he demanded we tell him whatever information he wants to know, I've devoted myself fully to researching ways to contact spirits. Because I've spent so much time online and at the library, I haven't been at Griffin's much—hence Tucker's presence here now.

"Are you almost done with that?" he asks, stopping his constant spinning and fixing his gaze on me. His eyes swirl slightly in his head.

I glance up. "I already told you—I can't hang out today."

He raises an eyebrow. "What? You got a hot date or something?"

I bite my lower lip. I haven't told him about my current involvement with Crystal—or the possible threat against her and her family. He'd want to help—which is actually admirable. There was a time I figured he was incapable of caring for anyone but himself, and he's proven time and again that's not true. Still, I'm not sure I should share what I'm up to. I don't know how Crystal would feel about him being around. Their relationship is complicated at best, and the few interactions I've witnessed between them have been strained to the point of discomfort for onlookers. Besides, if I told him what kind of threat Brody appears to pose, there's no guarantee he wouldn't do something stupid, like try to take Brody on himself out of some misguided attempt at bravado.

And there's also the other thing—the thing that lurks at the back of my mind, the one I try not to think about. But no matter how I try to ignore it, there it is, coloring all my rational thought about this matter: *I* need to be the one to help Crystal. Part of me thinks that by doing it, I'll somehow make up for the things I've done, I'll start to become the person I used to be. It's ridiculous, of course. But it doesn't change the fact I want—I *need*—to do this myself.

My phone buzzes. It's Crystal. She's just picked up Dana and the two will be over soon. I sigh. "If I tell you yes, will you go?"

"Nah. I'd stick around to see who it is." He flashes a wolfish grin and I can't help rolling my eyes. In an instant, his face grows serious, all traces of laughter and dizziness disappearing. "Is that it? Did you finally talk with Owen? Is that why you want me gone? Or is it something else?" He narrows his eyes. "You're not getting back together with Fox, are you? Because Dana Crawford seems to have her manicured nails plunged deeply into his flesh." He clicks his fingers. "Unless that's it—it *is* Fox, but you two are meeting on the DL because—"

I hold up my hand. "Enough with your conspiracy theories. If I were really having a clandestine meeting with some guy, do you think I'd be bringing him here? Jodi's downstairs, and my folks will be home soon." In January, Dad returned to the workforce after a five-year hiatus, and he and Mom usually arrive home around the same time each night. If Dad gets home while Tucker's still in my room, he'll likely throw a conniption, as I'm not technically allowed to have guys up here. Jodi and my mom have been more chill lately about letting Tucker stay for brief visits. I like to think it's because they trust me, or at the very least they realize nothing even remotely sexual is going to happen between the two of us, but I have a sneaking suspicion they're just happy I'm interacting with anyone at all right now. "In fact, you'd better leave before my dad gets home and skins you alive." I cross to

Tucker and grab his hands, heaving him out of the chair.

He reluctantly allows me to heft him to his feet. "You're no fun," he grumbles.

"And yet you continue to associate with me," I return, pushing him toward the stairs. He's about a foot from them when I pause, something he said clicking in my brain. "Wait—why would you think Fox might be showing up here? You said it yourself—he's with Dana now." He cut ties with me pretty quickly after Dana spilled all my secrets to him. Once he found out I'm not the girl he dated for years, that I have no memory of the two of us together, he seemed to make it his mission to move on with his life.

Tucker turns, an unaccustomed flush rising in his cheeks. "No reason."

If blood rushing to his face wasn't enough to make me think I was onto something, the slightly higher register of his tone tells me I'm right on. "What is it? Spill."

He begins with a shrug. "Well, you know how I'm still pretty new at the whole psychic thing."

I nod, already sensing where this is going. He's used this phrase numerous times in the last few months to excuse himself from fault when he does something he knows he's not supposed to. *I'm pretty new at this psychic thing... I didn't mean to make that guy to give me my order for free... I just wanted to see if I could convince the cashier my license said I was twenty-one...*

He puts up his hands innocently. "I may have scanned Fox's thoughts once or twice in English. And you may have crossed his mind on an occasion or two."

Panic rises in my chest. If Tucker's been in Fox's head, does he know the truth about me messing with time? No—there's no way. I dismiss the idea, taking a deep breath to slow the quickening pace of my heart. If Tucker had picked up on anything like that, he'd have said something already. This must be something else. "And?"

He shrugs. "Let's just say he's thought about the good ole times between the two of you."

It's my turn for my cheeks to flush. Fox and my alternate self were together for years. I'm not sure exactly what kind of memories he has from the relationship before I showed up. I almost want to ask what kind of images have been floating around in Fox's mind, but I stop myself. It's entirely possible I don't want to know. "Why would he be thinking about me?"

"Dunno," Tucker says. "It's probably a good thing Dana can't read his mind right now, though. Girl walks around like she owns him. I'm really not sure why he plays along with it. Well, I suppose I can think of a couple reasons."

I groan, rolling my eyes. "You always have to take things to the dirty place, don't you?"

"What can I say? Gotta stick with what I'm good at."

I'd be lying if I said my curiosity wasn't piqued by this information, but there's really no time to delve into it. Besides, what would be the point? Do I really want to know why Fox has been thinking about me? Actually, if it comes right down to it, he's not thinking of me at all, but her. He's thinking about the girl he was with before I showed up and messed with his life.

I shake the thought from my head. There's nothing to be done about that now. I can only move forward. Crystal and Dana should be here soon, and I'd rather they not find Tucker here. "Okay, it's time for you to take off."

He does his best puppy-dog face, but I'm unmoved. When he realizes he's getting nowhere, he relents and we make our way down the stairs. Jodi's in the living room, her computer perched on her lap, and Tucker makes sure to bid her farewell on his way to the door. I'm fairly certain Jodi doesn't think much of Tucker, but she's pleasant enough to him. I overheard her and my dad arguing in hushed tones once. She was trying to convince him that if he expressed disapproval about my new friends, I would only cling to them more. I don't think she's right—after all, I'm not spending time with him and Griffin as an act of rebellion.

Tucker pulls open the front door to reveal Crystal and Dana on the porch. Crystal freezes, her fist raised like she's about to knock. When her eyes lock on Tucker, she shifts uncomfortably. Dana touches her arm.

Tucker's eyes dart to me, something like accusation taking form there. I can tell he wants to say something to me, but he holds back. "I was just leaving," he murmurs as he brushes past the girls and lopes down the steps.

Dana presses the small of Crystal's back, urging her across the threshold. I feel like I should apologize, but I'm not entirely sure what for. I don't know exactly what happened between Tucker and Crystal, but I've spent enough time with Tucker to be relatively certain he didn't do anything wrong in the equation. It's obvious that unexpectedly seeing him rattled her, but it's not like I had any ulterior motives in him being here. In fact, I was doing my best to get him out before she arrived.

Dana greets Jodi as we walk past the living room. Jodi smiles warmly, a sharp contrast to her earlier reaction to Tucker. Yep, she doesn't like him at all. Jodi says nothing as the three of us head upstairs to my room. I didn't mention anything to her about Brody's visit, and I don't know whether Anya has brought it up. I didn't specifically tell her not to, but I wish I had. No need to worry her about this. Not yet.

As soon as we're upstairs, I indicate the small area by the bathroom where there's a couch. As Crystal and Dana settle themselves, I wheel my desk chair over to them.

Crystal seems to have recovered somewhat from her earlier shock. "So, what's the plan?"

It's not like I wasn't expecting this question, but it still puts me on edge. "I've been doing a lot of research, and it looks like the most straightforward thing would be to just contact Bess—not worry about your abilities for the moment."

Crystal's shoulders draw back and I know she's taking the news as well as I anticipated—which is to say not well at all. "No." Her tone is flat. "I don't like that one bit."

I was prepared for this. "When I came to you the other day, I wanted to help you figure out new ways to connect with magic and psychic abilities. But those things will take time to master, and right now we don't have that luxury."

Dana leans forward in her seat. "I think what Crystal is saying," she begins tentatively, "is that she's thankful for whatever help you can give her, but our goal hasn't changed. We both want our abilities back. How do we know you won't help us with the whole Brody problem and then leave us twisting in the wind?"

Even though Dana asked the question, I aim my response at Crystal. "I would think after all we've been through you would know you can trust me. I still have all those spells, and I'll help you master them. I'll do all I can to help you be able to cast small spells or maybe pick up on some thoughts, but right now our focus needs to be getting this information. These people are trouble, and they mean business. Brody wasn't making idle threats." I pause, waiting for one of them to ask how I know, but neither does. That's good, because I don't know how either of them would react if they knew I told Anya. If I'm honest, I'm still not sure how I feel about it.

Crystal huffs, crossing her arms over her chest. "Fine. Let's do it your way."

There is a resignation in her voice I wasn't expecting. Maybe these last few months have taken a toll on her, too. I pull out the notebook I brought with me from my desk. I've been scribbling down all the information I could find about contacting people beyond the grave. Some of it is probably nothing but fantasy, but I feel there are a couple of good contenders here. The one that looks the most promising is a spell that requires the help of a psychic. Luckily, I just so happen to be both a witch and a psychic. Although, really, I wish I didn't have to wear both hats for this. I'm not even sure how effective I'll be considering how long it's been since I've connected with another mind. Still, I have to try. I promised. "There's a spell I think might work. It's supposed to enable the caster to reach through the veil and contact people on the other side."

Before I can go on, Crystal reaches for the notebook. I almost don't give it to her. After all, it's not like she'll be the one doing the casting. But I know why she wants to see it. She's got more experience with spells than I do, first of all. And I suspect that part of it is also that she wants to feel useful. After I hand the book over, Crystal peruses the pages I indicate. She takes longer than is strictly necessary, and as we wait, I can't help my eyes being drawn to Dana. How are things going with her and Fox? Are things as straightforward as they seem to be when I see the two of them together? Or is there something else going on? How would she feel if she knew I crossed her boyfriend's mind?

Crystal finally hands the notebook back, nodding. "Seems legit."

"Thanks. I'm glad you think it looks okay," I say, even though I wasn't looking for her approval.

"There's just one thing," she says, being sure to meet my eyes. "It says you need at least three people." Her lips twitch. "Three people with abilities."

I knew that already, of course. But, really, what was I supposed to do about it? If the witches still meet together, I'm not aware of it. Even if they do, it isn't as if I can just commandeer them to help us out. There are the psychics, but my relationship with them is tenuous at best right now. Besides, if I don't have to get more people mixed up in this whole Amaranthine business, I'm not going to. "I think we can manage."

Dana eyes me suspiciously. "If you knew it took three people with abilities, why did you let Tucker go? He could've stayed to help." Crystal shoots her some major side-eye, but Dana doesn't buckle. "Shouldn't we be giving this spell the best chance at succeeding?"

"Tucker's abilities are still pretty unfocused," I say, partially as an excuse. While it is true in some respects, it's not the reason I didn't have him stick around. "I suppose I could've asked Griffin, but he's at work."

Dana slides her phone from her back pocket. "I can text Fox. I'm sure he'd be willing—"

"No," I say. Even if he would come to help—which he might if Dana cajoles him enough—his presence would only serve to distract me after Tucker's comment. Before she can mount a response, I press on. "I've got it figured out already. I'm a psychic and a witch, so that covers that part of the requirements. And as for having three abilitied people..." I stand and close the distance to my closet in two steps. In an old shoebox in the corner are some charms I made up after my initial meeting with the girls. I hand a satin bag filled with herbs and several types of crystals to each of them. "These should channel magical and psychic abilities."

Crystal cocks an eyebrow. "Should?"

"I haven't exactly tested them out."

"Maybe we should," Dana suggests. "You know—see if we can—"

I shake my head. "I'm not sure how much juice is in them. I've never tried to make charms like these before. If you try them out beforehand, there might not be enough energy left to help with the spell."

The hungry look that had been filling Crystal's eyes drains away and her expression sours. "So that's it, then? This is what we've got to look forward to? A life of you making charms with enough power for us to maybe cast a spell or read a thought?"

I hold my hand up. "Calm down. This is just a solution for a problem today. We'll worry about your abilities later."

It's clear from the look on her face that Crystal wants to argue, but she thinks better of it. "Fine. Let's try this."

Grateful she didn't decide to put up a fight, I offer a small smile. I'm not sure if the spell will even work. It's possible that we really *do* need three people to cast it. But there's only one way to know for sure. Before I can do it, Crystal turns to Dana to direct her about what to do. It's one thing I've always respected about Crystal: her ability to understand even complex spells and break them down for others to comprehend. I'm actually glad she's doing the explaining because I'm sure I'd miss something.

As she speaks, I lift my wrist and study the woven bracelet. The hemp fibers, which were originally scratchy against my skin, have worn smooth in the months since I made it. The Apache tears and snowflake obsidian glitter in the light from the nearest window. I have to take it off. Every time I've considered doing it before, I've stopped, afraid of what opening up myself like that might do. I've closed that part of me off so completely because I haven't wanted to know what people are thinking, and I haven't wanted them to be able to read me either. Still, there's no getting around it: I'm going to have to remove the charm in order to do this spell. A psychic is required for a reason: Apparently even magic has its limitations when it comes to connecting the dead with the living. I do my best to loosen the knot with the fingers of my opposite hand, but it's not easy. The simple solution would be to cut it off, but I can't do that. I have a feeling I'll want to be able to block out consciousnesses again once this spell is over, and I don't have another charm prepared. I finally resort to using my teeth to undo the knot. Crystal and Dana both stare at me, Dana's lip curled with distaste, but neither asks what the significance of the bracelet is.

I build a wall around my thoughts before removing the charm. A gentle pressure nudges at my mind, and I know I made the right move blocking myself off before breaking the protective spell. I'll have to drop the mental wall to accomplish today's goal, of course, but hopefully if I'm focused on Bess I won't be too assaulted by other sensations. "I'm ready."

Crystal begins the chant, but it's immediately obvious the power I've charged the charm with won't get her very far. Dana joins in, and I quickly link with the weak energy they're wielding. I can only hope it'll be enough.

Slowly, I drop my barrier. To my great relief, I'm not flooded with thoughts or emotions. I'm focused entirely on Bess. I don't know what she looked like, but Seth once said Crystal bore a resemblance. In my mind's eye, I pull up an image of Crystal dressed in clothes borrowed from another time—from Seth's time. I also allow memories to seep in from the night Bess took full control of Crystal's body, focusing on her behavior, her manner.

The spell was careful to warn the caster that it's imperative the search be specific. Opening up to just any energy on the other side is dangerous and can have some bad consequences, like possession. That's mostly why it calls for at least three people to cast the spell—for protection.

As we continue the incantation, my mind opens up to a bright white nothingness. For a split second, I'm afraid I've somehow slipped into a vision, but the blinding light doesn't recede. A hum fills me and I realize what's happening: This is where I can connect with souls. It's not a physical place, more another plane, maybe. There are no features here, just energy. The buzz in my head continues to build, along with a pressure against my mind. There are so many spirits around—how will I ever find just one?

I can't identify who is pressing. It seems focusing on Bess is enough to keep them at bay. But just concentrating isn't getting me anywhere near finding her. Am I even in the right place? Is there even somewhere else I could be searching? I'm not sure how long any of this is taking. It feels like I've been here for a long while, but this might be one of those situations where time passes differently inside the spell than outside of it.

The noise in my head begins to crescendo and I'm not sure how much longer I can hold on. I can barely sense Crystal and Dana anymore. It's possible the power in their charms is waning. If it disappears entirely, whatever protection they're providing will be gone, and who knows what'll happen to me then. I need to do something fast. If Bess won't find me, maybe I can find her.

The spell instructed to simply concentrate on the person, but maybe there's a nuance to the language I misunderstood. I've kept my consciousness firmly in my own head, but maybe I'm supposed to actively seek Bess out. It's worth a try.

I press out with my abilities with the intention of locating Bess somehow among the countless spirits swelling around. It only takes a split second to realize I've made a mistake. Once I'm outside of the protection of my own head, the buzzing morphs into sounds, voices, words. In an instant, a billion people are talking, each trying to be heard over the other. It's too much—I can't make anything out and I'm losing touch with Crystal and Dana. I'm losing touch with myself. One voice vies for my attention more than the others.

When the blackness overtakes me, I welcome it.

***

I'm floating in a formless void. There's no light, no sound. I'm neither warm nor cold. I simply *am*.

Pressure. I feel pressure—but how is that possible? I don't have a body. I'm simply floating... floating...

Sharp pressure. Vibration. Pain. A murmuring sound.

I come back to myself by degrees. Fingers dig into my upper arms and someone is calling my name.

Jodi.

It takes a considerable effort to open my eyes, and when I do, my room is so bright I have to close them again immediately. It takes several tries before I can focus on her face.

"Krissa? Are you with us?"

Jodi's voice is finally starting to make sense. There are other sounds in the room, too—whispers coated with concern. Crystal and Dana.

"What happened?" My voice is scratchy.

"You're an idiot, that's what happened." Jodi's face is pinched in anger. "The girls started screaming, and when I came up here, you'd fallen out of your chair and you were convulsing like you were having a seizure. Exactly what the hell kind of spell were you trying?"

I open my mouth but no explanation comes out. I don't want to tell her about Brody and the Amaranthine, but I can't come up with a plausible lie, either—not with my mind feeling all squishy.

"It's one I found online," Crystal says, her voice low and apologetic. "I'm sorry. Krissa said it didn't look right, but I made her do it anyway."

Jodi's eyes flicker to Crystal before returning to me. I can't tell whether she believes Crystal's story. An echo builds in my head, the way it always does before a person's thoughts clarify themselves in my mind. Jodi's wondering if she can cast some sort of protective charm to keep me from doing stupid things.

The corner of my mouth twitches. "I'll be more careful," I murmur. "I'm okay. Really."

Jodi's expression is dubious, but she stands, offering a hand to help me to my feet. "Something like this happens again and I tell your folks."

Although I'm not entirely sure what my parents would do if they found out I was being reckless with magic, I appreciate Jodi giving me a free pass on this one. It's because she feels guilty for pressing me to help Crystal and Dana. I scan the floor for my bracelet. I need to put it on again soon. Even with my brain a squishy mess in the aftermath of whatever just happened, I'm sensing Jodi's thoughts and emotions pretty clearly. Once I return to normal, there's no telling the kinds of stuff I'll pick up on.

My aunt turns to Crystal and Dana. "I think it's best if the two of you take off for today."

Crystal nods. "Of course. I'm so sorry."

Jodi gives a curt shake of her head. She wants to give us a warning, tell us not to take risks, but she's afraid if she does we'll just do spells like these somewhere else, somewhere she can't keep an eye on us.

As Jodi leads the way toward the stairs, I bend down to pick up my bracelet. The charm should still work—I didn't cut it. All I need to do is tie it back on my wrist and I should be able to block people out again.

When I stand, a memory swirls around in my head. There were so many voices echoing inside me, but one managed to be heard above the din. Alec Crawford, Dana's dad. He had a message for her.

She's at the top of the stairs now. Should I tell her? Of course. Were I in her position, I'd want to hear from someone I lost. "Dana."

She pauses, her foot on the top step. Her eyebrows draw together. "Yeah?"

I bite my lower lip. "Could you hang back for a minute?"

Dana glances down the stairs, presumably at Crystal, and gives a little nod. Footfalls continue to sound, growing quieter as Crystal and Jodi make it to the second floor. "What?"

"I have a message. From your dad." I try to ignore her sharp intake of breath. "I was trying to find Bess and he found away into my head and—" I stop. She doesn't need the details.

Her eyes dart around like she can't quite process what she's hearing. "What'd he say?"

I take in a breath, closing my eyes in an attempt to recall the words perfectly. "'Don't forget you're already whole. Don't chase after things you don't need.'"

Dana's lower lip trembles as the words hang in the air. Tears well in her eyes and she brings her hand to cover her mouth. Before I can say anything more, she's rushing down the stairs so quickly I'm afraid she'll fall.

Guilt swells inside me. That was a stupid move. I have no idea what kind of relationship she had with her father. Sure, after I lost my mom I would've given anything for one last message, but I'm not Dana.

The spell failed. I upset Dana. Even when I try to do the right thing I end up hurting people.

Chapter Twenty
Crystal

I sip my increasingly cold latte through the thin plastic barrier as I scan the contents of yet another website. I feel like I've exhausted all sites promising to increase magical abilities, so I suppose it's good that's not the focus of today's search. Instead, I'm looking for how to connect with a long-dead relative who recently possessed me.

Easy, right?

I tap the screen of my tablet in an attempt to make the text on the page large enough to read. This would be easier on my laptop, but third quarter grades just came in and my parents are not happy. My computer's on lockdown, only to be used for school-related assignments under direct parental supervision. They wanted my tablet, too, but I was able to convince them they'd already taken it when my grades began to slip. For the moment, they believe me.

That's why I'm here at Wide Awake Cafe instead of in my room. I'm out in public for a little privacy. How crazy is that?

After Krissa's epic failure contacting the great beyond the other day, we haven't made any further attempts. I should be nice. She tried. It's not her fault she started having a seizure or whatever it was. We should've had more people there—an actual witch and psychic at least. But, if I'm honest, I didn't want anyone else there any more than she did. So if I'm doling out blame for the spell failing, I can take a heaping mound myself.

My folks are having a date night tonight, and I'm under strict instructions to stay home and not have company. So naturally Krissa and Dana will be coming over to discuss next steps. If I play my cards right, I might even be able to have Krissa spell my homework assignments so they're completed in the blink of an eye. That should go far in convincing my parents I was a good little girl and followed their instructions.

The incantation on the site promises to bring lost loved ones close to the veil in order to communicate one last time. I don't know if this will work on many levels. First, Bess isn't exactly a loved one of mine. It's not like we ever really met. Having her in my head wasn't like having a roommate; we didn't chat. Besides, Bess already got a chance to communicate from beyond the grave. Would this spell work for someone who's already had that kind of experience? It's impossible to know, so I bookmark the site, just in case Krissa wants to give it a go.

I reach for the latte again, but a flicker in my periphery makes me jump, almost knocking it over. Standing beside me, clad in his signature leather jacket, is Tucker.

A smile tugs at the corners of his mouth. "Didn't mean to scare you." He shifts slightly, radiating a kind of unease. I've always saw him as self-assured, the kind of guy who couldn't care less what others think of him. To see him anything less than one hundred percent confident is a little disarming.

"It's okay," I mumble. I pull the paper cup across the tabletop, setting it up like a barricade between the two of us. I should say something else, but nothing comes to mind.

Tucker seems just as uncomfortable as I am. After a beat, he slides into the empty seat across from me. He doesn't ask for permission, which is much more like the guy I came to know. I remember like it was yesterday the first time he kissed me. He just came up behind me in the deserted stairwell I like to take between classes and grabbed me around the middle. I squealed—of course—but when his hot mouth found the curve of my neck, somehow I knew he wasn't there to hurt me. I fit against his body like I was meant to be there.

I take a hasty sip of my latte, doing my best not to cringe at the tepid temperature. I can't be thinking of the way Tucker makes me feel when we're together, not if I want my head clear.

"Didn't mean to ambush you the other night at Krissa's." He doesn't apologize for being there, for surprising me—of course he doesn't. That's not his way. He drums his fingertips against the edge of the table. "You know she and I aren't... You know, right?"

It never crossed my mind that Krissa and Tucker might be involved romantically or physically, but now that he's assured me they're not together, my mind can't help whirling with images. I give myself a slight shake to clear them. "Yeah. I mean, why would you be with her?" I don't mean it to come out as catty as it does, but there's no taking it back now.

His mouth twitches. Is he trying to hold back a smile? But then he's talking. "I think it's good the two of you are hanging out again. Maybe it's a sign things are changing. Getting better. For both of you."

I want to tell them they are, that I'm doing just fine, thank you very much—but it would be a lie. Instead I offer a small nod.

Some of the tension in his face drains. "Good. I'm glad to hear it." He leans forward, pressing his forearms into the table. "I know things were messed up before. I get it now."

I shake my head. Whatever he wants to say, I'm sure I'm not ready to hear it. I've seen this expression before—when I woke up from being possessed, in the days to follow. This hopeful look in his eyes isn't a good thing. "Tucker..."

"I was pissed when you broke things off with me the way you did. It hurt. But there was so much other stuff going on behind the scenes. There was the whole Seth thing, you being possessed. And I get that you've needed time to deal with everything. But when I saw you at Krissa's... It's been months. And stuff's still messy—I get that. I see it with K all the time. She's messed up over everything that went down. You are too. But it's not a problem. Nothing we can't deal with."

He stops short of telling me we can handle it *together*, for which I'm thankful. I don't know how I'd take such a romantic idea from him. "It's not that simple."

"Yeah, it is." He reaches across the table, stretching until he covers my hand. "I miss you, Crystal." He states it baldly. Simply a fact. There's no sappiness, no tear in the eye. That's not Tucker's style. "I've tried giving you your space. I figured you needed it. But, honestly, I don't want to wait anymore. I know you, and you're stubborn as hell. Probably why you and K were always so close—you're cut from the same cloth. I started realizing she's not gonna change until something pushes her, which made me think the same's true for you. So here it is. Consider this your push."

His fingertips stroke against the top of my hand gently. I want to flip my hand over, press my palm to his. I want to press more than my palm to him, if I'm honest. Being with him felt so good. But as fantastic as all the physical stuff felt, actually getting to know him was beyond what I ever imagined, too. He's funny, with a sharp, sarcastic wit. He's straight to the point—there's no subtext with him. Just like now. And he doesn't expect or want me to be coy either.

But that's part of what scares me. If he thinks I shouldn't be trying to get my abilities back, he won't pull punches. If he thinks I'm wasting my time, he'll let me know. What kind of stress would that put on us? And then there's the other thing. With Brody's threat hanging over my head, do I really want to start things up again with Tucker? At the very least, he's a distraction. Even now, instead of telling him to leave because I'm busy, I'm listening to what he has to say. I'm considering his offer. If we're back together, how much less time will I be spending on finding a solution to my problems?

I could tell him no. I could cut everything off now—tell him to find someone else. But my heart clenches at the idea. I've been doing my best to push Tucker from my head for months, to ignore him when he shows up to school, to tamp down memories when they surface in my mind. But despite doing that, I always knew he was there—a possibility. I'm not ready to shut that door entirely. I consider my next words carefully. "Okay... You've pushed me." I take in a breath, releasing it slowly before continuing. "Can you give me a little while to see where I land?"

Disappointment flashes across his face. He doesn't bother hiding it. But he also doesn't remove his hand. "I can," he says, his tone measured. "But don't expect me to wait around another four months."

"No—not another four months."

Tucker's eyes drop to my tablet. "I'll let you get back to whatever." He stands, regaining some of his signature ease and coolness. "See you around."

My eyes don't leave his form until he's out the door. Part of me wants to follow him, to wrap my arms around him, press him to the wall and kiss him the way we used to. But I know I can't. Not now.

Not ever if you don't figure out how to get the information Brody wants, a voice in the back of my head points out. With a sigh, I unlock the tablet's screen and tap the browser with my latest search results.

I'm clicking around on a new website when someone takes the vacated seat across from me. When I glance up, a smile touches my lips. I'm ready to tell Tucker I'll need a bit more time than this, but the words die in my throat.

It's not Tucker who sits across from me.

Brody folds his hands on the table, his posture straight, professional. He's dressed in a black jacket over a burgundy dress shirt, and I feel almost like I'm at a job interview. Or in the principal's office.

I fight against the swell of panic that threatens to claim me. What is he doing here? Is he following me? Suddenly even this public place seems too secluded. "What do you want?" I'm pleased that the words come out level and my voice doesn't shake.

He tilts his head, posture relaxing slightly. "Same as you. Just out for a coffee." He offers a smile, flashing his straight, almost impossibly white teeth. "I'll say, though, I was pleased to see you've got enough spare time on your hands that you can flirt. Must mean I'll be getting my information soon."

I fist my hands to hide the fact my fingers are trembling. "We're still working on it. It might help if you told me what you want to know."

"What, so you can cheat? No way. Bess knows exactly what I want to hear. When you make contact, she'll give you the information." He leans forward, like Tucker did just minutes ago.

Except this time I want to recoil, to put as much space between me and the man across the table as possible. I fight the instinct, not wanting to show weakness. "You know, I could arrange for that boyfriend of yours to meet a sticky end. Might help you concentrate without any distractions."

The panic that's been threatening since he sat down floods me. I try to swallow around the lump that's formed in my throat. "Don't hurt him. I'm working on getting your information. I just need a little more time."

"Funny," he says, his voice low, "that's the exact excuse you gave Tucker just now."

He smiles as I gasp at his use of Tucker's name. Before I can form a coherent question, demand how he knows—*what* he knows—he reaches across the table and picks up my coffee cup, taking a sip as he stands. He pulls a face. "A little cold, don't you think?" As he sets it back down, he steps toward me, standing much closer than he should, invading my personal space. "Don't waste time, Crystal. I don't like to wait."

I hold my breath until he drops my gaze and pivots, striding toward the door. He's barely outside before my phone is in my hand. I open the message app and type out a text to Krissa: *We need to figure this out NOW.*

Chapter Twenty-One
Krissa

I'm jittery when I pull up in front of Crystal's house. We were already planning to meet tonight, but after her run-in with Brody earlier today, I know she's probably antsier than I am. She's been texting throughout the day, demanding status reports. I'd have come over earlier, but she insisted I wait until her parents were gone. I get that we couldn't actually do spells with her folks there, so I'm not sure why she's being so picky about arrival time.

Crystal's green Spark is in the driveway, so it's obvious she's here. I wonder if she picked Dana up or if we'll have to go get her now. Or maybe she's managing her own ride. Maybe Fox will drop her off.

A hollow feeling forms in the pit of my stomach at the thought. I'm happy for him—I am. It hasn't bothered me at all that he and Dana are together. Well, not too much. I thought it was weird to begin with—just the speed with which they got together. One minute he's longing for a relationship with alternate-me, the next he's all cozy with Dana. I get that she's the one who told him the truth about me, that I'm not his Kristyl. I convinced myself his moving on was a good thing. Indeed, in the last four months I haven't spared much thought for the two of them. But after what Tucker was saying the other day about me crossing Fox's mind...

Dammit, Tucker.

I get out of my car and cross the lawn to Crystal's porch. For as cloak-and-dagger as she's being about this meeting, I'd almost prefer it be dark upon my arrival. But April isn't cooperating and the sky is still streaming with spring sunlight, even though it's after dinner.

Crystal's got the door open before I can even knock. Dana lurks behind her and relief sweeps through me. Fox won't be showing up anytime soon. One complication shelved—for the moment, at least.

"Get in here," Crystal snaps. "What took you so long?"

I raise an eyebrow. The decorative analog clock on the wall almost directly ahead of me indicates I'm right on time, but I don't bother pointing it out.

Dana catches my gaze and rolls her eyes. "Ignore her. She's in a mood."

This might be the first unsolicited thing Dana's said to me in months. I offer a conspiratorial smile. This is progress.

Crystal stalks down the hallway, beckoning for us to follow. When I enter the bedroom behind Dana, Crystal is already sitting cross-legged on her bed. Dana takes the chair in front of the desk, so I sit on the chair Crystal clearly dragged in from the dining room.

I don't bother with small talk. I shrug the drawstring backpack from my shoulders and open it, removing the Barnette grimoire and a notebook I've been jotting things down in. "I think I know what went wrong with the spell the other day. I opened myself up because I couldn't connect with Bess. That's when things went crazy. But I think the reason I couldn't connect has nothing to do with not being open enough. I think what I was missing is a personal connection to her."

"What does that matter?" Crystal asks. "The spell doesn't say the psychic needs to have a personal connection—"

"But it *does* describe having a loved one present," I say. "When I first read it, I figured it was because that was the person who would want to talk to the spirit. But the more I thought about it, the more I figured it'd be kind of obvious for that person to be there, so why mention it? Unless it's a key component to the spell."

"Well, we don't exactly have a loved one handy," Crystal says. "Unless you want to connect with Seth first and have him help find her. Something tells me that'll end badly."

Irritation flares and I do my best to tamp it down. She's being difficult, but I don't think she's doing it on purpose. I can't say I wouldn't be acting the same way if some dude from a cult searching for eternal life took time out of his day to harass me. "I don't think it has to be a loved one."

"I'm confused," Dana says. "Isn't that just what you said the spell needs?"

"I think what's required is a personal connection. And there's no one connected to Bess like Crystal."

"Yeah, we know," Crystal grumbles. "I was possessed."

"But you're also a distant relative," I remind her.

Dana's face scrunches in concentration. "I still don't get it. Crystal was part of the spell last time. If your theory's right, you should've been able to connect because Crystal was there."

I sigh. I didn't think I'd have to explain this much. "But I was the one trying to find Bess last time. I was connected to the two of you for more energy. I wasn't letting Crystal help me find Bess—not specifically. I think we should try again, but this time I'll let Crystal kind of lead the search."

Crystal rubs her hands together. "All right. Let's do it."

I hand out the same kind of charms to Crystal and Dana as they used last time—except these are bigger. I've filled the bags with more herbs and crystals and I've spent every spare moment in the last few days charging them. I even asked Tucker and Griffin to help. They both rolled their eyes at my reluctance to tell them what they were for but helped anyway.

This time when I cast the spell, I tap into Crystal's mind. I've already instructed her to conjure anything she can related to Bess, and her head is spinning with fuzzy memories and sensations. I do my best to guide her consciousness forward, to let it lead, when my psyche arrives in the blinding white place. But no matter what I try, the results are no better than they were the first time, and I refuse to open myself up again, fearing what happened last time will repeat.

When I finally end the spell, disappointment is etched on Crystal's face.

Dana helps me tie my bracelet back into place. "We'll figure it out," she assures Crystal.

"Yeah, right." Crystal doesn't sound convinced. She checks the time on her phone. "You guys need to get out of here. My parents said they'd be out until ten, but you never know with them." She scoots off the bed and strides toward the door, but I block her progress, forcing her to look at me.

"We *will* figure this out," I say. "This spell didn't work. That's fine. I'll find another."

A hard look sets in her features, and her lip curls like she wants to tell me off, but before she can her face falls. "Thanks, Krissa."

I want to spend more time reassuring her, but I can tell by the way she's ushering us toward the door it would be bad for her if her parents came home before we left. As I climb in my car to drive home, I know one thing for sure: I'm going to do anything to keep my promise to her. I thought for sure this plan had a chance, but since it didn't work, I'll find another way.

I have to.

Chapter Twenty-Two
Crystal

It's already been a rough morning.

My parents and I met up with David Cole for breakfast to celebrate his birthday. David Cole, a man that five months ago I'd never laid eyes on, but who in this reality was married to my aunt Crystal. Since in my reality my aunt died nearly twenty years ago, and in this one she died soon after I found myself here, I never really got to know her husband. That means I had to spend the last hour and a half pretending to recall memories of birthday parties spent with my uncle David and my aunt Crystal—events that never happened for me. It's been exhausting.

The only benefit of the morning has been the fact that both my parents have been too preoccupied to bother me much about my grades. Mom caught me with my tablet yesterday so now I'm in trouble for lying as well as for flunking half my classes. But not a word about either of those things has been uttered since we pulled into the restaurant parking lot. David Cole is still adjusting to life without his wife, and my parents seemed determined to make this a light, happy occasion. Even now, on the car ride home, neither my mom nor dad has spoken a word directly to me. They're both up in the front, talking in low voices about how David looks and speculating about how much he's eating.

I'm itching to get back home, even though I don't know how much progress I can make. Now that my access to the internet is basically cut off, I'm not sure how I'm going to find time to research ways to contact Bess, let alone figure out how to get my abilities back. Maybe I could convince my mom that I have some research to do at the library. I'm not sure she'd buy it, but it might be worth a try.

I stare out the window as different scenarios play in my head. I recognize exactly where we are—just blocks from home. After our right at this intersection, it's a straight shot to our street. Dad complains because he always seems to catch a red light, so it surprises me when he accelerates as he approaches.

"What the...?" he murmurs.

Mom tenses. "Honey, slow down—"

I glance through the windshield. The light is red, as usual, but our car is picking up speed.

"I can't get the car to stop." Dad's voice is tight with panic. I hear a soft *thunk, thunk, thunk* as he repeatedly slams on the brakes.

We're ten yards away. Five yards. We're going to blow through the light. I scan the cross street for oncoming traffic. There's a big four-door truck about to pass through the intersection.

We're going to crash.

I brace myself with one hand against the back of my mother's seat and the other gripping the door handle. I squeeze my eyes shut, preparing for the impact.

A horn blares and breaks screech, but there's no collision. Although my eyes are closed, I can feel the movement of our car as dad maneuvers away from the danger. A jolt bumps my body, but the force is not that of a crash. When I open my eyes, I find we've jumped the curb on the other side of the intersection. The car is finally at a standstill.

"Is everyone all right?" Dad asks.

"Yes, I'm fine," Mom says, her voice shaky. "Crystal?"

It takes a moment before I can speak. "I'm okay."

Dad runs a hand through his hair as he blows out a breath. "I don't know what happened. The car just wouldn't stop. It was speeding up."

"You're not planning on driving home, are you?" Mom asks.

Dad shakes his head. "I need to call a tow truck. Clearly there's something very wrong."

I replay the scene in my head. No joke something went wrong. It would be one thing if the car just wouldn't stop. That could be blamed on faulty brakes. But the car was speeding up. What on earth could cause that?

Eyes prickle the back of my neck. I'm being watched. As Dad pulls out his cell phone and calls for a tow, I scan the vicinity. My heart begins thudding in my chest. Standing on the corner opposite the one we jumped is Brody. Beside him is a man I don't recognize, but just the sight of him is enough to make me tremble. It's not that he looks frightening in a classic way or anything, but something about him radiates danger. His dark brown hair is long and brushes his shoulders. It's stringy, like he hasn't washed it in a few days. That, plus his scrubby mustache and chin hair and the oversized layers of clothing he wears, gives him an unkempt appearance.

I know even before Brody jerks his head to the side that he wants me to go to him. Doing my best to swallow around the lump in my throat, I reach my trembling fingers toward the door handle. "Um, I need to stretch my legs. I can't stay in this car right now."

Dad waves a vague hand as he talks with the tow truck driver. Mom calls, "Stay close," as I open the door and climb out.

Brody and his companion have disappeared just beyond the corner. I make my way in that direction, doing my best not to rush, just in case my mom is watching.

Brody's lips curls into a smile when I catch up. "So nice of you to join us."

"If you wanted to talk with me, there are easier ways." I'm pleased that my voice sounds stronger than I feel.

The smile on Brody's face doesn't fade. "I'd say the time for talking has long passed. I told you what I want, and yet you still haven't delivered the information to me. I'm beginning to think you don't believe I'm serious. My friend and I are here to show you how very wrong you are."

Now that I'm closer, I take another look at Brody's companion. He looks young, in his mid-twenties like Brody, but he gives off the vibe of someone who's seen a lot—none of it good. There's an iciness in his eyes that makes me shiver. "I'm doing the best I can."

For the first time, the smile slips from Brody's lips. "Either your best isn't good enough, or you need proper motivation. I thought when we spoke at the coffeehouse you understood just how far I'm willing to go, but apparently an object lesson is in order." He nods toward the man beside him. "I had Kai use some restraint with your parents just now. Consider this a warning. Next time, your mom and dad might not be so lucky."

I fight to suppress a shiver. They were behind the accident. Of course they were. There's nothing wrong with my dad's car—this man, Kai, made it behave that way. "I'll get you what you want. Don't hurt my family."

"That is entirely up to you," Brody says. "I want to be very clear: I will kill everyone you love if you continue to hold out on me. And if I still don't get what I want, I'll kill you too."

Kai straightens beside him, and Brody inclines his head kindly. "Apologies. Kai will be the one doing the killing."

At this correction, Kai's posture relaxes, as if he's pleased it's clear who will be doing the dirty work. I wonder if he's able to speak, or if he's just used to Brody doing the talking.

"You don't need to kill anyone, and I don't need any more object lessons. You just have to trust me when I say I'm doing everything I can to get you what you want."

Brody folds his arms across his chest. "That's just it. I don't trust you."

Before I can mount a defense, he turns and starts up the street, away from me. Kai offers a leer—a promise of nasty things to come—before following behind.

However bad I thought things were, they've just gotten worse.

Chapter Twenty-Three
Krissa

"Heads or tails?" Jodi calls from behind the register.

I glance up from the bundles of herbs I'm restocking. My aunt holds a shiny quarter between her thumb and forefinger. If she's explained what we're flipping for, I wasn't paying attention. I'm finding it increasingly difficult to keep my mind from drifting when I'm at work. Every time my hand passes over an herb or crystal—heck, even the homeopathic supplements—my head starts spinning with possible applications for the items. And there's the fact that I've gotten two texts from Crystal since my shift started, each basically telling me I need to figure out how to contact Bess ASAP.

Yeah, like I haven't been working on that.

Jodi is staring at me expectantly. "Uh—heads."

She nods before flipping the coin in the air. She catches it deftly with her right hand before slapping it on the back of her left. When she peeks at it, she grins. "Heads. Looks like you're going to pick up the pizza."

I vaguely remember her asking me for topping preferences a bit ago. I didn't realize she'd actually put in the order. "Yeah, sure."

Jodi rolls her eyes as I approach. "Well, of course 'sure.' You can't argue with the almighty decision-making power of the quarter."

I do my best to offer a smile. No matter how withdrawn I've been these last months, Jodi's never changed the way she interacts with me. While Dad's been more apt to act all surly and in control and Mom's more gentle, like she's afraid the wrong word will send me over the edge, Jodi behaves the same way she always has, despite the fact I don't return the favor.

I'm a crappy niece.

But she doesn't know, whispers a voice in the back of my mind. *If she knew what you did and how you feel about it, she wouldn't treat you like this. She'd think you're a monster.*

I stumble on my next step toward Jodi but recover quickly as I stuff the voice back down into the depths. I can't let myself think like that. What's done is done. All I can do is move forward—which is exactly what I'm doing in helping Crystal.

I can be a good person again. I'll prove it.

Is it just my imagination that Jodi's scrutinizing me a little more closely than usual as I take the bill from her hand? I'm probably imagining it—it's not as if she can read my thoughts. I force my lips into what I hope is a more natural-looking smile. "Promise not to eat it all before I get back."

Her expression from a moment ago—was it concern?—disappears and is replaced by a grin. "You'd better not or I'm liable to munch on your arm."

"Cannibalism?" I ask, starting for the front door. "That's a little intense, isn't it?"

"Clearly you have no concept of the hunger burning in my belly," Jodi calls after me as she moves from behind the register to pick up on the job I left unfinished. "I'll go full zombie on you," she continues as I pull open the door. "And after I've had my fill, I'll sell what's left. You'd be surprised the number of spells that call for a tongue or an eye or a kidney..."

I fight back a snort as Mrs. Winters enters, a horrified look washing over her age-lined face. A woman of at least seventy, she's a regular who comes in for tinctures and herbs for her many ailments—most of which Jodi is convinced are imagined. As Jodi continues to ramble on about specific uses for human organs and Mrs. Winters' eyes go wider and wider, I can't contain a bubble of laughter. Jodi glances up, blanching at the look on the older woman's face. I step out onto the street as Jodi begins sputtering out an explanation for what our customer walked in on.

It's with light spirits I head down the street toward the pizza parlor. I don't remember the last time I was able to joke with my aunt. I didn't realize how much I missed it.

Maybe I've squandered these last several months by shutting myself off for no reason. Maybe I'm more like the person I want to be than I think. Is it possible I've been stuffing my real self down beneath the surface, convincing myself things must be different because of what I've been through? Because of what I've done? People who knew what happened tried to talk with me about it. Owen, Felix—even Lexie and my dad. I refused to discuss the topic, afraid of the direction the conversation would go. Maybe it was wrong to do that.

Maybe it's time for a change.

After a quick glance in either direction, I jog across Main. Technically I don't need to cross for another block; I do so now out of habit. The coffee shop is just ahead and I definitely am there more frequently than the restaurant. Unbidden, my gaze searches through the front window as I approach, a half-formed thought about stopping in for drinks to accompany our pizza buzzing in my head. But when my eyes land on *him*, I freeze in my tracks.

Sitting at a high-top table the two of us occupied on more than one occasion is Owen, his head down, his attention fixed on the textbook in front of him. The thumb and index finger of his right hand tap out a beat in time with whatever is being piped through his earbuds. Even at this angle, I can tell he just got a haircut—it's styled slightly differently than usual to compensate for the loss in length.

Typically I'm not one to search for hidden meaning in everyday events, but Owen's presence in the shop without the usual throng surrounding him just as I'm thinking about how I should've talked to him back when I had the chance feels like a sign. Before I can talk myself out of it, I'm pushing open the door and striding purposefully toward him. Maybe this is the universe telling me things don't have to be as complicated as I've been making them, that I'm not so far gone as I've come to believe.

Owen's music is so loud I can hear muffled reverberations even over the hiss of the espresso machine's steam wand and the hum of conversation from other patrons. He's so focused on his math book he doesn't notice my approach, and I'm standing at his side a full ten seconds before he finally looks up.

"Krissa?" He jumps with surprise when his eyes land on me. He quickly casts his gaze around, like he's afraid someone in one of the small clusters of people at nearby tables might have seen his reaction. He tugs at the wires of his earbuds with one hand as he turns the music off with the other. "What are you doing here?"

He has every right to be shocked at my sudden appearance, so I try not to take offense. I honestly don't remember the last time I approached him. In the weeks following the battle with Seth, it was Owen who did the approaching. I was the one who did the pushing away. There are so many things I could say right now—so many I probably should. There will be time later for apologies, but right now I need to get the thing between us off my chest. "I'm ready to talk."

Owen's brow knits, his usually clear blue eyes clouded with confusion. "You're ready..."

"To talk, yeah," I finish, nodding as I slide into the empty seat adjacent to him. "You tried to get me to so many times and I just..." I take in a breath, hoping it will help to quell the guilt surging in my chest. "But I'm here now, and I'm finally ready. And when I saw you sitting here, it was like I was *supposed* to come talk to you and—"

He cuts me off with a slight shake of his head. "Don't get me wrong—I'm glad you're finally ready to open up to someone," he begins, except he doesn't sound glad at all. His voice is tight, almost pained, like every word is a struggle. "I hope you can process everything you've been going through. But..."

My breath hitches as I wait for the rest of his sentence. I didn't have a chance to fully imagine how I wanted this conversation to go, but this is certainly not the trajectory I would have wished for.

He takes in a breath and releases it slowly. "I don't think I'm the best person for you to open up to. Maybe once, but..." He breaks eye contact, rubbing the back of his neck.

I'm having a hard time breathing. The air seems thin. "How can you say that?" My voice comes out higher and shakier than I intend. I swallow before continuing. "You know me better than anyone."

His eyes flick to mine for a brief moment. "Maybe that was true once."

The word *maybe* stabs through my stomach like an icy dagger. "Of course it's true."

The corners of his mouth twitch. "If you're serious about talking with someone, I'm sure Griffin or...Tucker...would be willing to listen." He struggles so badly with Tucker's name I'm surprised he doesn't choke on it.

My heart sinks. Is that what this is really about? Owen never liked Tucker, and his distaste bloomed into full-blown hatred the night Tucker almost attacked me. But that was in my old reality—the one this Owen remembers but never actually experienced. The Tucker here isn't perfect, but I've never seen him act maliciously. It took me a while to accept this version for who he is and forget about what his alternate self was like, but it seems Owen still hasn't moved past it. Is that where this resistance is coming from? Something in me relaxes. If he'll just let me talk, I can explain why I've been spending time with Tucker and Griffin, why I turned to the two of them and away from Owen. "I don't want to talk to them. You're the one—"

"Krissa." He breathes my name so gently that in another circumstance I'd be convinced it would precede a kiss. But it's obvious from his body language—his subtle leaning toward the back of his chair—that he has no intention of brushing his lips against mine. "I can't do this right now."

The air presses itself from my lungs as if I've been sucker-punched. It takes several tries to gulp in a breath. "Then when?"

He rakes his upper teeth over his lower lip. "I don't know."

His response does nothing to soothe me. "How can you not know?"

He runs a hand down his face. "Don't you understand how hard the last four months have been for me?" he snaps, drawing the attention of one of the baristas. He lowers his voice when he continues. "I barely remember my life from this reality anymore. I had to sit through a *very* uncomfortable talk with my dad where he asked if I was on drugs because I couldn't remember some family trip we apparently took a couple summers back. Except there was no trip in your reality, and it's the only one I can remember. There's been a hundred times I've needed to talk to you, but you completely shut me out. So I'm doing the only thing I can: I'm trying to move on. I'm trying to figure out my place now. At first I thought it was by your side but..." He shakes his head.

My stomach lurches violently and I'm afraid I'll be sick. "And now?"

"And now..." He blows out a breath. "What if I give up the life I'm starting to cobble together here only to have you shut me out? I don't know if I can take you choosing your ex-boyfriend's brother and the guy who attacked you over me again."

That's not fair and he knows it, but I doubt pointing out the inaccuracies in his statement will win me any points. Besides, the sentiment is true enough. I'm not sure what else there is to say. I press my palms into the edge of the table to help myself to my feet. "Okay. I'll give you time. I think it's the least I can do, considering all the time you've given me." I want to press further, find out when he thinks he might be ready, but I don't want to push my luck. Owen simply nods and, with considerable effort, I turn away and stride on unsteady legs toward the door.

It was foolish of me to think things would go back to how they were before just because I announced I was finally ready to talk. I can't expect Owen to be able to switch gears that quickly. He's respected me enough to give me space, even though it's probably hurt him every day. I dig my nails into my palms. This was a stupid move on my part. I disregarded entirely what I've been doing to him these last few months. I thought pulling away was protecting him from the person I feared I was becoming, but I never considered he might still need me.

The door opens just before I reach it, revealing the straight white teeth and blonde spiral curls of a girl who seems vaguely familiar. I stand back, allowing her to pass, and as she does it hits me. She's Laurie, the girl who's been spending so much time with Owen lately. Indeed, she makes a beeline for his table. A smile breaks across his face as she approaches.

I have to turn away before she reaches him. What if he stands and hugs her—or worse? I can't see it or I might fall apart—shatter into a billion shards right here on the coffee shop's floor.

Maybe it doesn't matter how much time I give Owen. Maybe I'm already too late. I've put him through so much in the six months we've known each other. He deserves better than what I've been able to give. Perhaps this is for the best. He should have something pure and uncomplicated, and maybe this Laurie girl is just the person to give it to him.

Chapter Twenty-Four
Sasha

I've been spending so much time at Allegro Bread I've got a regular seat. What's more, I'm starting to recognize other customers. There's a rowdy bunch of seventy-something men who sit at a corner table meant for four. They commandeer chairs from surrounding tables as more join their ranks. I've counted as many as eight crammed around the small square table before. They mostly argue politics and flirt with the store manager when she comes out to check on things. Then there's a heavy-set woman in her forties with frizzy brown hair who shows up with a new mystery novel each time I see her. She devours the story and her sandwich with fervor. There's also a man who shows up in a business suit and a wireless earpiece which he uses to talk to clients, presumably, as he clicks through pages on his laptop.

I wonder what these people think of me. I usually meet Anya here, but occasionally Elliot shows up, too. Do we seem to them to be a happy little family catching up with each other? Or can they see when I force a smile or pretend to be engaged in the conversation? Do the others in the restaurant even notice us?

Lately lunch dates have been consumed by one topic: The search for Nate. I haven't had any luck breaking whatever enchantments kept the castaways hidden, but that hasn't stopped Anya and Elliot from looking. Elliot was convinced earlier this week that he'd located him, but his suspicions ended up proving incorrect. He was crushed to learn the car salesman living in Illinois wasn't his relative. In our long relationship, I've shared in plenty of Elliot's joys and pains, but this is the first time I can remember having to fake an emotion for his benefit. In truth, I was glad when he told us Mr. Nathan Standish of Peoria was not, in fact, his uncle. I know Uncle Nate never manifested abilities—that's why he was cast out of the Devoted—but there's ordinary and then there's pitifully ordinary, and Nathan Standish definitely falls into the latter category. Still, I painted on a disappointed face and patted Elliot's shoulder. I promised to help him continue the search for a man who, in all likelihood, will want nothing to do with us if we ever do find him. I know if I never manifested abilities, I wouldn't want to reminded of that failure.

Elliot and Anya arrive within about a minute of each other and are separated by only one person in line to order food. I nibble at the apple that came with my still-untouched sandwich. I'm not really hungry. I haven't had much of an appetite since Elliot confronted me about contacting the Amaranthine.

By the time my sister and best friend join me at the table, Anya is practically quivering with suppressed excitement. Elliot looks mildly exasperated. "Okay, we're here now," he says as they sit. "Are you finally going to spill what you're so amped about?"

Anya tries and fails to scowl at him. "It's just tearing you up you're not strong enough to break into my head, isn't it?"

He holds his hands up. "I'm practicing restraint because we're practically family, but if you want me to go full bore, just let me know."

She rolls her eyes. "Uh-huh," she sighs, clearly unconvinced of his psychic prowess.

Although I have no doubt the two could carry the conversation themselves, I decide to interject, knowing a lack of participation on my part could read as disinterest, and the last thing I want is for either of them to be suspicious of my intentions. Elliot already figured out I'm the one who brought the Amaranthine to Clearwater, and for the moment I'm pretty sure he believes I'm willing to help keep Crystal and everyone else safe. I don't want to give him any reason to doubt me. "Since I'm not psychic, do you think you could just tell us the old-fashioned way what's got you so happy?"

A bright smile flashes across Anya's face like she's been waiting for me to ask. "I didn't want to get your hopes up, not until I was sure, but I've been in contact with someone recently."

The curve of my lips is too forced, so I take a sip of my pop and nod encouragingly. Has she found another Nate candidate? For Elliot's sake, I almost hope she's found the real deal this time, because I don't know if I can watch him go through another disappointment.

Elliot's eyes stray to me for an instant before he says, "Don't leave us in suspense."

Anya shakes her head, her dark hair swishing around her face. "I'm sorry, it's just... I still can't quite believe it. I didn't want to say anything until I was positive, and now... The person I've been in contact with..." She pauses, taking in a breath as she reaches across the table to cover my hand. "It's Misha."

I freeze. That's not at all what I was expecting her to say. Elliot mentioned they were looking for her, of course, but neither of them have said anything about it since then. There's been plenty of talk about the search for Nate, but none about finding my other sister. But I suppose it was foolish of me to think they weren't looking.

Anya and Elliot are both staring at me, and I realize I still haven't reacted to the news. I open my mouth to respond, but nothing comes out. I take a few pulls from my straw before trying again. "Misha. Wow."

"I'm sorry for springing it on you like this," Anya says, her eyes moistening. "I didn't want to get your hopes up if it wasn't really her."

Get my hopes up? If I'd realized Anya was actively searching, would I really have been hoping she'd find Misha? Since her exit from my life, I haven't spent much time thinking about her. Not long after she left, Anya also disappeared—but I was told Anya had been killed by a mob of ordinary men when she left our community on a regular errand. I mourned the loss of my eldest sister more than Misha's leaving. After all, Anya actually had abilities. Misha was different—not really one of us.

But now that it's possible I'll see her again, I can't stem the flood of questions that surge in my mind. Where has she been for the last thirteen years? What's her life like? Did she ever think about the Devoted? About me? Is she glad she left, or did she miss her family terribly? Did she believe it was for the greater good she was cast out, the way we were always taught?

Not missing a beat, Elliot pulls Anya into a hug. "This is amazing! How long have you been in contact? I can't believe you've been able to keep this a secret! Does she want to reconnect? I mean, I assume so, because you're telling us…"

He shoots off questions in a rapid-fire fashion and I stop trying to follow along. I might see Misha again. I never thought that would happen, never considered it as a possibility. But now here it is.

I have no idea how I feel about this. From the way Anya and Elliot are grinning like idiots, I know how I'm *supposed* to feel, but I can't help the tight knot of apprehension in the pit of my stomach.

Does Misha even want to see me? Anya left the Devoted of her own accord. I stayed. I'd still be a part of that community if everyone but Elliot hadn't died.

"There aren't any firm plans yet," Anya says, jarring me back to the conversation. "Misha's still processing all that's happened. She never anticipated seeing any of us again, but it was still a blow to find out our parents are dead. She's built a life for herself. She's got to figure out how we might fit into it."

"Then there's a possibility she won't want anything to do with us?" I ask, keeping my voice measured. The thought simultaneously brings a wave of relief and a pang of disappointment.

"There is," Anya says bracingly, misreading my tone. "But I have a feeling she'll want to meet with us. It just might take her a little while to come around."

I'm not sure what the right response to this revelation is, so I just nod.

Anya pats my hand before removing hers and launching into an account of how she found Misha. I nod vaguely at intervals as I take bite after bite of my sandwich. It's not that I'm hungry—having a full mouth keeps me from having to add to the conversation. I chew each mouthful mechanically, far longer than is strictly necessary. The whole time, my head buzzes with conflicting thoughts and emotions. I can't land on how I feel at the prospect of seeing my sister again.

It's not until Elliot takes over the conversation that I tune in to what's being said. "Yeah, it was crazy," he says, obviously in response to something Anya asked. "I was probably half a mile down the road when it happened, but I still saw it. The Jamisons' car sped up at the intersection and ran the light. Almost got T-boned."

His eyes catch mine for the briefest moment as he reaches for his drink, and my stomach swoops. I get the distinct impression there's more to the story than he's saying.

"Goodness," Anya breathes. "Was anyone hurt?"

Elliot takes a pull from his straw before responding. "Didn't look like it. When I drove by, Mr. and Mrs. Jamison were out of the car, talking to the other driver, and Crystal was walking around." He stretches out his arm to set his plastic cup back down but overshoots, brushing his knuckles against my fingertips for the briefest moment.

The contact is so fleeting I doubt Anya noticed, but it was enough. Although I'm not psychic, Elliot and I spent countless hours figuring out how to send thought messages to each other when we were younger. When it was my turn as sender, the results were always hit or miss, since not only did I have to clear my mind of all other ideas, but Elliot also had to reach into my head to pick up what I wanted him to know. Elliot, on the other hand, has pretty much a perfect record for planting ideas into my brain. This time is no different. The inside of my skull seems to reverberate with a thrum like guitar strings being strummed for a moment before the sensation fades, leaving only Elliot's words: *I know an unnatural attack when I feel it. It was the Amaranthine. Crystal must not have given them the information they want yet. I thought you were helping her.*

My gaze drops to the table. Even though I promised Elliot, I haven't made contact with Crystal yet. Although it's tempting to simply hang back and wait for the Amaranthine to do her in, if I do, I run the risk of losing Elliot. I still want my revenge, but not if it costs me my best friend.

I resolve to throw myself into my research. I'm positive there's a way for my plan to work. Elliot will think I'm helping, and, in a way I will be. I'll be helping Crystal ruin Krissa's life.

Chapter Twenty-Five
Krissa

I ignore Crystal's texts for much of the day because I'm still upset about Owen and not really in the mood to answer her incessant questioning about what my next plan of attack is to contact Bess. But when I finally check my messages as Jodi drives us home after the shop closes, I feel like the worst friend ever: She and her family were in an accident earlier—one caused by the Amaranthine.

There might not be as much time for trial and error as I'd been anticipating. I figured as long as we were doing *something* Brody would be patient and give us the benefit of the doubt that we were doing our best. But this move changes things.

Elliot warned they were dangerous.

As Jodi turns onto our street, I tap out a quick text to Crystal. *Sorry for radio silence. At shop all day. Researching as soon as I'm home. I'll text with any news.*

While I hope my pitiful excuse is enough to appease Crystal, it does nothing to assuage the guilt that swells for ignoring her all day. Isn't this exactly what got me where I am now with Owen? I shut him out because I had too many things going on inside my head. I can't do the same thing now. I'm trying to undo my mistakes.

Jodi's not an idiot, so I know she realized something happened when I went to pick up the pizza, but, being Jodi, she hasn't asked about it. Instead, as she pulls into the driveway, she keeps up the constant stream of one-sided banter she's engaged in since we got into the car. Lucky for her it's a short drive. I tune in to her anecdote as she cuts the ignition. It takes a second for the words I only half heard since the ride began to join up with what she's saying now and another for me to make sense of everything. "Wait," I say, cutting her off. "You had a boyfriend?"

My aunt pauses, her hand on the door. When she turns, her expression is bemused. "You were paying attention?"

For some reason, the surprise in her tone makes me laugh. Not just a giggle, but an all-out belly laugh with my head tipping back and everything. When my snickers subside, Jodi's eyes are on me, a smile curving her lips.

"It's been a long time since I've heard you laugh like that." There's a note of sadness in the way she says it that threatens to darken the moment, but she moves on quickly. "Yes, I had a boyfriend. I've had several, actually. Why do you sound so shocked? It's not like I'm a nun or anything."

"I know," I say quickly, my mind spinning into panic mode. For a moment I'm worried I've given away something alternate-me would have known, but Jodi isn't looking at me like I'm crazy or forgetful. "It's just... When's the last time you were in a relationship?"

Her shrug is nonchalant, but there's something that tightens in her face. "Um... I think the last *real* relationship ended just before you and your mom moved in. Then for a while I kind of dropped out of the dating game—what with a teenager to help raise and all. I've been on a few dates recently. Nothing to write home about—which is precisely why I haven't talked about them."

Her hand goes to the door again, but I'm not quite ready to drop the subject. "Has there ever been anyone special? Someone you thought was the one?"

Pain flickers across Jodi's face and I regret asking the question. Still, I can't help wanting to know the answer. "Once," she says at length. "A long time ago. But he chose my friend over me and..." She raises her hands as if to say *oh well.*

I open my mouth, ready to ask if this guy was David Cole, but I stop myself just in time. In my reality, David Cole dated Crystal Jamison's aunt before she died in a house fire, then moved on to marry Shelly Tanner—another member of Jodi's circle. In this reality, since Crystal Taylor didn't die that night two decades ago, David ended up marrying her instead of Shelly. But, of course, I shouldn't know that. Instead, I simply say, "Okay."

Jodi takes this as her cue to exit the car without further interrogation. Although I'm glad to know a little bit more about my aunt, I'm sorry for making her uncomfortable. Maybe I can make it up to her somehow. Maybe after I put in a few hours of research on the Bess problem I can come downstairs and we can watch a movie together. I'll even let her pick and not groan when it's a romcom from before I was born.

I'm trying to remember whether we have popcorn in the cupboards as Jodi pushes open the front door and steps across the threshold. She stops short and I bump into her. "What the—"

My parents stand in the hallway just outside the dining room, identical grins stretched across their faces. They look almost manic, and for a moment I'm afraid something is terribly wrong. But then Mom is ushering us inside, rushing past me to close the door. "Take off your shoes," Mom urges.

I'm glad for the reminder, because their odd behavior has thrown me off. It takes Jodi a second to respond to Mom's prompting, too, and after she kicks off her flats, she approaches my dad, who is sweeping his arm toward the dining room. Jodi glances over her shoulder to catch my eye, but all I can do is shrug. I've got no more of an idea what's going on than she does.

I consider how much easier things could be if I removed the bracelet charm. The desire to be able to figure out what's going on in my parents' heads only intensifies when I enter the dining room and find a bottle of champagne in the center of the table surrounded by four of Jodi's "fancy" glasses—flutes left over after one of Clearwater High's proms. Shelly Tanner was the senior class adviser that year and foisted a half-dozen off on Jodi when she couldn't fit any more in her own cupboards.

Jodi asks the question that's racing through my mind: "What's going on?"

"We have an announcement," Mom says, easing up behind us and slipping an arm around each of our waists as Dad strides past us to the table.

"And champagne?" Jodi asks.

Dad grins his response, grabbing the bottle by the neck. He picks up a kitchen towel that had been hanging over the arm of one of the chairs and drapes it over the top of the bottle, holding it in place. "We think our announcement merits some celebration."

"Well, don't leave us in suspense," Jodi says. While her tone indicates she's playing along, there's a tightness in the set of her jaw that hints at apprehension.

Mom squeezes us both gently before removing her arms and easing between Jodi and me. As Dad begins to tug at the cork through the towel, Mom turns to face us. "When Ben left five years ago, I knew he did it because he believed it was what was best for our family. But I don't think either of us could really anticipate what that time apart would do to us as individuals or how those changes would affect our relationship. The last four months have really been a process of getting to know each other again to see how—and if—we still fit together."

A knot tightens in my stomach. *If* they still fit together? That doesn't sound good. I thought things between them were back to normal. They stopped being overly formal when they talked to each other ages ago, they go out at least once a week for a date night. They're sharing the same bedroom, for crying out loud. But what if I've misread the signs? What if in my distraction I've been assuming things are getting better between them when they haven't been? "Wait—are you two getting a divorce?"

A loud *pop* explodes through the air and Mom, Jodi, and I jump. Jodi even lets out a squeal.

"Sorry, sorry," Dad mutters, although the wicked smile creeping across his face indicates he is anything but.

Mom swats his arm playfully as he removes the towel from around the bottle. The cork falls to the ground as he tosses the damp cloth onto the table. Once the first flute is full of the sparkling, pale, honey-colored liquid, she turns back to me. "No, we're not getting divorced. Quite the opposite, actually. This summer will be our twentieth anniversary, and we've decided to celebrate by renewing our vows."

Jodi reacts first. She squeals and wraps each of my parents in a hug—first Mom, who's closest, then Dad, who does his best not to spill the champagne.

I try to emulate her exuberance. This is good news—better than good, really. Still, even as I pin a smile to my face and embrace each of my parents in turn, something doesn't sit right in the pit of my stomach. I try to figure out what it is as Jodi rattles off questions about the ceremony and the guest list and a second honeymoon, and I even miss an opportunity to call Dad on his hypocrisy about me drinking as he presses a flute brimming with bubbly into my hand.

It's not until later, long after I've finished the second glass of champagne Mom insisted I take, after I've heard so much talk about ceremony elements like colors and flowers and dresses that my already woozy head spins, that something finally clicks into place. I'm upstairs in my room, poring over scans from an old grimoire I found within the depths of the internet when it hits me so hard it takes a full five seconds to catch my breath: I can't be happy for my parents because I'm jealous. They hardly communicated at all for five years. Even when they did, it consisted of one-sided coded messages from my dad. When he came back, he and my mom barely knew how to talk to each other. And then there was the whole world of awkwardness that came with the knowledge that Dad spent his five years away with Anya, who is about as far from unattractive as a woman can get. Still, my folks have found their way back to each other. They belong with each other. I know they're supposed to be together—the same way I'm supposed to be with Owen. I've messed things up, but maybe not beyond repair. Maybe it'll take four months—or four years—but one day Owen will see we're meant to be.

Chapter Twenty-Six
Sasha

My feet are sore when I finally get back to my apartment. After lunch, Elliot managed to persuade me and Anya to see a movie. He also convinced us that it would be a crime not to purchase some concessions, so we gave in and got a huge tub of popcorn and three separate jumbo boxes of candies—not to mention the bucket-sized drinks. By the time the film was over, the three of us could barely pry ourselves from our seats. Anya insisted we "walk it off," and walk we did. At first, we just paced back and forth in front of the theater, but eventually we ventured further, circling the entire parking lot so many times I lost count.

Every step up the stairs leading to my door feels impossible, but I press on because the only way I'll be able to sit on something relatively comfortable and take these blasted shoes off is if I can reach my couch. After what feels like an eternity, I make it to the top and fumble a few times before I slide the key into the lock. I wish I had a bathtub. Some days, a shower stall just doesn't cut it. I'm going through a mental checklist of items in my house to determine whether I have something large enough to soak my feet in when I swing open the door.

And stop dead in my tracks.

Straight ahead, lazing on my couch as if he owns the place, is Brody. He glances up from the screen of the computer—*my* computer—perched on his lap. "Ah. Sasha. So nice of you to join me."

Every instinct in my body urges me to run, to slam the door

behind me and put as much distance between the two of us as possible. Instead, I take in a breath and shove those ideas down deep as I enter the apartment. "Was I expecting you?" I know without a doubt I wasn't, but I don't want to start this off by getting defensive. Not that I'm paranoid or anything, but after Brody showed up in town, I set up some protective enchantments around the apartment. The fact that he's in here now means he's more powerful than I anticipated.

He snaps the laptop closed and sets it on the floor beside him. "If you weren't, you should have been."

He doesn't elaborate as I cross the room. The couch is really the only place to sit, and as much as I don't want to be that close to Brody, standing seems a more aggressive pose, and I'm not exactly itching to pit my abilities against his. I have to walk past him to get to the open end of the couch, the one closest to the window overlooking Main Street below. "I, um, heard about what you did—with Crystal's family and their car. Well done. Really. I bet that lit a fire under her."

Brody doesn't respond. Instead, his dark eyes follow me as I settle onto the cushion. I try to match his relaxed posture, but my body just won't uncoil. I feel exposed under his gaze and I wish I were wearing more layers so I could adjust them to cover as much of my exposed flesh as possible. When I got up this morning, shorts and a tank top seemed the perfect choice to complement the warmest day of the year so far, but now I wish I were wearing long pants and a sweatshirt. And maybe a hat.

I feel like I did as a little kid when Elliot and I would get into trouble for doing something we weren't supposed to. Usually it involved using our abilities too close to a population of ordinary. Elliot's mom would make us stand in front of her and she'd just stare, not saying a word. Eventually either Elliot or I would break and confess to whatever transgression we had committed. One time we hadn't done anything wrong, but Elliot's mom stared us down for so long I almost started making up things just to get her to look away. Now, as then, I want to tell Brody whatever he wants to hear just so he'll avert his gaze.

After what feels like ages, he takes in a breath, his nostrils flaring. "I don't know what you're playing at. You brought me here with the promise of providing crucial information, and yet here I am, having learned nothing." He leans forward, resting his forearms on his thighs. "Do not underestimate me, Sasha. Crystal Jamison may be the one who can get the information, but you're the one who brought me here. My patience is wearing thin. Next time, it might not be Crystal's family we go after—it might be yours."

I inhale a sharp breath and Brody's lip curls.

"Yes, we know about your sister Anya. And that guy you're always hanging around? Elliot, is it? And I believe you have another sister. Didn't Anya just find her? It would be tragic if something happened to her before you were able to have a reunion."

My fingers twitch. Spells jockey for position in my mind—the kind I learned in preparation of Seth's coming, the ones capable of inflicting pain. But I don't cast one. He's obviously powerful, and if I attack him, it could be the last thing I do. Then what might he do to Elliot? To Anya?

He stands, his bearing that of a man whose business is complete. "I recommend you do all that's within your power to get me that information." With one last predatory smile, he turns and strides to my door, letting himself out.

As soon as the door clicks closed behind him, the adrenaline that's been coursing through me since I first saw Brody on my couch ebbs and I sink back into the lumpy cushions. This isn't what I signed up for. My plan was simple: Bring the Amaranthine here and lead them to Crystal Jamison. If she couldn't deliver, people Krissa cares about would get hurt. But now it's my friend, my family, in the cross hairs.

Crystal needs magic, and there's a way for her to get some. At least I think there is. There was talk from time to time about a spell that could give powers to someone without them. Mothers and fathers would speak about it in hushed tones when the possibility arose one of their children would become a castaway. No one ever went through with it, though, because the price was too steep, the consequences too dark.

But those dark consequences won't be mine to deal with, they'll be Krissa's.

I glance down at my throbbing feet. As much as I'd love to sit, to try my hand at locating the spell I want somewhere online, I don't have time to waste. There's one place on earth I'm positive I can find what I need, even if it's the last place I ever expected to step foot in again.

Chapter Twenty-Seven
Krissa

I think I might have a way to contact Bess. Crystal might not like it, but I'm past the point of caring. I haven't run this idea past her because it's easier to ask forgiveness than permission.

I plan to do it first thing in the morning, since Lexie is in my first hour English class, but all the seats surrounding her are already full by the time I enter the room. It would be possible for me to use a confusion or persuasion spell on those sitting nearby to make them move, but Dana and West are also in the class and I don't want to tip either of them off that I'm doing something out of the ordinary. Dana might tell Crystal and West... Well, West might not care at all, if I'm honest. Still, there's a chance my behavior might pique his curiosity, and the last thing I want is for him to find out about the Amaranthine. I don't want him involved in this. It's bad enough I'm mixed up in it, as that puts my family in danger.

I wait until after class to make my move. I intercept Lexie on her way to her locker, hooking my hand in the crook of her arm and tugging her down the hall.

"What the—" Lexie glances at me before letting out a sigh. "Oh, it's just you. Why are you kidnapping me?"

A smile tugs at the corners of my mouth. I'm relieved she didn't just shake me off. "I need your help. Actually, Crystal needs your help."

Lexie curses under her breath. "Why is she sending you? Why isn't she asking me herself?"

I lead her down the hall toward a seldom-used stairwell. Crystal takes it occasionally, but never between first and second hour, so I figure she won't disturb us. "She didn't send me. She's not the kind of person who asks for help."

"Don't I know it," Lexie mutters. She pushes open the fire door that closes the stairwell off from the rest of the hall, holding it for me. I nod thanks as I walk past her. "What's this about?"

Since I came up with this idea yesterday, I've run through countless scenarios in my head about how to explain everything. Part of me thinks the less Lexie knows the safer she'll be, but is Lexie really safe at all? As Crystal's cousin, Brody's very presence threatens her. Still, no point in frightening her unnecessarily. If this works, we can get Brody's information and he'll leave us alone.

Before I can begin my explanation, the doors we passed through moments ago swing open. My whole body goes on alert. I expect Crystal to walk in after us, to demand what we're talking about, so I'm surprised when it's Felix who appears. "What are you doing here?"

He tilts his head to the side. "I could ask you the same thing."

I eye him closely as he walks further into the stairwell, positioning himself at Lexie's side. "Stalker much? This is a private conversation. You don't need to be here."

He glances at Lexie. "I'm sure she doesn't mind."

Lexie tugs at his shirtsleeve, casting a glance in my direction. "What are you doing here?" Her voice is softer than I expect it to be.

"Try not to get too riled up. Believe it or not, I'm not keeping psychic tabs on you. But I did sense the two of you were wandering down here, so I came to check it out."

Several things click into place in my mind. The first is how casual Lexie is as she touches Felix. Also, there's the familiar way he's talking with her. I was so distracted back when the witches and psychics were bound together that I didn't pay too much attention to the fact that the two of them were spending more time together. Back in my old reality, Bria once mentioned that Lexie and Felix were into each other but hadn't made a move. Are the two of them together now? How could I not have noticed that?

If they're together, it makes sense that he would be more aware of her, but that doesn't explain why he'd come after her if he realized she was with me. Unless it does. A flush rises in my face as it occurs to me what his presence implies. "You don't trust me," I accuse. "What do you think I'm going to do? I just need to talk to her—she's not in any danger."

Felix takes a step toward me, holding up both his hands. "Whoa there, crazypants. It never entered my mind you might want to hurt her. When I realized you guys were wandering off together, I was curious. I just want to see what's up."

I scrutinize his face. Is he lying to me, just trying to calm me down? I dismiss the idea. It's too out of character for him.

The warning bell sounds through the hall. Only a minute until second hour begins. I need to make this fast before we all end up with detention for being tardy. I could insist Felix leave, but I know him well enough to be sure he wouldn't go without a fight. Figuring Lexie will probably just tell him anyway, I decide to go for it. "There's this group of witches—the Amaranthine—who found out somehow about Crystal being possessed. They believe Bess knew something—some information they've been searching for. They want her to connect with Bess to find out what. We haven't had any luck, and I think it's because Crystal doesn't have abilities anymore. I'm fairly certain we need someone with a biological link to Bess in order for the contacting spell to work. Since Crystal can't manage, that leaves you, Lexie. Can you help?"

Lexie's face scrunches with concentration as she takes in my words. "And why exactly do we care what this Amaranthine group wants? Why not just tell them we don't have the information?"

I hesitate before answering. I don't want to tell her how dangerous they are, but I do have to give her a reason. "Suffice it to say they won't leave her alone until they have whatever it is they're looking for."

Lexie considers this. My reasoning is vague, but it seems to be enough. "I'll help. When do you want to do it?"

I release a breath I wasn't aware I was holding. "Today after school if I can get it set up. Would that work for you?"

She glances at Felix. "I kind of already have plans, but I think I could get out of them."

Felix shakes his head. "You're not getting rid of me that easily. I'll come, too."

The tardy bell rings and Lexie leads the way out of the stairwell.

"No," I say quickly. "I mean, it's a spell. You're not a witch. You won't really be any help."

Lexie nods toward a door to the right. "This is me. I'll let you two figure this out."

Before she can duck into her classroom, Felix tugs her hand until she's facing him again. He brushes a swift kiss across her lips before releasing her. I have to look away.

Felix rejoins me as I hurry toward my science class. "It's a spell, yeah, but I figure it won't hurt to have an extra psychic around if you're seeking out someone's consciousness."

"I *am* a psychic, in case you forgot."

Felix tugs on my hand, forcing me to stop and face him. "I know. I know you're not connecting to minds anymore." He taps a finger against the bracelet on my wrist. "Now, I'm sure you can take that off to do the spell, but I'm guessing you really don't like to. I'm also guessing you're a little out of practice. I think you know as well as I do I can help you on this."

There's no point claiming he's not right. As much as I still want to be the one who solves this problem for Crystal, I have to accept that I might be part of the reason the spell isn't working to begin with. It probably would be beneficial to have another psychic on the case. Besides, he already knows what's going on, so it's not like his presence will put him in any more danger than he's possibly already in. "Okay. You can come."

"Thanks for the blessing, but I was going to come anyway." He grins, waggling his eyebrows. Wow, I've missed him. He splits off, heading down the hall to his classroom. As I walk toward science, I can't help the swell of gratitude that rises inside me. Now I can only hope my plan will work.

Chapter Twenty-Eight
Sasha

I never intended to come back here. When I originally left, I assumed it was because the Devoted would take our rightful place in Clearwater when Seth purged it of the ordinary. After everyone died, it was because going back would be too bitter a reminder of everything I'd lost.

As the beat-up Civic rambles over the cracked asphalt leading to the center of our out-of-the-way settlement, I can't help remembering all the times someone cast a spell to repair a pothole when it would appear. But there's no magic here now, and I jerk and jostle inside the car no matter how slowly I go.

The protective enchantments around the town have no doubt broken, yet I'm not surprised to find the area completely vacant. This place was chosen specifically because no one has any reason to come through here.

No one but me.

I park outside the meeting house at the center of town. It's a long, squat building made of brown bricks that Elliot and I used to call the poop house due both to the color and the unfortunate aroma that would inevitably tinge the air during longer sessions. I could never figure out why no one ever cast a spell to make the place smell better.

The houses are laid out in concentric circles around this point. There are no businesses or office buildings. We never needed them. That's the beauty of living in a town full of people with abilities. If something breaks, magic can fix it. If you can't do it yourself, ask your neighbor. Water and power? The psychics persuaded the appropriate local departments to run the necessary plumbing and wiring and mixed up their heads so we never saw a bill. Anything we couldn't or didn't want to make ourselves, we'd go to the nearest town to procure.

I park the car and climb out. I've made a mental list of which houses to check for the information I seek. I may have to branch out, as I'm working on the imperfect memories of a child, but at least I've got some places to start.

The Malloys had four children. The first two ended up as castaways, and when it looked like the same fate might befall their third, they mentioned it. Influence. Elliot and I were over, playing with the two younger kids, when I left the room to ask for a drink of water. That's the first time I remember overhearing the word. They noticed me before I heard too much, but I got a sense the conversation was serious and very, very secret. I never even told Elliot. Within a few months, both kids manifested and I forgot all about it until the day I forgot my sweatshirt at the meeting house. I was more than halfway home when I remembered, and by the time I made my way back, I figured everyone would be long gone.

I was wrong.

The five settlement leaders were still there, and they weren't happy. The atmosphere was tense. I should have left immediately, but I heard that word again. Influence. Miranda Stevens was trying to make a case for casting the spell, but the other leaders questioned her sanity. They likened use of the spell to unleashing a demon.

I start at the Malloys' house. There are no locks on the front door and I let myself in. The floor plans of all the homes are virtually identical, so even though this isn't where I lived, I automatically know where everything is.

It's disconcerting walking through the living room. My skin prickles like I'm a child expecting to be caught doing something naughty, even though I know there's no one here. I start in the master bedroom. It's the most likely place for parents to hide something. The room is in slight disarray. There's a pile of dirty laundry on the floor, as if Mrs. Malloy had been collecting it to wash before being interrupted. The bed is unmade. The coating of dust on the dresser is the only indication that the house's inhabitants haven't stepped out recently to return later.

The people who lived here are dead, still I feel like a thief when I start ransacking drawers. I check everywhere I can think—under the mattress, tucked up beneath drawers, in the back of the closet. I scour the floor for loose boards and try every spell I can think of to reveal something hidden. The rest of the house gets the same treatment, and by the time I'm done, I'm convinced there's nothing related to Influence here. It's possible they never had physical information. Perhaps they'd only been discussing something overheard.

My spirit sinks with each step toward Miranda Stevens' place. What if I don't find anything there either? What if these people had just been talking about old wives' tales they'd heard? Or, worse, what if I'm remembering everything wrong? If the spell I'm seeking is little more than the fabrications of an overactive imagination, where does that leave me?

But my fears turn out to be unfounded. Tucked in a black velvet bag in the back of Miranda Stevens' china cabinet is a thin leather grimoire tied with a thong. The cover is still supple to the touch, unlike some I've seen that have cracked with age. I wonder how old it is. Although each page is filled, there aren't many spells contained within, as each one is complex and accompanied by words of caution. It seems nothing within is to be undertaken lightly, and each carries serious consequences.

I understand now why no one in the Devoted ever worked this spell. Magic comes from nature and the ability to wield it is inborn. Every person has natural limitations. To get around that, Influence can't draw its power from nature. Spells cast using Influence come from somewhere else, somewhere darker. And if what's written on these pages it true, Influence can drive a person to madness.

Perfect.

***

I feel like a stalker, sitting in my Civic across the street from the Clearwater High parking lot. I put a tracking spell on Crystal's car, so technically I could be sitting at home waiting, but I'm too keyed up to be locked in my stuffy apartment. Besides, if she stops somewhere quick—like at a coffee shop or a gas station—I need to be able to show up without too much time elapsing.

When the bell finally rings at the end of the school day, it doesn't take long for students to start pouring out of the building. I don't bother scouring the faces for Crystal's: Her bright green car is more than a little conspicuous. It's not until it starts moving that I bother to start my engine.

At first I'm afraid she's going to go straight home, but I'm pleasantly surprised when she pulls into the parking lot of the library. I can't help smiling at my stroke of luck.

I take care to allow enough time to elapse between when she enters the building and when I do so she won't notice me walk in. By the time I'm inside, Crystal is nowhere in sight. Panic threatens to swell, but I remind myself there are only so many places she could be. I look up and down some aisles before noticing her in the computer section. Instead of using her own laptop, she's logged in to one of the library's machines. There's a man in his sixties sitting with his face mere inches away from the screen a few stations away from her, but the spot right beside Crystal is open. I adjust the ropes of the drawstring backpack on my shoulders before making my way to her side.

She minimizes her browser window when she realizes there's someone near her. Yeah, that's not at all suspicious. She attempts a subtle glance in my direction—probably to determine whether the patron settling beside her will be nosy enough to read over her shoulder—but all pretense of nonchalance evaporates when she recognizes me. A pinwheel of emotions scroll across her features—surprise, curiosity, fear—before she settles on one. Hostility.

"What are you doing here?" she snaps, careful to keep her voice low so as not to draw attention to either of us.

I consider a quip about it being a free country or how it's a public library, but I bite back the words, figuring my snark won't win me any favors. Picking a fight with her won't help when I try to get her to listen to me, to trust me. I'm already fighting an uphill battle there as it is. "Are you checking out dirty pictures or something? You closed that window pretty fast when you thought someone might be looking."

Crystal squirms in her hard plastic chair, but I know it's not because my accusation is right. If she's smart—and I'm giving her the benefit of the doubt on this one—the information on her screen is far less salacious and far more interesting. "It's none of your business," she mutters, doing her best to pin me with an icy glare.

Even if she still had magic I wouldn't feel threatened by her. I get the sense she's more bluster than action. I fight the part of me that wants to prove just how weak her threats are. I've got more important business today. "Maybe not," I agree. "But that doesn't mean I can't help."

Incredulity colors her expression—as I expected. "Why would you want to help me?"

"I don't," I say easily. "But my sister told me about your problem."

Crystal's disbelief is replaced by panic. Not wanting to let her continue on the fast train to Freak-Out Town, I press on.

"She said you lost your magic." I make sure to keep my voice low. Although Gramps a few computers down seems totally engrossed in whatever he's attempting to read, too many years of being drilled about how dangerous it is for outsiders to learn about our abilities is difficult to fight. "I didn't even know that was possible. I can't imagine how awful it is."

Crystal sneers. "So, what? You come here to rub it in?"

I shake my head. "No. Like I said, I can help."

"Yeah? Well, you also said you didn't want to."

The corner of my mouth quirks up in a half-smile. I can't help it—this couldn't be going better if I'd scripted it. I'm ready for this. "I've lost everyone—except Anya and Elliot. And they've decided to stay here in Clearwater. That means I'm going to stay here, too. But things are harder than I thought they'd be. I grew up in a community where magic was a part of everyday life. I'm having trouble adjusting to life around all these ordinary people." I sigh for effect. "Your friends are the only ones with abilities, and you all hate me—not that I blame you, necessarily. I was willing to do anything for Seth. But I came out on the losing side of that battle." I press my lips together. That last part was a little harder to say out loud than I anticipated. "Seth's beloved was from the Taylor line. If I can help you, it's like... It's like I'm doing something he would've wanted."

Crystal studies me for a long moment. An internal struggle plays itself out across her face. I may not be a psychic, but I've always had a talent for reading people, and I know my words are having the desired effect. She doesn't want to trust me, but she's curious about what I might know. "I'm listening," she says at length.

I waste no time slipping the drawstring bag from my back.

From it, I pull the flimsy two-pocket folder I picked up to put copies from the grimoire in. When I hand it over, Crystal weighs it in her hands before opening it. She scans the first of a dozen pages. I did my best to copy only information about the spell and nothing about its consequences.

Her brow crinkles. "Influence? Never heard of it."

"I'm not surprised. This is old magic, and it takes some serious power to do the spell. Obviously you'll need a witch to do the casting." When she glowers, I backpedal: "One who's in, you know, top form, that is."

Crystal shoves the folder back at me, not even bothering to close it. "No. Look—thanks but no thanks." She stands and takes a step away. "I appreciate the offer, but..."

I grab her arm before she can move any farther. She stiffens at my touch but doesn't pull away. "Hey. If you don't want to do this just because you don't trust me, I think you should reconsider. If you want to get magic back, this spell *will* give it to you. Now, you can waste your time and continue to search for other things that won't work if you want. And you'll have the same two choices then that you do now: Trust me enough to try this, or stay the way you are forever."

I don't wait for her to respond. While she stands stock-still, allowing my words to sink in, I'm the one who rises and leaves.

Part of me wants to stay to see where she's leaning after she processes, but I know I can't press her. She can't feel like I'm pushing her to do this, not if I want her to go through with it.

I ignore the voice in my head questioning the wisdom in my plan. This spell is dangerous, but I convince myself I won't have to deal with the consequences. That'll be a job for Krissa. There's no way she'll stand idly by as the Influence takes over her friend. And as she watches helplessly as her friend descends into madness, she'll be consumed by guilt. She'll live with the enduring pain that comes from not being able to save someone she would do anything for.

Chapter Twenty-Nine
Crystal

After Sasha left, I sat back down in the hard plastic chair and stayed at the library until Dana sent a text to ask whether I was picking her up. I got so distracted poring over the pages Sasha provided I completely forgot I was supposed to meet Krissa at Griffin's apartment at five.

My mind swirls the whole time I'm in my car. Influence seems straightforward enough: It's a way for people without abilities to acquire them, a way for them to *influence* the world around them. Instead of using stones and charms to channel magic, from what I can tell, this spell would make a person a conduit for energy to pass through.

I hate to admit it, considering the source, but this spell might be just what I've been looking for.

Dana is subdued from the time I pick her up until the time we pull into the parking lot of Griffin's building. I'm not surprised—there's not much she can do to help with my current predicament. I like to think she's coming out of a sense of loyalty and friendship, but I have a sinking suspicion her motives aren't entirely that pure. More likely she wants to be present on the off chance Krissa's able to do something to reconnect us with our abilities.

I trip over an uneven spot on the sidewalk as we approach the door nearest Griffin's address. I've passed by this place hundreds of times in my life, but I've never really noticed it. The rectangular red brick structure hidden behind a row of three large trees seems designed to blend in with the surroundings. There are only six units, with three on the ground floor and three stacked neatly above. I press the button beside *Holloway* and wait for a response.

We're buzzed in, and Dana and I make our way up to the second-floor unit. The door opens before I get a chance to knock, revealing Krissa and, to my great surprise, Lexie.

"What's going on?" I ask as Krissa ushers us inside. It's not what I wanted to ask, but I figure demanding what my cousin's doing here will only make tempers flare.

Lexie grins like she knows what I'm really thinking. She stands by a mud-brown couch. "Easy there, cuz. I'm here to help."

I fight the urge to ask what Krissa was thinking involving Lexie in this. Whether I like it or not, Lexie's already involved. She's part of my family, which means Brody could target her as easily as my parents.

Dana throws up her hands. "Okay, I'll bite. No offense, Lexie, but why do we need her? When you said we were meeting here, I assumed Griffin was gonna be your extra witch power. Why is Lexie here?"

Krissa sweeps her hand toward the dilapidated couch. "Why don't you sit down?"

We do as she requests. When Lexie, Dana, and I fill in the spots on the couch, Krissa settles on the coffee table in front of us. I can't help noticing just how comfortable she is. How much time does she spend here? And where is Griffin? A flush from the bathroom answers that question.

"I'm still convinced a personal connection to Bess is what we need," Krissa begins. "We tried using Crystal's link, but it wasn't strong enough. And I think I know why."

"Because I don't have magic anymore," I supply. I don't need a road map to come to her conclusion. "That's why you asked Lexie. She's also blood related, but she actually has abilities."

"We wouldn't need Lexie if you'd just help us get our abilities back," Dana mutters, her voice easily carrying across the room.

"I *will*," Krissa says, her voice soft but firm. "But right now, getting in touch with Bess is the priority."

The water from the bathroom tap shuts off, accompanied by a

solid thud—a sound I always associate with old plumbing. The door opens and I turn, expecting to see Griffin—except it's Felix Wolfe who emerges. He lifts his chin in greeting before taking a seat beside Krissa on the table. This time I can't contain my question. "Okay, what's *he* doing here?"

If Felix is offended by my tone, his face doesn't register it. "Nice to see you, too, Crystal."

Krissa shoots him a look like she's warning him not to poke a bear. "Psychic support," she answers. "I'm a little out of practice and could use the backup."

I'm about to ask what she's talking about, but my mind dredges up a detail from every time we've attempted this spell so far: Krissa always removes her bracelet. I never thought to ask about it. Is it possible she's somehow cutting off her mind-reading abilities? And if she is—why?

Krissa checks the time on her phone. "We should get started. Griffin's working late at the garage today, but I don't know how long this'll take and I'd rather be done before he gets home."

"Wait—he's not even here?" Dana asks. "I figured he was in his room or something. Do you have, like, a key?"

Krissa shakes her head and I roll my eyes. Of course she doesn't need a key to get in here. I know Dana was new to the whole world-of-magic thing and she didn't have her psychic abilities for long before they dissipated, but sometimes her lack of understanding is embarrassing. "He knows we're here," Krissa assures us. "He just made it clear he wanted us gone by the time he got back."

Dana nods vaguely, but she still looks mildly confused. "So, what? Are you two...dating now?"

Krissa snorts like the question is ridiculous, but I can't help noticing how Lexie and Felix perk up as if the same question has been buzzing in their heads. Krissa picks up on this, too, and makes a show of rolling her eyes. "No. By no stretch of the imagination."

"Oh," Dana says, a distinct note of disappointment clinging to the syllable. "That's too bad. If we ended up marrying brothers, we'd be sisters like we—" She stops short, mortification painting her features. I almost feel sorry for her, and not just because she's given voice to the desire I've already picked up on: The way she talks about Fox, if I didn't know any better I'd think the two were already planning a wedding. But I do know better—I've seen them together. And although I'd never admit it to Dana, he just doesn't look the same when he's around her as he did when he was with Krissa.

It's Lexie who breaks the awkward silence. "If we're on a clock, we should probably get to it."

The tension that's built up in both Krissa's and Dana's shoulders drains at the same moment, like they're two separate parts of the same being. An image flashes in my head of a younger version of the two of them with their arms slung around each other's shoulders. It was a picture in my alternate-self's middle school yearbook. In this reality, the two of them used to be friends—before this reality's version of me formed the circle and brought Krissa into it. Dana was a casualty of that transaction. It's not something I usually think about. Is it difficult for Dana to spend as much time with me as she now does? Despite knowing I'm not the same girl, does she sometimes think of me that way?

Krissa begins giving directions. I pay minimal attention since this isn't my first time doing this spell. The only differences I detect are that Lexie, not I, will be the link to Bess; and Felix, not Krissa, will be handling the psychic end of things. Dana and I are still provided with charm bags for helping to work the spell, but I sense they're mostly for show. While I've felt a trickle of energy the other times we've tried this, the power from the charged herbs and stones is nothing compared to the magic I used to be able to tap in to so easily. With assistance from Lexie and Felix, Dana and my pitiful contributions will be nothing more than sprinkles on an ice cream cake: Not very useful.

I do my best to swallow the bitter taste that rises in the back of my throat. I feel so useless—something I'm entirely unaccustomed to. Since Saturday, the accident Brody and Kai caused has replayed through my head so many times I've lost count. A jumble of emotions swirl in my mind about the event, but more overwhelming than the fear that something could have happened to my parents and the anger that Brody would make so bold a step is the shame tinging every moment of the memory—shame that I'm completely incapable of keeping my family safe. Not only do I not have the magical power to fight against Brody, I can't even be useful in getting the information he wants.

Krissa leads us in casting the spell, and I do my best to clear my head and focus on the task at hand. Despite my limitations on the abilities front, I can immediately sense a difference in the upswing of power surging this time. It's an odd sensation, connecting to others during a spell: Although everyone remains separate, for the most part, it's still possible to feel the thrum of another person's magic—like different currents of electricity. Even when only aided by the charm bags, a pale echo of the hum reaches me. Lexie's magic and Felix's psychic abilities join with Krissa's vibrant thread to form something greater and more complex than any of the three are alone—like a chord played on a piano.

Like the first time we tried to connect with Bess, I'm a mere passenger, adding what juice I can to the effort. I have no sense of whether things are going well, only how much energy is being drawn from me. Unlike that first time—or even the second—the demand on what I have to share never increases. The addition of Lexie and Felix must be providing Krissa with everything she needs.

An icy wave crashes over me, marshaling every nerve ending to high alert. My eyes, which have been closed for the duration of the spell, spring open, but what fills my vision isn't Griffin's sad apartment, it's a bright white nothingness so dazzling and brilliant I bring my hands up to protect myself. But even when my palms press flat against my face, the light doesn't abate. Despite how uncomfortable and overwhelming these sensations are, they're also familiar, like I've been through this before. The feeling of my fingers against my forehead, my palms cupping my cheeks, fades, and I have the oddest sense that I'm a helium balloon being allowed to float to the end of its ribbon tether.

As suddenly as it came on, the ice is gone, replaced by a vague soreness on my left shoulder. Voices press in around me, but they're garbled, like they're coming to me from underwater. It's not until hands grip me—too many to be from one person—that I come back to myself enough to open my eyes.

"What happened?" The voice is sharp, tight—almost accusatory. Lexie's.

"I... I..." Krissa stammers.

Felix's is the first face I'm able to focus on. His head is right above mine, and upside down. How can that be? Unless... I force my muscles to tighten and relax and determine I'm lying on the floor. My first instinct is to sit up—who knows how dirty this place is—but I can't make my body comply. "She's okay," Felix says, a note of certainty in his tone. "She's clear."

"Are you sure?" Lexie demands, her hands sliding around my shoulders and tugging me upright. "I asked Krissa to check her out last time and she said the same thing."

My head spins. What is she talking about? Last time what? I can't make sense of what's happening.

Lexie manages to right me, pressing my back into the lumpy fabric of Griffin's couch. Felix brushes her shoulder with his fingertips. "Babe, give me a little credit here."

The gears turning in my head grind to a halt for a split second. Babe? Are these two together? Since when? But I can't let those questions overwhelm me for the moment. There are more pressing matters. "What's going on?" My voice comes out scratchy, like I haven't had anything to drink in too long.

Lexie opens her mouth to answer, but Felix is faster. "Short story? We found Bess."

Despite the fact this is what we were trying for, Felix's face isn't a victorious one. His expression is hard, pinched.

Dana beats me to the obvious question: "Did you get the information?" She stands aloof, just behind Krissa, looking small and scared. She doesn't appear to be as bad off as I am, and I wonder just how much of what happened to me she sensed.

"No," Felix says flatly. "I think Krissa was right—we needed a blood relative with abilities to find Bess. But..." He shakes his head as he blows out a breath. "It was like she couldn't actually connect with Lexie. And before I knew it, she found you and rushed right through me to get to you. But it was too much—she started to overwhelm your system almost immediately, so I broke off..." He runs a shaky hand through his hair. His expression finally cracks, revealing just how ragged the encounter left him.

Krissa's brows draw together in concentration as she listens to Felix's report. She didn't sense this the way he did, of course—she kept her bracelet on this time. But when he's done talking, something seems to click for her. Her shoulders square and she catches my eye. "Looks like the plan's changed."

Felix nods. "I agree."

Dana and Lexie exchange glances, expressions confused at the turn the conversation has taken. "What changed?" Dana asks.

The pieces click together in my head. "You need a relative with abilities to find Bess, but Bess won't connect with Lexie. And when Bess went for me, it was too much for me to handle without abilities."

Krissa nods. "We have to find a way to get your magic back if we want to get that information."

Breath rushes over my parted lips. It's exactly what I want—my magic. I have to bite my lower lip to keep from mentioning the Influence spell Sasha gave me. If I bring it up right now, Krissa will demand to know where I found it. If I tell her the truth, there's no way she'll even entertain it. If I decide to trust Sasha's intentions and information, I'll have to make Krissa think the research came from me. I don't want to lie to her, but it may come down to that if we can't find another option.

Chapter Thirty
Krissa

The drive home from Griffin's house is silent except for the low murmur of the radio. I've been lost in my own head since we split up outside Griffin's building. I'm glad Felix convinced me to let him drive because I'm sure if I were behind the wheel right now I'd run a red light—or worse. I keep going over different scenarios in my head, but no matter how I slice it the end result remains the same: Crystal needs magic if we're going to get this information. And I don't mean energy that's been charged into herbs and stones, like she's been using. The charm bags she and Dana were using today were the strongest I could make, but they were no match for Bess when she tried to connect.

The song that's playing goes quiet, but I don't think much of it. I assume Lexie is changing the channel until she turns to face me.

"Lex..." There's a hint of warning in Felix's tone.

She bats at him without taking her eyes off me. "So, whatever happened between you and Owen?"

The question is so blunt, so out of nowhere and without preamble, my first instinct is to deflect. I could ask her what she means or simply say nothing, shut down the conversation before it starts, but there's something in Lexie's face that gives me pause. In this reality, she's been a girl capable of harming others, someone driven by a desire for more power—someone I haven't considered a friend. But in this moment, I'm reminded of the girl I knew in the other timeline, the one who accepted me into the fold without question, who smiled easily and was generous in spirit. Guilt tugs at my heartstrings. How long has it been since she's changed? Did it begin the night we could've lost Crystal? Or was it subtler than that? Is it Felix who's bringing out the side of her, or has it always been there?

Felix catches my eye in the rearview mirror, but I give a tiny shake of my head. I don't need him to intervene. "I thought we might have something. I guess I was wrong." It's not quite the truth, but it's not as far from a lie as I would like it to be. Despite what I decided the night my parents announced they were renewing their vows, I haven't approached Owen again. I want to believe we're supposed to be together, but what if I'm wrong?

Lexie squints like she's trying to discern from the look on my face if I'm leaving anything out. "You two seemed to be getting cozy before—you know... Before the circle was unbound. I was surprised that things didn't last long. You seemed to be really into each other. And you—I don't think I saw you like that with Fox for a while."

I bite my lower lip, trying to think of a way to end the conversation. "Sometimes things just don't work out."

Lexie nods, and I'm glad to see she finds this an acceptable answer. What I don't anticipate is Felix piping up.

"How can you say that?"

Lexie shoots me a confused glance before turning to him. "You certainly have a pretty intense opinion considering you didn't want me to bring it up."

From my spot in the backseat, I can see the tension in Felix's jaw as he clenches his teeth. When he speaks, I can tell he's choosing his words very carefully. "I just don't understand how after everything that happened you can think there's not supposed to be something between the two of you."

The wrinkle of confusion etched between Lexie's eyebrows deepens, but I know exactly what Felix is talking about. The original keeper of my secret, the only one I told about me ending up in this alternate reality, Felix knows my history with Owen. He also knows about how Owen spontaneously began remembering a life he didn't live—the life we shared in the other timeline. I can't explain what happened. I don't know why Owen remembers what he does. At first, Owen was convinced there was a reason behind it. He thought that no matter what reality we found ourselves in, we were supposed to be together. But things have changed so much since then. If our last conversation is an indication, he is as much at a loss for these transplanted memories as I am.

I'm relieved when Felix pulls his car to a stop in front of my house. I unlatch my seatbelt and have my hand on the handle before Felix even has a chance to throw a farewell over his shoulder. Before I can push the door all the way open, Lexie's fingers feather against my shoulder.

"Look, I know I'm not a psychic, so don't laugh at me, but I have a feeling about you two. I think whatever stopped you before can be overcome." Lexie offers a small smile. "I get that it doesn't mean much coming from me, but I really think the two of you are meant to be."

I manage to nod, and even that is a struggle. My lungs squeeze tight in my chest, and I fight to take in a breath as I climb out of the car and cross the yard to the front porch.

It's true Lexie is no psychic. She has no special insight into past, present, or future. Then why did she feel such a strong urge to tell me she thinks Owen and I belong together? Is it possible she heard about our interaction at the coffee shop this weekend? If so, could she just be saying this as a way to somehow hurt me, embarrass me? I shake away the thought. I can't see Felix spending time with someone like that. I have to believe Lexie's words weren't malicious.

After this weekend, I'm hesitant to believe what she's saying is a sign. Maybe it's more like a nudge. I promised to give Owen time, but maybe that's not what's best for either of us. I need to tell him everything, but I'm not sure how. Even worse, I have no idea what he'll say. All I know is I have to try—I can't give up on us yet.

Chapter Thirty-One
Sasha

I open my freezer and stare blankly at the sad cardboard boxes stacked within. I know I should eat, but I have no desire—not that any of these so-called meals has the ability to kindle one. I suppose I'm just hoping that one of the names will stick out, despite the fact that I know how similar Salisbury steak and chicken Parmesan taste.

It's been a struggle to eat since Brody's visit. Every time I look at the spot on the couch where he sat, my stomach swoops with shame and dread. This isn't how things were supposed to go. In my mind, contacting the Amaranthine would only cause Krissa pain. The reality couldn't be farther from the truth. I never expected Brody would threaten Elliot and Anya. My revenge was supposed to make me feel better, but all it's accomplishing now is making me feel sick.

My front doorknob twists and my heart rate ratchets up. I close the freezer door and scan the vicinity for something to use as a weapon. I could, of course, cast a spell for defense, but depending who is on the other side, it could be easily deflected.

It's not until the door swings open that my tense muscles relax. A sigh of relief escapes my lips. "Elliot."

He grins, closing the door behind him. "Of course. Who else would it be?"

I force what I hope looks like an easy smile and cross the apartment to meet him. "What's up?"

"It's about dinnertime. Have you eaten? I was going to see if you wanted to come out with me."

Although I'm not hungry, the thought of getting out of this apartment is appealing. "You're just in time. I was about to make dinner."

He pulls a face. "Glad I saved you."

I don't bother feigning hurt at his implied insult. Elliot knows I'm a disaster in the kitchen. Despite my magical prowess, I've never been good at even simple domestic spells. "What did you have in mind? I noticed an Italian place the other day that might be good."

"I've got another idea." He jerks his head in the direction of the door. I don't bother asking him to elaborate. Sometimes he likes to pretend he's all mysterious, and I find it's best to play along with him when he's in that mood, otherwise he whines about how difficult I am.

I take care to lock the door behind me despite the fact that if anyone truly dangerous wanted to get in, a simple lock wouldn't stop him. Our feet clatter down the metal stairs that open up to the parking lot behind the bookstore. Elliot's car is parked beside mine.

"I'll drive," Elliot says, making a beeline for the driver's side of his car.

I could point out that he's stating the obvious, since I don't know where were going, but I hold back. Usually I tease Elliot as easily as breathing, but I'm not in much of a mood for it right now. Guilt clenches my stomach. He's in danger. My best friend is in danger because of me. I can't engage in our usual lighthearted banter because I'm afraid of what the Amaranthine might do if they don't get what they want soon.

If Elliot notices anything off in my behavior, he doesn't mention it. Once we're both buckled in, he puts the car in gear and starts out of the lot. We drive in comfortable silence until we're off Main Street. I know Elliot is about to talk before he even opens his mouth. When he starts to shift in his seat and rub the back of his neck, it's a clear tell. "I know I've said this before, but I'm really glad you're reconnecting with Anya."

I nod, not sure where this is going. Elliot knows I'm the one who contacted the Amaranthine, but it seems he hasn't put together how my interest in making nice with Anya is an attempt to make others think I'm putting my past behind me.

"It's precious, right? You know, the people we have left?" Elliot keeps his eyes on the road as he speaks. "I know I'm glad to have the two of you. I'd be lost without you."

I pretend to brush a tear from my cheek. "Aw, dry your eye," I tease.

"No, I'm serious. Family is important."

The measure of playfulness that had bubbled within me evaporates. I nod solemnly. "Of course. It's very important." What else am I supposed to say? If I disagree, Elliot will see it as more than suspicious. I only wonder why he's talking like this. It's not entirely out of character for him, of course, but tonight the topic seems loaded. I consider asking him what's got him so riled up, but I think better of it. What if he got some bad news about his uncle Nate? That might be why he's suddenly so concerned about the family he has left. If that's the case, I want to give him the space to tell me in his own time. There's no sense pushing.

We drive in a heavy silence for the next several minutes. The area we are in is familiar, but I suppose the streets of Clearwater are becoming that to me. Familiar. Not quite like home. I don't know that I'll ever think of this town that way. But at least I'm slightly more comfortable here now than I was when we first arrived.

When Elliot finally pulls into a parking lot, I groan my displeasure. "Allegro Bread? Are you kidding me? Don't we eat here enough?"

Elliot spares a glance in my direction just long enough to stick out his tongue. "Oh, come on. The food's not bad."

He doesn't exactly address my questions, but I let it slide. I know him well enough to be sure there's a reason he's chosen this place, and based on the fact that he won't come out and say it, I can infer some possible reasons. The most obvious is that there might be an employee or regular customer here that he thinks is cute. That's something he wouldn't share with me—not because it would be weird due to how close we are, but he doesn't know how

I would react if I learned he had a thing for an ordinary girl. *I'm not sure how I'd react to that scenario.*

After Elliot parks, we head into the restaurant and stand in line to order our food. I watch him closely the whole time, but he doesn't appear to be giving any undue attention to anyone in the vicinity. Still, he does seem hyperaware of our surroundings. He's on edge about something.

It's not until we get our food and find a table that our conversation picks up again. "I'm thinking about getting a job." As he says it, Elliot watches me to gauge my reaction.

I gape, sure I heard him wrong. "A job? Why?" It's not as if the two of us need money. In the Devoted, our way of life was mostly communal. While families had their own separate homes and money for purchases outside the community, everything we possessed was shared. When everyone died, Elliot and I were left the soul heirs of everything belonging to them. Technically, the land and buildings in the town where we grew up are ours, but it's not as if we could live there. The place is both too empty and too full of memories. And, frankly, even if we didn't have more than enough money to support ourselves, we have abilities in a world full of ordinary people. There's not much we can't get even without funds.

Elliot purses his lips. It's clear he was prepared for my reaction. "I think it'd be a good way to meet people." I open my mouth to respond, but he talks over me. "The only people I really know are you and Anya. Well, I suppose there's Krissa and her circle, but I don't exactly expect them to accept me with open arms."

I roll my eyes. "Like you want to be friends with them anyway." The darkness sweeps over my mood before I can dial it back. I take in a breath and try again, forcing a smile. "Sorry. Okay, so you want to get a job? What on earth are you going to do? What kind of marketable skills do you even have?"

Elliot holds up his hands, a slightly bewildered look on his face. "I have no idea. It's just a thought. But it's a big world out here, and I'm sure I can find something to do. And if I don't exactly have the qualifications... I bet I can persuade someone to give me the job anyway."

This time my grin is genuine. "That's my boy." I'm about to start listing off job suggestions—pool boy and rodeo clown topping the list—when a familiar form catches my eye. Anya. I suppose I shouldn't be surprised she's here—she seems to like this place as much as Elliot does. I lift my hand to wave for her attention, trying to convince myself as I do it's because ignoring her would draw Elliot's suspicions, but I freeze with my arm halfway up. Anya's not alone. I attempt to draw in a breath, but the air around me seems to thicken and I can't gulp it in. There's no mistaking my sister's companion. It doesn't matter that it's been thirteen years. A hundred could have elapsed, and I would still recognize her. "Misha?"

Anya's eyes widen in surprise when they land on me. She didn't expect me here. Her gaze slides to Elliot as she approaches our table, a knowing look on her face. Misha is temporarily obscured as she follows behind our sister, but once Anya reaches the table, Misha finally catches a glimpse of me and Elliot. She nearly drops the tray holding her food, and it's only with Anya's help the food makes it to the table unscathed.

Misha's unburdened hands fly to her mouth and moisture gathers in her eyes. "Sasha?" Her voice is high and tight, like she's trying desperately to hold herself together. "I didn't think... Oh my..."

Unable to form a coherent thought, Misha abandons speech in favor of leaning across the table to pull me into a tight hug. I'm frozen. I don't know what to do. Thirteen years is a long time. Anya said she found Misha, but I never expected this. Somehow, I never actually expected to see her again. Suddenly, I'm seven years old again, listening to my parents explain how it's best for our community, for our way of life, if Misha goes away to live with the ordinary. My parents sat stony-faced and told me my big sister wasn't good enough to live with us anymore.

I believed it. I had no reason to doubt my parents, to doubt they knew what was best. They told me to forget about Misha, the sister who braided my hair and played my silly make-believe games with me, so I did. I buried her memory into the back of my mind and shoved it down forcefully any time it would surface. I never thought I'd see her again, but here she is.

My body can't react to her embrace. At once I want to fiercely hug her and roughly shove her away. Although I know they're gone, I can't help wondering how my parents would react to this moment. Would joy and affection swell in them, or would they be ashamed that their ordinary daughter dared to show her face in their presence? I asked about her only once after they sent her away. It was after Anya disappeared, after I was told she had been killed. All I remember is that Mom and Dad seemed oddly unaffected by the news. In my seven-year-old mind, I suppose I understood they must be in shock. When I asked if they missed Anya, my mother quickly replied that of course they did. She went on about how Anya had so much promise, so much to give to the Devoted. She lamented that Anya's abilities wouldn't strengthen our number. Then I asked about Misha—I asked if she was sad about her middle daughter. I'll never forget the venom that crept into my mom's voice. She insisted she had only two daughters, me and Anya. It was as if Misha's failure to manifest abilities was a reason to erase her from existence.

If my parents were here, they probably would have gotten up and walked out by now. But here I stand. Somehow, the fact that I haven't left when my parents would have tells me everything I need to know in the moment. My arms snake themselves around Misha's back and I squeeze her with all my might.

"I've missed you," Misha whispers in my ear. "Not a day has gone by that I haven't thought of you."

The fact that I can't say the same stabs me through the heart like a dagger. Tears sting my eyes and I do my best to blink them back. I can't echo her sentiment, but I can tell her something true. "I'm glad you're here."

It's a long time before Misha and I finally release each other. She fawns a bit over Elliot, about how grown-up he looks. He looks as happy as if we had found a member of his own family, which, I suppose, is kind of what has happened.

When we all finally take our seats, our food sits ignored as Misha answers question after question about where she's been for the last thirteen years. She tells us about the family she was placed with, about how there had clearly been some kind of spell work involved to make them believe she had lived with them for years. She went to normal high school and then on to college. She's a social worker at a high school. She's also married, which is the only thing I find as surprising as her appearance here. I have a brother-in-law, and he's ordinary—just like my sister.

The four of us laugh and smile and brush away tears as they form. The whole time, a thought nags me: If Seth were still alive, I wouldn't be having this reunion. Misha would still be lost to me. Would having him still here be worth never seeing my sister again? In this moment, I can't answer that question.

But there is one thing I know for sure: As pleased as I am to see her again, Misha's reappearance right now only puts her in danger. Brody already knows she exists and that we found her. There's no way he doesn't already know she's in town.

I figured I could give Crystal the information about Influence and let her draw her own conclusions. I realize now the folly of that plan. What if she takes too long? What if Brody doesn't wait as long as I think he will? I need to press her to move forward before Brody makes good on his threats. Elliot's right: Family is precious, and I can't let the Amaranthine take it away from me.

Chapter Thirty-Two
Krissa

I know I should be spending all my free time figuring out how to get Crystal the abilities she needs to contact Bess, but I can't make myself focus. I have to talk to Owen. I know he wanted time, but maybe he won't need it if he knows exactly what's been keeping me from him. If he knows why I pulled away, he might understand. And if he understands, maybe we can move forward and put the past behind us.

I'm a ball of nerves at school. Owen and I are in second hour together. It's not ideal, but the idea of waiting until later in the day puts me on edge. I want him to know as soon as possible.

My plan is simple, if inelegant. Obviously, the middle of science class isn't the most ideal place to have the kind of conversation I want to have. The benefit here is that Owen is a psychic. The bracelet I wear keeps me from linking with the minds of others, but I've successfully taken it off and been able to use those abilities in the spells I've cast to try to find Bess. Of course, when I worked those spells, there weren't many people around. My hope is to compensate by taking the bracelet off but keeping it near so I can grab it if I start to be overwhelmed. But hopefully that won't be necessary. I'll sit at an open desk by Owen and simply touch him. It's how we used to share thoughts when we were first learning. For some reason, physical touch assists in the mental link. Since I'm out of practice, the contact can't hurt. In addition to keeping the information strictly between us, I'll be able to explain myself much more quickly and thoroughly this way than I would ever be able to out loud.

I don't even bother feigning attention during first hour. Mrs. Buchanan and I have a tacit agreement: She won't bother me as long as I turn in my assignments. Since I can do spells to assist with the work part, that leaves my class time pretty open. I need that today. I couldn't concentrate even if I tried.

I have to fight to keep myself from running straight to science class. Part of me wants to. If I get there too late, there's a chance the seats near Owen will be filled. That's a simple enough problem to solve, but I'd rather not resort to using magic against unsuspecting classmates. An alternative is to show up right away and take a seat near Owen's before they fill. But there's a danger there, too. What if Owen sees me and chooses another seat? If I move my seat to be by him, he may refuse to listen to me at all. I'm already not respecting his wishes, so I don't want to push him any more than I have to.

Instead, I'm left with option three: Waiting for Owen to arrive in class and hoping I get there before the spots by him are taken.

I take an unnecessarily long time at my locker, keeping my eyes trained down the hall. When I catch Owen approaching, I start slowly toward the classroom door. When one of his guy friends stops him, I cut toward the nearest room to buy time.

I'm not sure whose class this is—it's not a teacher of mine. I'm blocking the doorway for anyone who may want to enter, but I don't care. I'll take dirty looks if it gets me what I want. I watch as Owen talks to the sandy-haired guy. If I take off my bracelet now, it's possible I could peek in on the conversation. I resist the urge. It doesn't matter what they're talking about. My only concern is this guy will keep him too long, and by the time the two of us make it to science, there won't be two desks together.

I'm not paying much attention to what's going on inside the room until I catch a snippet of chatter. Two girls sitting along the wall beside the door are deep in conversation about prom. I can't see them from my position, but when Owen's name comes up, I know who one of the girls is: Laurie.

"It's still, like, a month away," one girl says, her voice soothing. "Nothing to be worried about."

"I keep trying to drop hints, but Owen just changes the subject every time I bring it up," says Laurie, sounding put out.

"I bet he's planning some big promposal and it's just not ready yet. He doesn't want to talk about it because he doesn't want to spoil the surprise." The friend is talking as if she's the font of all wisdom. I would roll my eyes, except my stomach is clenched and heat begins building in my limbs. They're talking about Owen—my Owen—asking this girl to prom. If I'm honest, I haven't given much thought to the dance. I certainly haven't considered that Owen might be thinking of going.

"Maybe you're right," says Laurie, sounding a bit more hopeful.

"Of course I am," her friend says. "There's no way he's not asking you. Just don't worry about it."

"Easier said than done."

A rushing sound fills my ears, drowning out the rest of their conversation. I've seen this girl with Owen, I've even considered the idea that they might be together, but to hear this conversation—this confirmation—is more than I can handle. Is it possible Owen really has moved on? Is it possible he didn't tell me when we spoke before simply to spare my feelings?

I've been so foolish. Of course he wouldn't wait around for me. I've given him nothing to wait for. He's right: I ran away from him, straight to two guys who, put together, aren't half the man he is. My plan now seems so foolish and flawed as to be completely laughable. I really thought this was going to work. How could I be so blind?

The answer is obvious: I'm completely self-centered. If I weren't, I would have realized what my choices were doing to Owen. He was right—his life is in turmoil because he remembers a reality unknown to almost everyone else he encounters. I could have been there for him, but I pushed him away. I thought it was for the best, that I never really considered what was best for him.

I can't stay here anymore—and there's no way I can sit through science now. Maybe I should just leave. It's not like I'm in any state to be here today anyway.

I dart into the hall, careful to keep my head down in case Owen is still around. Before I've made it three steps, I collide with someone.

Hands grip my shoulders gently. "Um. Sorry."

The voice is so stilted and awkward it takes me a minute to place it. When I do, heat rises to my cheeks as I remember Tucker's information about how I cross his mind. "Fox."

I don't know if it's because of the tone of my voice—higher than usual—or the look on my face—embarrassed—but instead of continuing on his way down the hall, Fox locks his eyes on mine. "I, um... How are you?"

It's the first time he's spoken directly to me in months. I could easily blame this on my self-imposed isolation, but I know it's more than that. He's been avoiding me as much as I've been avoiding him. "I'm good," I say automatically.

His lips twitch. "Liar." He shakes his head and runs a hand through his hair. "I might not know this version of you, but I can still read your face."

"It's nothing," I insist. "I thought... It doesn't matter. It's nothing." I wish it wasn't so hard to talk to him. Despite what he may think, I do care about him. Maybe it's not in the way he wants, but my feelings are real nonetheless. My alternate self was such a big part of his life for so long—I hate that he feels he needs to treat me as a stranger. "You and Dana seem happy."

I regret the words as soon as they pass my lips. Like I'm the person he wants to discuss his love life with.

His eyebrows draw together and his lips purse, but the tightness passes quickly. "We are," he says, nodding, but I get the sense there's more he's not saying. Before I can ask, he takes a step back. "I should get going to class."

I nod. "Yeah," I agree, but before the words are past my lips, he's striding down the hall, away from me. I sigh. Maybe I should ask Tucker exactly what kinds of thoughts have been crossing Fox's mind. Perhaps knowing that could help me understand what he needs from this version of me. But even without asking, I already know. He needs me to be *her*, the girl he loved, but I'm not. I'm supposed to be *me*, the girl Owen loved—but I might be too late for that, too.

I start down the hall again, my eyes glued to the floor. Someone nudges me gently in the shoulder.

"We've gotta stop meeting like this," Felix says.

Despite my state, or perhaps because of it, the sound of his voice is enough to calm me by a few degrees. "Sorry." I do my best to keep my eyes down. But this is Felix I'm dealing with, and whether I like it or not, he knows me better than almost anyone.

"Hey, what's the matter? You look like you want to punch something." He dips down just far enough to catch my eye, and when he straightens, my gaze follows his face. "You okay?"

I don't know what to tell him. It's obvious I'm not okay, and I don't have the strength to lie. "I was going to talk to Owen. But... I changed my mind. I don't think it's a good idea." I decide to leave out my awkward interaction with Fox.

Felix's shoulders sag. "I'm sorry Lexie brought that up."

"So you don't think I should talk to him?" I'm so mixed up right now, I need to know I'm doing the right thing. Five minutes ago I was so convinced that talking to Owen was for the best, but now it seems like the worst of all possible options. I need an opinion from someone outside of my own head.

Felix doesn't answer right away. "I think you've done a lot of work to put distance between the two of you the last few months. Jumping in to have a serious conversation with him might not be the best idea—not if he's not prepared for it. Tell you what—how about I talk to him? I can kind of set the stage..."

I shake my head. "No. Don't do that. I think... I think I waited too long. Owen might finally be getting his life back together, and I don't want to destroy it again."

Felix's jaw tightens. "Destroy is a pretty strong word."

"But not incorrect." I press my lips together. "Thanks for wanting to help. Look, I gotta get out of here."

"Want me to skip with you?"

My chest constricts at his offer. Felix is so good—almost too good. How can he have forgiven me so easily for having treated him so poorly? I don't deserve a friend like him. And as much as I don't want to push him away again, I also don't want to pull him down into my darkness. "I think I'd rather be alone. Thanks, though."

It's obvious from his expression he doesn't like that idea, but as the warning bell sounds overhead, he sways on his spot. "You've still got my number."

I nod. "I'll use it if I need it."

His lips twitch like he wants to say something else, but he just gives his head a small shake before starting toward his next class. I dart down the hallway in the other direction as quickly as I can without arousing suspicion. I could just hide out in the bathroom all hour, but I suddenly feel claustrophobic. I don't want to be in this building. I'll leave. I have to. I need to put some distance between me and the conversation I overheard. Owen has moved on. I need to find a way to be happy for him. He's figuring out how to make a life here in a reality he doesn't remember. My reality has changed, too. No longer am I an innocent girl, a target because of the abilities I didn't know how to control. Now I'm something more, something darker. I'm a young woman capable of murder without remorse. I can't believe I let myself forget that. I can't believe I let myself think it might be okay to put that behind me, to interact with normal people as if I'm the same person I was before Seth died. When I plunged the knife into his heart, I killed two people: Seth and the girl I used to be. Of course Owen doesn't want to be with me anymore—I'm someone different now. I won't forget that again.

Chapter Thirty-Three
Crystal

Krissa wasn't in school today, and she ignored my texts until after lunch.

To say I was experiencing heart palpitations until she finally responded would be an understatement.

Worst-case scenarios kept popping through my brain: What if she doesn't want to help now that she knows the only way to do so is by first giving me my abilities back? What if she never intended to help me do that in the first place? What if she can't do it now—or flat out refuses? What will happen to my family?

But when she finally got back to me, she didn't express anything that made me think she would go back on her promise. On the contrary, she assured me the reason she was absent was to spend the day doing research.

I found it harder than usual to concentrate during school. I wanted desperately to be wherever she was, helping her. This is my life, after all. No one is more invested than I am. Still, I can't afford to be skipping classes. Gone are the days when I could simply cast a spell to make a teacher believe I was in class, and there's no way I can get around having to do whatever assignments are set. I'm constantly finding new ways that a life without magic completely sucks.

It's not even like I can throw myself into research once the school day ends, either. Today is Mom's short day and she's home from work just as I arrive from school. Since my grades haven't rebounded as quickly or as well as she and my dad had hoped—indeed, as I had promised—she insists I sit at the kitchen table and work on my assignments. At first I claim I have no homework, but that quickly backfires when she pulls up the online grade book and starts rattling off a list of things I'm still missing.

I'm stuck at the table until just before dinner, allowed to rise only to help set out plates and flatware and to hug my dad when he gets home. When the meal starts and I finally am permitted to put my books away, Dad quizzes me on what I've been working on. My answers are basic at best, my mind elsewhere.

"Is this about a boy?" My dad's abrupt question startles me out of my preoccupation with twirling spaghetti onto my fork.

"Is... What?" I get the feeling I've missed a crucial part of the conversation. After Dad stopped asking me specific questions about what I've been working on, I began to tune him out. He and my mom started down the path of lamenting how my poor grades will look on a college transcript and wheeling out the tired argument of what will I do with my life without a good education. That's the point at which I always zone out, but now I wish I'd been paying at least a little attention. "What boy?"

Mom and Dad exchange glances. "You tell us," Mom says. From the tone of her voice, I can tell she thinks she's caught wind of the truth.

I'm not sure exactly what to say. Tucker isn't the kind of guy a girl brings home to her parents. I never talked about him in the brief time we were together, and since they never asked specifically about him, I assume my alternate self never mentioned him either. I curse myself for not paying better attention to the flow of our conversation—if I had, I'd have a better idea how to proceed now. They think I'm having guy troubles. What I say next is crucial. I'll either be able to help explain away my poor grades lately, or I'll bring down an inquisition about whatever guy is distracting me from my studies. I'm not sure which course is my best option at this point.

Dad takes my silence as his cue to impart some parental wisdom. "You know, sweetie, you're young and there will be plenty of time to date when you get older. I know it may seem like the most important thing in the world to have a boyfriend, but, trust me, sometimes they're more trouble than they're worth. Now, I know you and your friend Kristyl have always had a kind of friendship-slash-rivalry going on, but just because she's had a steady boyfriend for years doesn't mean you should, too." As he talks, he twists his fork around, gathering a spool of spaghetti. As he brings it to his mouth, it strikes me how little they actually know about my social life. First of all, I haven't referred to Krissa by her given name in months—when I mention her at all. And then there's the glaring untruth that she's still in a relationship. She and Fox have been finished for months. How is it possible my parents don't know that?

I'm about to point these facts out when Dad begins sputtering. He clutches at his throat and his eyes bulge. It takes a moment for me to figure out what's wrong—he's choking on a mouthful of spaghetti.

Mom is on her feet in a second, immediately at my dad's side, urging him to stand. I watch, frozen, as she stands behind him and wraps her arms around his middle. Dad's face is turning progressively redder, and I can see the panic in his eyes. What if Mom can't dislodge the food? Am I going to watch my father die? Should I call 911?

Mom performs the Heimlich maneuver on Dad, but nothing changes. How long can he go like this before he passes out? And what happens if he does? I've never felt more powerless. If only I had magic, I could solve this problem in the blink of an eye. I've raged at my lack of abilities before, but never quite like this. I'm completely helpless. My father could die, and there would be nothing I could do about it.

Tears prickle my eyes. My dad could die.

There's a horrible gagging sound and a mashed glob of noodles and sauce shoots out of my dad's mouth. It's completely repulsive, but I ignore it. I ignore the spittle-flecked bits of food surrounding Dad's lips when I run to embrace him. His chest heaves as he takes in frantic gulps of breath, like someone stuck underwater too long.

He strokes my hair, murmuring, "It's okay, it's okay." It strikes me that I should be the one doing the comforting, but I don't stop him. It seems his words are as much for him as they are for me.

When he finally releases me, no one seems particularly interested in finishing the meal. Without being asked, I start clearing the table. Our conversation about my grades and boys is long forgotten as my parents replay the event, trying to figure out how Dad managed to choke on something that is not traditionally considered hazardous food. I don't much care to hear the replay, so I excuse myself to my room. Ten minutes ago, I couldn't wait to be free of the dinner table and my parents' watchful eyes so I could go through the last round of notes I printed out at the library, and maybe text Krissa to see if she found anything that looks promising. Now I'm not sure I'll be able to focus at all.

I run my hand over my face as I walk into my room and close the door behind me. It's not until I've perched on my bed that I realize I'm not alone. Kai stands against the wall, one foot pressed against it, looking like he's waiting for something. My mouth drops open wide, but the scream building inside me never reaches the air. I clutch at my throat, trying to figure out why my voice box isn't working.

Kai tilts his head, his unruly hair sweeping across one of his eyes. "What? You thought your dad just happened to choke tonight?"

I stop trying to scream. Of course I thought my dad choking was a simple accident. It never crossed my mind to consider another option. When I try to speak again, I'm pleased to find my voice works. "That was you?"

"Of course." His voice is low, gravelly, like he's not accustomed to using it. "I told Brody he should let me kill your dad, but he disagreed. Unlike Brody, I don't have as much confidence that you're taking us seriously. We've given you plenty time."

I fight to keep my panic in check. This man almost killed my father tonight. While part of me wants to run at him, to hit him, to make him hurt, I'm afraid any such action would cause more harm than good. As I realized just moments ago, I'm useless. I can't protect my family—not like this. "I've been doing everything I can to get that information—you have to believe me."

"No, I don't. I think you and your friends don't intend to give us that information at all, and that you're stalling for time."

I shake my head. "That's not it..."

Kai silences me with a jerk of his chin. "In any event, even Brody's getting impatient. He's giving you five days. Believe me, this is more than he gives most people. The only reason I can think that he's being so kind is since you're related to Bess. But even Brody's got limits. Unless you give him what we want, I'll be back and there'll be nothing anyone can do to stop what I unleash against your family."

My mind struggles for something to say in response but comes up completely blank. Kai watches me for another moment before pushing himself off the wall and striding to the door. Panic floods me. Is he going to go do something to my parents right now? If not, how will I explain the appearance of this stranger in my room? But before he crosses the threshold, Kai waves a hand in front of his body and the air around him begins to shimmer. A split second later, he disappears from sight entirely. My bedroom door closes, seemingly of its own volition, and it's only then I find I can breathe.

Five days. That's not much time. We can't keep doing things by trial and error. We have to figure out how to get this information, no matter what it takes. I can't let Brody or Kai or anyone else hurt my family.

I stand on shaky legs and cross to my desk, where I open the drawer I've been keeping my research in. The folder Sasha gave me is thick with pages of copies I haven't looked through in full yet. If I'm honest, I never intended to look through them at all. How can I trust anything coming from Sasha?

I take the folder back to my bed and start spreading things out in piles. My fingers hesitate as they brush against the paper. If what she said is true, this spell will get my abilities back. Does she have any reason to lie? While I don't clearly remember the horrible things she did in town before Seth died, the stories have been recounted to me enough times that I feel like I do. I don't know if I want to accept help from someone who could torture her own sister.

But that sister seems to have forgiven her. The last time Dana and I were at the shop, I overheard Jodi talking with Anya about how she and Sasha have been spending time together for the last few weeks. Does that mean Sasha's turned over a new leaf?

I sink my teeth into my bottom lip. I want to do it. I want to forget the source and convince Krissa to work this spell for me. But things that seem to be too good to be true often are, and this certainly falls into that category.

There has to be another way to get my magic back. And if there's not... I guess this Influence thing can be a matter of last resort. If it comes down to it, I'll trust Sasha if it means I can keep my family safe.

Chapter Thirty-Four
Krissa

My fingers tremble with anticipation as I mix together the herbs Anya scrawled out on the back of an envelope. The solution was so simple I can't believe it didn't occur to me sooner. If Crystal needs magic in order to cast a spell, I can give her mine—the same way the circle passed its abilities to my dad the night Seth died.

Well, not exactly. I went to Anya's for information on the finer points of casting the vessel spell, but she quickly shot down that idea. My dad spent five years learning how to take in and hold on to the abilities of others. She likened it to training for a marathon—he had to build up a bit at a time to be able to control that much power since he didn't have any inside him to begin with. The vessel spell isn't like when the witches drew power from Seth's crystal or when the circle was bound and we could borrow energy from each other. In both cases, those involved had abilities to begin with—something that is apparently key in being able to use more. Even though Crystal used to have magic, the fact that she doesn't anymore means flooding her system with something like the vessel spell would overwhelm her. Instead, Anya suggested a transference spell. Instead of taking on the combined powers of a group of people, Crystal will borrow the abilities of a single person.

Me.

The downside is I can't choose to give away *just* my magic. During the spell, my psychic abilities will be drawn out, too, but I can direct them to Dana so she can help with contacting Bess.

"We should be ready in just a minute. Then you guys should

have what you need to cast the spell," I say, sprinkling the last element into the clay bowl Crystal found among her aunt's belongings after she died.

"But it's not permanent," Dana says from her spot on the coffee table opposite me. I convinced Griffin to let us meet at his apartment again. He agreed and even offered to be the third person the spell calls for, since I'll be unable to assist. He didn't even ask what we were trying to accomplish. I get the feeling he misses being a part of the circle and is looking for an excuse to use magic for something other than everyday tasks.

"No, it's not," I agree. The spell's purpose is merely to allow someone without abilities the use of another person's.

Dana huffs, crossing her arms over her chest. "Then it's *not* exactly what we need, is it?"

"Could someone tell Drama Barbie to tone it down?" Griffin grumbles over the distinct snap and hiss of an aluminum can being opened. When he enters from the kitchen, he's taking a long drink of beer, despite the fact he's over a year too young to legally have it.

Dana shifts, apparently uncomfortable at Griffin's disapproval. "I'm just *saying*," she murmurs.

Griffin lifts his chin at Crystal. "So, I bet this is tons of fun, right? Hanging out with my little brother's current and ex-girlfriends? Be honest now—how many catfights have you had to break up?"

Without looking up from the incantation I'm reviewing, I flick my wrist and send Griffin's bed pillow careening from his room until it smacks him on the side of the head. He chokes and sputters as the beer can he was drinking from slips from his hand, spilling amber liquid down his clothes as it falls to the ground.

"Dammit, K!" he snaps. "Learn to take a joke."

"Learn to not be a dick," I counter easily. I probably shouldn't be so mean—he is doing us a favor, after all. But he makes himself a target so easily and so often that sometimes I can't help myself. "Here," I offer, finally glancing up. I take in the damage wrought when the can fell and focus on the liquid spotting his clothes and pooling on the floor. After a beat to concentrate and another wrist flick, I use my abilities to gather all the beer into an undulating orb level with Griffin's navel. "Want me to put it back in the can?"

He snorts, but his expression is a mix between gratitude for not having to go find a clean outfit to change into and awe at the ease with which I've solved his problem. "I'll just get another." He pivots and strides back into the kitchen. I send the glob of liquid after him, directing it to the sink.

Dana's mouth hangs open. "How did you...?"

"It's a psychic thing. Telekinesis." I catch her eye and hold her gaze for a beat. "I'll teach you how to do it when we get your abilities back."

Any fight that remained in Dana's eyes evaporates and I force the tiniest of smiles. This can't be easy for her—just sitting around while I try again and again to help Crystal get whatever information the Amaranthine are looking for. There's really nothing she can do to help, so I can only assume her presence is out of loyalty to Crystal, out of friendship. I know she wants her abilities back, and the fact is that's not my main focus at the moment. It's possible she doesn't trust I'll do what I said I would. Not that I can blame her: I don't really have the best track record for truth-telling in this reality.

I turn my attention to Crystal, who has been unusually subdued during this whole exchange. "You ready to give this a try?"

She nods, but her movements are stiff, almost mechanical. It's only with great effort she turns to meet my eye. There's something veiled in her expression, like she's hiding something from me. I'd ask, but I know her well enough to be sure she won't tell me something unless she really wants to. Maybe there's a reason she's holding back—like Griffin's presence. And if he catches wind that she's keeping a secret, I'm fairly certain he'll harass her until she either tells or got so mad she leaves.

Griffin cracks open another can as he reenters the room. "You ready for me?"

I nod and he moves to the coffee table to help Dana pull it away from the couch. He has his faults and is a jerk more often than not, but there's a reason I've stuck around him these last few months. Despite his flaws, he does possess a good heart—even if it's difficult to find most of the time.

I slide off the couch onto the floor and sit cross-legged there. When I nod, Crystal, Dana, and Griffin join me.

I take in a breath, ready to start, when Crystal rests her hand on my forearm. "Do you really think this'll work?" she asks, her voice small.

I want to tell her it will, to give her a guarantee, but I know I can't. This isn't the first time I've been certain that something would get us the result we need. "I think there's a good chance," I say finally.

She gives a solemn nod before breaking eye contact. I take this as my cue to begin the spell. After reciting the first part of the incantation, I light the bowl full of herbs on fire. They burn up with a bigger puff of smoke than I anticipated, and I hope we don't set off an alarm.

As the pungent cloud rises from the clay bowl and snakes into my nose, a bubble of warmth brews in the pit of my stomach. With each breath in and out, it grows, pushing outward until it fills my entire body. The sensation is uncomfortable, but not unpleasant.

Until I begin the next part of the incantation.

As I form each word, the heat inside begins to boil, rolling outward and popping against the cage of my flesh. My voice is high and tight in my ears, but I don't stop. It's not as if I haven't experienced pain before, and this isn't quite as bad as when Sasha tortured me.

Yet.

My vision begins to swim, but it doesn't blur things enough for me to miss the concerned looks painting the faces before me. I press on, straining to get each word out as the boiling sensation gives way to the feeling of razor blades against my skin. With each phantom cut, a measure of power leaves me. The fact that the spell is working is the only thing that keeps me going. I can take this punishment—I *should* take it. I can't experience the acute stab of guilt for ending Seth's existence, but I *can* feel this. And better than simply absolving me from my lack of remorse, this agony will actually do some good—it will save Crystal and her family from the wrath of the Amaranthine.

When I'm sure I can't take any more pain or I'll black out, I do—or at least it feels as if I do. My vision goes dark and what little noise reaches me sounds as if it's coming through water. The only reason I know I haven't passed out is because my mind is still spinning and I'm aware of the position of my body in space. I'm still sitting propped against the couch. The quiet, garbled sounds of voices provide a kind of white noise that I sink into as I take stock of myself. I've felt like this before—empty, incomplete—most recently the night my dad enacted the vessel spell and siphoned away my abilities to use against Seth. Is this how Crystal feels all the time? No wonder she's been working so hard to find a way to get her magic back.

I wish I could monitor the progress of the spell she, Dana, and Griffin are working. I didn't realize donating my abilities would cut me off from my senses. I anticipated being able to guide them if they needed it.

Pressure builds against me like a stiff wind. It's not until hot slices tear up my arm that I realize what's happening: My abilities are returning. My instinct is to push back—there's no way they've contacted Bess and gotten the information yet. But no matter how much I focus on keeping the power outside of my body, it rushes inward through the invisible cuts in my skin like water being sucked down a drain. The accompanying heat is so intense I'm sure my flesh and muscles are melting like hot plastic.

I'm not sure how much time elapses before I'm aware of hands gripping my shoulders, of voices calling my name. I have to blink a few times before anything comes into focus.

Crystal's face hovers in front of mine. I assume the two blotches of color behind her are Dana and Griffin. "Are you with us? What happened?"

"I..." My throat is too dry to continue. A cool glass is pressed into my hand and I gulp some water before continuing. "I don't know. I didn't do anything—my abilities just came rushing back in."

Crystal curses but offers an apologetic look. "I'm sorry, it's just—we were close. We found Bess, but I didn't get a chance to actually connect." She presses her lips together like she's debating her next words. "Could we... Do you think we could try again?"

Griffin's face comes into focus as he inches nearer. His expression is livid, his eyes fixed on Crystal. "Are you joking? There's no way she can do that again."

"He's right," I agree before Crystal can retort. "I think the earliest I could possibly try is tomorrow. It's just... I don't think I could do a simple spell right now. I'm wiped."

Crystal runs both hands over her hair, blowing out a breath. "And if it doesn't work tomorrow? What then? We try again the next day? No."

Dana places a small hand on Crystal's shoulder. "If it doesn't work tomorrow, we'll try something else. Something has to work. It just might take some time."

"That's what I don't have." Crystal fixes her stone-blue eyes on me. "Four days. That's all I've got left before..." Her face screws up and she blinks rapidly. "They're going to hurt my family."

Griffin's expression hardens. "The hell are you mixed up in?" His tone is sharp, but it's clear he's not mad at her. His eyes dart the way they always do when he's thinking quickly. "What about me? If Krissa can't do the spell again today, let me try it. You can borrow my magic and—"

I shake my head. "It won't work." He shoots an irritated glare at being interrupted, but I ignore it. "No offense, but I think we both know I'm the stronger witch. If I couldn't handle this spell, you don't stand a chance. We're just going to have to find another way—and fast."

***

Griffin flat out refuses to let me drive home. Although I feel more like myself after the four of us talk about possible options to help Crystal contact Bess, he insists I let him take me back to my house and gets Dana to agree to follow behind in my car. I figure it's no use fighting. Griffin can be remarkably stubborn when the mood strikes. I almost opt to ride with Dana, afraid Griffin will take the opportunity to read me the riot act for not looping him in on everything happening with Crystal, but all he does is call me an idiot for not asking for help and leaves it at that.

Jodi's car is in the driveway and I'm thankful for small favors. Although I've grown pretty adept at mixing teas for most occasions, I'll need something much more potent than usual if I stand any chance of doing research tonight. All I want to do is climb in bed and sleep for the next week, but I know I can't.

"Jodi?" I call as I push open the perpetually unlocked front door. "Put the kettle on. I'm going to need—"

The sentence dies in my throat when I pass from the hallway into the living room. It's not Jodi who sits on the couch, it's Owen. He's leaning forward, elbows on thighs, chin resting on laced fingers like I've interrupted him in deep thought. He straightens his back as he takes in my dumbfounded expression. "Jodi let me in."

I scan the room, half expecting her to pop out and yell "surprise." It would make about as much sense as Owen's presence at this point.

"She's not here," he says as if reading my thoughts. My fingers flutter to the bracelet to make sure it's still in place. "Miss Tanner came to pick her up. They're meeting some friends for a movie. And your parents are at dinner."

My head nods of its own volition and I'm afraid it'll float away like a helium balloon. Owen is here. In my house. What could he be doing here? Oh, no... Does he want to tell me about taking Laurie to prom—soften the blow in case I hear it at school and go nuts, shooting off spells rapid-fire like an insane scorned lover? Or is it something else?

A half-smile turns the corner of his mouth, but it fades quickly. He pats the cushion beside him and waits until I'm crossing the room to continue. "Felix talked to me."

My muscles go rigid as I lower myself onto the couch. "I'm sorry. I told him not to."

He brushes his fingertips over the back of my hand for an instant. "I'm glad he did. After everything I said at the coffee shop, I was afraid you'd pull away again. I shouldn't have said... I regret some of the things I said." He sits further back on his cushion, angling himself toward me. After studying me for a long moment, he blows out a breath. "It's been really hard calling her Miss Tanner, you know? Instead of Mrs. Cole? Especially now that she's the principal."

This turn in conversation jars me. Is this why he's come? Does he need to talk to someone about the other reality, the one I lived and he remembers? I'm not sure how to respond, so I remain quiet.

"Sometimes I think about the harvest dance—you know, when she died?" he continues. "It's crazy how something could be one way there and another way here, but so many other things are the same in both timelines."

I finally find my voice. "Is that what you want to talk about?"

His expression clouds. "I still think of you that way—as the new girl in town with this...*spark*. The girl I couldn't ignore," he says, not really answering my question. "But you've changed, haven't you? You're not her anymore."

My cheeks heat and I scoot away from him, closer to the opposite end of the couch. Of course I've changed. That girl may have had her faults, but she never intentionally caused a person harm. The times before I moved to Clearwater when flare-ups of my abilities hurt someone, I was eaten up with guilt, even when I didn't understand I was the cause. But after I took a man's life with my own hand, I felt nothing. Is he here to rub my face in how hard my heart has turned? "No, I'm not," I agree through clenched teeth.

Owen flinches at my tone but presses on. "A lot has happened to both of us... I think I—*we*—need to accept that if we ever want to stand a chance of moving forward."

The anger and irritation coursing through me evaporates in an instant. Moving forward? Is he saying what I think he's saying? No, I must be misunderstanding him.

There are a million questions I could ask, but only one bubbles to the forefront of my mind: "What about Laurie?"

His face tightens at the sound of her name. "She likes me. I mean, it's pretty obvious. But I don't like her—not like that. We were assigned to work on a history project together and I think because I'm a nice guy she read something between us that's not there."

Did she ever. I wonder if he realizes she's expecting a "promposal" any day now. "Why haven't you just told her you don't feel that way?"

"I don't know if you've noticed, but friends have been kind of thin on the ground for me. The people I was hanging out with before I got the other memories... I don't really have a connection with them. I try, but...it's hard. Bria and West are polite, but they don't remember me like I remember them. It's better with Felix, but he's been busy with Lexie—finally." He offers a genuine smile, but it fades too quickly. "We used to be friends. I mean, I thought we were."

His accusation stings. "Of course we were," I insist, leaning in closer.

"You completely shut me out." His voice is measured, but I can still detect an undercurrent of hurt. "Friends don't do that—friends rely on each other. But you didn't. You pulled away and I couldn't figure out why. Don't you trust me?"

"Of course I—"

Owen shakes his head. "You told me you were ready to talk. I'm ready to listen now."

I open my mouth, but nothing comes out. There's so much to say, I have no idea where to start. I could simply do what I was planning at school—take off my bracelet and push information into his head, but now that he's here and willing to listen, that course of action seems too impersonal. But how do I tell him how very different I am from the girl he almost kissed the night of the harvest dance? How do I explain I've become a remorseless killer? And what if telling him changes the way he looks at me?

Owen nods like I've confirmed something he suspected. He stands and strides toward the hallway, but he turns back before he's completely out of the room. "Laurie thinks I'm going to ask her to prom. I really doubt I'll be going at all, but if I were, she wouldn't be the girl I'd choose. Right now, there's only one person I want to be with. But I can't promise that'll be the case forever." His mouth twitches like he wants to say more, but after a second he seems to think better of it. "Talk to you later," he murmurs as he starts for the front door.

His footfalls recede and the door creaks gently as it swings open and closed. When it latches shut, I curse aloud. What's wrong with me? He gave me the chance I've wanted and I completely blew it. This whole day has been a disaster. Not only could I not help Crystal get the information she needs, I'm apparently not even capable of helping myself.

Chapter Thirty-Five
Sasha

Feeling like a stalker is not nearly as awkward as it should be. That fact should disturb me more than it does as I sit in my parked car just down the street from Crystal's house. If it wasn't for the chill in the April air, I'd be outside, where it would be easier to intercept her before she gets in her car and takes off for school.

She still hasn't figured out whatever the Amaranthine want to know. Brody's casual walk-by of Hannah's Herbs last night while I visited with Anya was enough to confirm that.

The front door to her standard-issue single-story house swings open, and I'm out of my car before she's off her porch. She catches sight of me as she crosses the well-manicured yard to her car—I can tell because she picks up her pace. She digs her keys out of her purse, but before she can press the button to unlock the doors, I murmur a spell that makes the metal in her hand heat up, giving her no choice but to drop everything.

She doesn't bother bending down to pick them up, content to scowl as I approach. "What do you want?" she asks, her voice venomous.

I fight the urge to remind her she's no match for me in her current state. I want to keep things as friendly as possible and I'm already off to a crappy start. "Sorry," I say, the word grating my throat on its way out. "I didn't know how else to get you to stop and talk to me."

She crosses her arms over her chest. "I repeat: What do you want?"

She doesn't trust me, and I don't have sufficient time to build that relationship, so I play the only card I have. "I know you're in danger."

Her eyes widen. "How do you...?"

I can't very well tell her the truth, that I brought the Amaranthine to Clearwater, so I lie. "Elliot told me about the accident you and your parents were in—and about how you talked with some guys afterward. It seemed weird to me, so I did a little digging and found out the kind of people they are. If they're talking to you, it means you have something they want, and if they're threatening your family, it must be because you haven't given it to them."

Her gaze hardens. For a moment, I'm sure she's going to tell me to buzz off—or perhaps something slightly more colorful—but then her shoulders sag. "Nothing we've tried has worked. It looks like I need magic to get the information, but unfortunately I'm not a witch anymore." Her tone is laced with bitterness.

I bite back a smile. She's touched on exactly the topic I wanted to discuss. "About that. Have you read over the information I gave you?"

Guilt mixed with defiance flickers across her face. "I've looked at it."

Her noncommittal answer is less than helpful. I decide to give her the benefit of the doubt. "If you've looked at the spell, you probably realized it takes a *lot* of power—maybe more than all the witches in Clearwater could provide, and that's assuming they'd all help."

She narrows her eyes. "And this is supposed to help me how?"

I take in a breath through my nose before responding. I don't want to snap at her—she'd probably ignore everything I have to say on principle after that. "You might not need the help of a bunch of witches if you can convince just *one* witch to perform the spell during a celestial event. That way, she could channel the power and—"

"I know how it works," she snaps. "I'm not an idiot."

All evidence to the contrary. I fight to keep my face neutral—pleasant, even. "There's a lunar eclipse tomorrow night.

If you can convince—" I stop short. I almost said Krissa's name, but I don't want her to know just how much I'm aware of her current situation. "If you can get one of your friends to do the spell then, that person should be able to harness enough energy. And even if none of them will—I could do it, if you wanted."

Too late I realize I've crossed a line. Crystal's expression darkens to suspicion. I could kick myself. Now she's probably wondering why I'm pressing this so hard. After all, why would I care what the Amaranthine do to her? To backpedal now would only make her more suspicious.

She bends at the knees and taps her keys once to test their temperature before picking them up. "Thanks for your concern, but I've got things under control." She presses the button to unlock her car and I watch, mute, as she circles to the driver's side.

I could lie—tell her I'm doing this for Anya. But then she might talk to my sister about it. Or I could tell her I'm desperate for her friends to like me—but I doubt she'd believe that for a second. Or I could go with the truth, tell her my loved ones are being threatened, too. But before I can do anything, she's in her car. All I can do is stand and watch her drive away.

Chapter Thirty-Six
Crystal

Bridget hasn't changed her seat in sixth hour all year, so I know it's my fault we don't sit together anymore. After I lost my abilities, I tried pretending things were the same as always, but difficulties emerged almost immediately. First, Krissa slowly stopped talking. She withdrew mentally long before she moved to the complete opposite side of the room. When Krissa stopped interjecting into our conversations, I was left to listen to Bridget wax on and on about all the things she was learning from Anya about writing spells. I tried to be happy for her: Like the Bridget from my reality, this one was never particularly good at working spells without the help of an outside force. But since she learned of her talent for crafting her own, it seems she's been unstoppable.

But I couldn't be happy for her. I was too jealous. Maybe it's awful of me, but it's the truth. And one day when she was absent, I told the long-term substitute she and I had been in a fight and asked if I could sit somewhere else. When Bridget returned the next day, I lied about it. Like a coward.

For the past several days, Krissa and I have been sitting together during history class, and every day my stomach is a knot of guilt. Bridget has noticed, of course, and I've seen the hurt flash in her eyes more than once. As she glides into class today, she keeps her head resolutely turned from us.

I could tell her what's going on—enough people know already—but I don't want anyone else involved unless it's absolutely necessary. The deadline Kai set is quickly approaching and I don't want to give him any more targets.

Krissa slips in the door just as the tardy bell rings and stealthily makes her way down the aisle to the empty desk beside me. Her stealth is unnecessary, as Mrs. Jennings is nowhere to be seen.

The classroom buzzes with voices, students taking full advantage of a few extra moments to gossip and finish up conversations. I'm thankful for the noise—it makes it easier for Krissa and me to talk without being overheard.

I've been screwing up my nerve all day. Despite having had several chances to mention the Influence spell to Krissa, I haven't. Every time I'm about to, I stop. I think part of me is afraid she'll be able to tell I'm lying about where I got the information. If she knows it's from Sasha, I can't imagine she'll entertain it for even a moment. But I'm growing desperate. I'm willing to try anything. Sasha's appearance at my house this morning only underscored how incredibly screwed I am. Although I didn't tell her, I *have* gone over the spell in great detail, and I already realized the kind of power it would require. I've been considering calling on the circle—Lexie and Griffin have already thrown their hands in to help, after all—but Sasha made a good point about the eclipse. If someone were drawing on its power, she wouldn't need the help of the whole circle, especially if that someone were as strong as Krissa.

"I spent all last hour in the library," Krissa says, scooting her desk closer to mine.

"You skipped health again?" I can't help raising my eyebrow. I don't think she's been to her fifth hour in a week.

She shrugs. "Mrs. Stanton thinks I have permission to be out of class, and I've been keeping up with the assignments. Don't worry about it."

I'm far from being worried; a wave of envy surges in me. I'd love to be skipping right along with her. Being cooped up in classrooms for endless hours every day makes me feel useless. But I can't risk cutting class, not with my parents breathing down my neck about missing assignments. If I could work a spell to confuse my teachers just enough, and if I could use magic to complete my assignments like I used to, it wouldn't be a problem. But I can't do either of those things. It's hard not to be jealous of Krissa because she can. "Did you find anything?"

Her face provides the answer before her lips do. "I'm only finding things we've been over before. I swear I've been on any site that looks the least bit legit, and *nothing* looks like it's got the oomph to do what we need. I'm willing to try the transference spell again, but I was texting with Anya and she says it could take weeks before you can hold on to my magic long enough to fully connect to Bess." She offers upturned palms.

Her almost carefree gesture rankles. I shove down my irritation—she's doing everything she can to help, and I know it. She's taking this threat seriously. Still, the fact remains that if something bad happens, it happens to me, not to her. "I don't have much time left."

"I know." She leans across the aisle and scoops my hand up in hers, squeezing my fingers with gentle pressure. "We'll figure this out. I won't let anything happen to you or your family."

As she releases me, I try to convince myself she's telling the truth. But desperate times call for desperate measures, and I'm pretty sure we've reached that point. Before I can talk myself out of it, I pull the folder Sasha gave me out of my backpack and slip it onto Krissa's desk. "I might've found a way."

She stares at the folder before turning to me, her brow knit in confusion. "What's this?"

I open my mouth to answer, but Mrs. Jennings chooses this moment to make her appearance. The buzz of voices, which has climbed to a volume rivaling a rock concert, halves as people start to notice her. She stands at the front of the room expectantly as she waits for everyone else to stop talking. Substitutes don't generally command enough respect for this maneuver to work, but Mrs. Jennings made it clear when she arrived just after winter break that she wouldn't put up with any nonsense from us.

"Okay, everyone," she says when the last strains of conversation die down. "Sorry I'm late, but I was finishing up a meeting with Miss Tanner in the office."

A few guys up front send up a chorus of *oohs*, like she's just admitted to getting in trouble. She offers them a good-natured grin.

Krissa isn't paying any attention to what's happening at the front of the room. She's opened the folder and her eyes skim its contents. As much as I want to watch her, to gauge her reaction, I tear my gaze away, giving her the space to draw her own conclusions.

"I told you when I first started that there was a possibility I wouldn't be finishing out the school year with you guys," Mrs. Jennings continues. "Today, Miss Tanner told me she hired a permanent teacher for this position."

Some girls up front whine and ask why. I tune out the answer. Mrs. Jennings has been decent so far as subs go, but it doesn't matter to me who's teaching the class. I try to watch Krissa out of the corner of my eye as she flips a page. My attention doesn't snap back to the front of the room until a familiar name passes Mrs. Jennings' lips: Mr. Martin.

Even Krissa's head pops up at this. She and I exchange glances. It can't be—can it? Mr. Martin was our history teacher back in the other timeline. Is it possible the guy who's taking over this job is the same one?

"Oh," Mrs. Jennings says, glancing toward the hallway. "Speak of the devil. Mr. Martin, why don't you come in and meet your sixth hour?"

My jaw drops as a portly man in his forties walks in. His dull brown hair is combed forward strategically to hide the fact that it's receding, and his bespectacled eyes dart shrewdly. It's the same guy, all right. Krissa catches my gaze, her brown eyes wide. I'm not sure how to respond. We stare blankly ahead as Mr. Martin addresses the class about his vision for the rest of the year. Miss Tanner hovers by the door, obviously waiting for him to finish. She's probably giving him a tour of the school or something. But when Mr. Martin's impromptu speech is over, he waddles over to the teacher's desk, his lip curling into a sneer at the state of disarray. He beckons for Mrs. Jennings to come over and the two of them start talking. Miss Tanner joins them and the class begins buzzing with low voices again, like a hive of bees.

"Wow," I breathe.

Krissa nods. "Right?"

It's strange how things that are different from our timeline shift to match it. "It's like some things are meant to be," I murmur, half to myself.

Krissa raises an eyebrow. "What do you mean?"

I shake my head, trying to order my thoughts. "Nothing—just... Miss Tanner wasn't the principal when we found ourselves in this timeline," I say, being sure to keep my voice low. Not that it's entirely necessary—there are empty desks surrounding us and the nearest pair of boys is engaged in conversation about some car in a magazine one holds. "My aunt was. But now Aunt Crystal's gone, like she was before. Mr. Martin's going to be our history teacher. Miss Tanner is the principal. And I overheard my parents talking the other night about how David Cole is spending more and more time with Miss Tanner now that my aunt is dead. Like maybe they're meant to be together, but the things we changed derailed it."

Krissa stiffens at my use of the word "we." I guess I can't blame her—I'm the one who saved my aunt from dying in a house fire almost twenty years ago. I'm the one who affected the timeline. All Krissa did was cast the spell that took us back in time. She presses her lips together. "Do you really think some things are... fated? No matter what?"

I can't tell from her tone what her opinion is. "Maybe?" I offer. I guess I haven't thought much about it myself. "I mean, it kind of seems that way, doesn't it?"

She shakes her head. "I don't want to believe that. In the other reality, my mom died in a car crash, and Jodi... Jodi was cursed. The same curse that killed our principal at the harvest dance. If there are things that are meant to be no matter what, does that mean the three of them are going to die here, too?"

I suck in a breath. I knew Krissa's mom died in our old reality, of course—that was the reason she came to Clearwater to live with Jodi. But there's something about Miss Tanner's death in that timeline, about Jodi's illness, that I've only recently come to understand. At first I thought I was just having nightmares, but then I realized I was experiencing memories. "It was because of

Seth," I murmur. "The curses, I mean. The shard of quartz I wore as a necklace... It connected me to whatever bit of Seth's soul was still in it. I think that's why I was so obsessed with finding the crystal in the first place. But I've had these...dreams. In them, I can remember a voice in my head—Seth's voice—when I'm touching Miss Tanner's hand in the hallway the day you found my necklace, and in Jodi's shop one day when I was picking up some supplies. He's chanting—they're words I don't understand. And then I can feel this...surge rush out of my hand."

I hold my breath as I wait for Krissa's reaction. She stares for a long moment, her face scrunched as if she can't comprehend the words I've spoken. When I'm about to ask if she heard me, she exhales noisily. "You're telling me Seth was behind the curses? He used you to kill Miss Tanner and curse Jodi?"

I flinch at her bald summary. "Yeah," I say tentatively.

The corners of her mouth twitch upward. "That's actually a relief. Part of me has been just waiting for something like that to happen again. But I guess it makes sense now that Jodi was never cursed in this timeline—Seth never had a reason to do it." She closes her eyes, shaking her head. "If he was aware on some level of what was happening in the outside world in the other reality—and he must've been if he used you to cast curses—then it was his plan to push me to help you with the spell to get the crystal from the past. He was manipulating the situation before he ever appeared in our lives."

A kind of relief and pain mixes on Krissa's face as she processes this information. Mr. Martin's voice reaches my ears over the rumble of conversation, and I glance up long enough to catch his grumpy expression as he surveys our class. It looks like he's not pleased with his decision to become our teacher. Well, that seems in line with what I remember of him from our reality, at least. He turns his attention back to the desk and jabs a thick finger at the open textbook lying there. Mrs. Jennings is wearing the same expression she does when someone tries to explain why they don't have their assignment—a kind of forced compassion not quite masking an undercurrent of oh-my-goodness-stop-talking.

Krissa's still unfocused after my admission, and I take the

opportunity to direct her attention back to the papers on her desk. "What do you think about this?"

It takes a second before she shakes her head, coming back to herself. "Influence. It sounds familiar, but I don't know why. Maybe I've come across it in the Barnette grimoire."

The possibility both comforts and alarms me. If she's seen it in her family's grimoire, that only lends credence to the possibility of it doing what Sasha claims. Then again, I know she's been through that book at least once in an attempt to find something to help me, and she's never mentioned this spell before. "Do you think it'll work?"

Her attention is back on the pages in front of her. "The spell seems complex—like, *really* complex. And the power needed is well beyond anything I can do."

She hasn't answered my question. "But do you think it'll get my powers back?"

She purses her lips as she rifles through some of the papers. "Unclear. This doesn't seem to be a spell for getting lost powers back. Honestly, I'm thinking it's something that just doesn't happen. But clearly the intent is to get magic from *somewhere* for a person to hold inside and use. I just can't figure out where it's supposed to be pulling it from."

I wait for her to go on, but she doesn't. "Do you think it'll work?"

She shrugs, meeting my eyes. "I'm not sure. There's something off about it. I want to do some more research—see if I can figure out why it sounds so familiar."

I tense. "We don't really have time for research. In case you forgot, I've only got three days left before Kai makes good on his promise. Maybe less. You didn't see the guy—he's completely unbalanced. And, Krissa, I don't think he'll stop this time. I don't think he'll do something just to scare me—I think he'll actually..." I can't make myself finish the thought—*kill someone.*

"I get that," she says quickly. "But we can't just jump into this. Like I said, I can't cast this spell by myself anyway."

"There's an eclipse," I say before she can come up with more reasons not to do it. I bite back my next words at the last moment.

I almost tell her Sasha said the event would provide enough power to cast the spell, but I reword my sentence. "Tomorrow. If you can harness the energy of the eclipse, you'll be able to cast the spell."

"Maybe," she says, sounding thoughtful.

Before we can continue, Mr. Martin finally removes himself from behind the desk and trundles after Miss Tanner as she leaves the room. He doesn't give us so much as a goodbye, but no one seems particularly offended. The door is barely closed when my fellow classmates begin expressing their displeasure at the prospect of Mr. Martin being our teacher for the rest of the year. Mrs. Jennings hushes the dissenters and assures us he'll be wonderful before transitioning into the day's lesson.

I don't get a chance to talk to Krissa about the Influence spell before the end of the hour, and she gives me the folder with all the research when the bell rings. "Don't you want to hold on to it?"

She shakes her head. "I want to check into it on my own a bit. I think it's safer with you for now."

I shove the folder back at her. "You should keep it so you can plan for how to do it." I'm being forceful and I know it, but Krissa's reasoning makes no sense. The information isn't any safer with me than it is with her. I've already been over it enough times to be familiar with it. Besides, I'm not the one who'll be working the spell. If she won't take it, is it because she doesn't plan to do it at all?

She gently pushes it back. "I want to see what I can find in my grimoire. Okay?"

Although she inflects the last word like a question, it's obvious it's intended more as a warning. I glare at her for a moment before folding the file in my arms. "Okay," I agree, my voice tight. She nods and starts up the aisle toward the door.

I hate being reliant on someone else for anything, but especially something magic-related. Am I imagining things, or is Krissa more reluctant to cast a spell that would give me magic than she was contacting someone beyond the grave? Why is that? Is it possible she *doesn't* want me to have powers back for some reason?

If that's the case, I'll have to find someone else who *is* willing to help.

Chapter Thirty-Seven
Sasha

My stomach is a nervous knot as I walk up Main Street.

Only a couple of blocks separate my apartment above the bookstore from the coffee shop, and with every step I take, I can't help wishing there was more space between the two points. Then I'd have more time to prepare, more time to figure out what to do, how to act, what to say.

I'm meeting Misha at the coffee shop.

It won't be the first time I've seen her since Elliot brought me to ambush her meeting with Anya at Allegro Bread: Anya had us all over for dinner last night. But this will be the first time I'll be alone with her. When she suggested this outing last night, I agreed because I knew I had to. How would it look if I told her I didn't want to see her? And I don't *not* want to see her—I just have no idea how to interact with her one on one.

I suggested Elliot join us, but he politely declined being my buffer. My sister wanted to spend time alone with me, and he refused to interrupt. He ignored me when I pointed out he'd done that exact thing when we crashed Anya's meeting with Misha at the restaurant.

Things will be fine. In all the time we've spent together so far, Misha's done nothing to indicate she harbors any ill will toward me for being cast out of the Devoted. She doesn't really like to talk about it. That makes it hard for me to tell anecdotes of my childhood. I'm sure she has no interest hearing funny memories of our parents, the ones who let her be taken from them. Instead, I make a list of different questions to ask her about her life. Despite the fact I was conditioned to believe the world beyond our community was basically a worthless, steaming pile of uselessness, my time in Clearwater has piqued my interest. I might as well learn what I can. It's not as if I can go home again, anyway.

The coffee shop's front windows are painted with colorful flowers and cartoon bunnies, apparently in celebration of it finally being spring. All the shades are drawn against the afternoon sunlight. I take in a breath as I place my hand on the door. This will be fine. I'll get through it. I may even have some fun.

I allow a little bubble of hope to bloom in my chest. If Misha can put our complicated history behind her, so can I. Maybe we can even move forward. I push open the door and scan the room for her familiar figure. It only takes a moment to find her—she's so similar in appearance to Anya and me; it's obvious we're sisters. Even a casual observer would notice.

But it's not a casual observer who's made the connection. My throat goes dry when my eyes land on a second familiar form in the chair across from Misha.

Brody.

My first instinct is to scream—to warn Misha to run or to tell Brody to get away from her. I fight back the urge to do either. The last thing I want is to make a scene.

Misha's lips are curled in a smile and she's laughing at something Brody is saying. I take in a few deep breaths in an attempt to slow the rapid cadence of my heart before crossing to the table. I have to get Misha away from Brody somehow. I'm still formulating a plan when she catches sight of me and stands.

"Sasha!" Misha opens her arms wide to embrace me. I step close to her, considering using the opportunity to whisper a warning, but she doesn't give me the chance. "Brody, this is my sister—the one I was telling you about." She releases me from the hug and sweeps a hand in his direction. "This is Brody. He saw me sitting alone and decided to keep me company until you got here. Isn't that sweet? People in small towns are so welcoming."

I have to force my response around the lump in my throat. "Great."

Misha doesn't seem to notice anything off in my tone. "Anyway, Brody, it was so nice to meet you. Thanks for chatting with me."

He grins, flashing his white, predatory teeth. "No problem at all." When he turns his eyes to me, there's a hard edge to them. "Very pleased to meet you, Sasha. I was going to get something. I'd love to keep you company in line."

His invitation makes my skin crawl, but I don't dare turn him down. Misha gives me a surreptitious thumbs-up as he brushes past me toward the line at the counter. I try to give a smile, but my face feels frozen, like it might crack under too much pressure.

Brody waits until we're safely in line, several yards away from Misha, before speaking. "I'm a little hurt you didn't mention your sister was coming for a visit." His smile remains in place as he talks, but the hard glint remains, reminding me just how dangerous he is.

"We haven't been in contact since I was little," I say quickly. "She's nothing to me. No abilities. Worthless." I parrot the words I heard the Devoted say so many times, willing myself to believe them, for them to come out like they're true.

Brody tilts his head to the side. "All evidence to the contrary."

"I have to keep up appearances for my other sister," I say.

"And yet the lovely Anya is nowhere in sight."

I fist my hands, digging the nails into my palms in an attempt to keep any other part of my body from showing just how angry and scared I am. I want to hit him. I want to do something to show him I'm not some weak girl he can just threaten—but I know doing so would only incur his wrath. Brody's not in Clearwater alone. He has at least one person with him—perhaps more. In fact, he might have people stationed around the coffee shop now—I don't know. Too risky to try something here. Besides, how would I explain things to Misha? Elliot already figured out I'm the one who brought the Amaranthine to town. He's willing to forgive me—so long as I appear to regret my decision. Will Anya accept my apology so readily?

"Leave my family alone," I say, being sure to keep my voice low. The patron ahead of us has earbuds plugged into his ears, but that's not to say he couldn't overhear us if we talk too loudly.

"You'll get your information. I have a plan."

"A plan? Oh, I love those." But Brody looks far from amused. "I need results, Sasha." He hisses my name like a snake. "I've given your friend Crystal a deadline."

I gulp at his emphasis on the first syllable. "As long as it's after the lunar eclipse, things should be fine. She'll need its power and then, I promise, she'll be able to access the information."

A woman in her thirties clad in yoga pants steps away from the counter and earbud boy strides forward to place his order.

"Your promises mean little to me," Brody says as we ease into the space vacated by the boy. "Misha would be such an easy mark. It would be so simple to snap her neck, just to prove to you I'm serious. Usually I save the killing for our assassin, but I might make an exception in her case."

"You don't need to do that," I say quickly. "I know how serious you are. I'm sorry you don't have your information yet. If it were up to me, you'd already have it."

The smile finally slips from his lips. "You think I don't understand there's more going on here than you're letting on. You didn't bring me here to help me. Few people are suicidal enough to contact the Amaranthine without immediate intel—and no one has ever approached us asking for nothing in return. Everyone wants something—power, protection. But not you. You intend to keep your hands clean. I understand that desire. But I also know how to take matters into my own hands when it's warranted. I don't know if you have that resolve."

"I do," I insist, temper flaring. Brody knows nothing about me, about what I'm willing to do to get what I want. He has no idea I once tortured Anya, the sister I now hope to protect—all in Seth's name and for his sake.

Brody's lip curls and he leans in close. "Then prove it."

Earbud boy slips away from the counter just then, and Brody steps out of line, striding straight for the door. Gulping, I advance toward the counter and manage to place my order. By the time I make it back to the table, Misha is grinning like a fool.

"He's cute. Did he ask for your number?" she asks, leaning forward across the table. Before I can answer, she launches into a description of how he sat down across from her and what they talked about. I do my best to feign interest, but Brody's presence haunts me like a ghost.

I don't want to admit it, but maybe Brody's right. Maybe I haven't been willing enough to take matters into my own hands. I have my reasons, of course—I can't seem too eager for Crystal to do the Influence spell or she'll want to know why. She might even ask sticky questions, like why the Devoted didn't avail themselves of the spell instead of sending family members away. I don't know how well I can navigate that without her being able to see right through my lies.

No matter what, Crystal needs to do the Influence spell. With magic, she'll be able to get the information the Amaranthine need and keep her family—and mine—safe. I'm not concerned with what happens to her after that. Any other consequences will be Krissa's to deal with.

Now I just have to figure out how to get Crystal to trust me enough to do the spell.

Chapter Thirty-Eight
Krissa

I twist my father's ring around my finger as I carefully leaf through the pages of the Barnette grimoire. I'm supposed to be at work, but my mind's too big a jumble after talking with Crystal in sixth hour. Devin said she could cover for me for an extra hour and a half before she had to leave for her night class, for which I'm grateful.

Crystal seems intent on doing this Influence spell. She clearly spent a lot of time combing through whatever grimoire she found it in; she's got all the information I'd need to cast it. Then why hasn't she mentioned it before now? Any other time she came across something that might help, she immediately texted me and Dana—she didn't wait until she had a folder full of scanned pages for me to read.

I know Crystal wanted me to take the research, to read over it, to plan out how to work the spell—but I couldn't do it. Something nags at the back of my mind. I'm sure I've seen reference to Influence before. I just can't remember where.

I skim through page after page in my family's grimoire, but none of the spells are even remotely similar to the one Crystal showed me. When I make it all the way to the end, I close the book and open the cover to the first page. I wonder if there's an easier way to do this. There has to be. Magic seems to be able to speed up everything.

Jodi's at work, so I can't ask her if there's a spell for what I want. It's probably better that way—too many sticky questions. So far I've managed not to mention the Amaranthine to her, and I want to keep it that way.

Bridget has been having success writing spells—I know because she's in the shop frequently looking for new elements to try out. If she can do it, maybe I can, too. I feel comfortable enough with my magic to attempt a spell even if I don't know that one exists. I close my eyes and take in a breath, still absently stroking the smoky quartz set in my ring. I call up the word Influence in my mind's eye and hold it there. I need my abilities to guide me to the mention of that word in this book. I need to know whatever information there is about that spell.

I stretch out my right hand and hold it, palm down, over the book. "Show me Influence," I whisper.

For a beat, nothing happens. Then a soft rustling sounds, like dry leaves skittering across the sidewalk in an autumn breeze. When the soft swish of pages dies down, I open my eyes. The book is open to a page about a third of the way through. I can't hold back my surprise as I lean over the yellowing pages. I can't believe it worked. I skim the fading spidery handwriting gracing the page. It's not a spell—it's more of a diary entry. I read it three times just to be sure I haven't missed anything. The lines are a recounting of a man named Solomon Brown. According to the author, Solomon used his Influence to persuade a lady in the town to become his wife. Later, he used that same Influence to become mayor. The events do not appear to have taken place in Clearwater, and the retelling gives the impression that this story is more morality tale than history.

I'm disappointed. I was hoping for something more specific. I don't even know that the reference here is to the same Influence spell Crystal wants me to perform. One thing I've noticed from reading through this grimoire is that people tended to capitalize words that wouldn't be capitalized today. Perhaps the person here is referring to some actual kind of influence—or maybe even a psychic ability to persuade someone.

I wish there was a way I could get more insight into what the author was thinking. If I could feel the author's emotions, maybe I could get a sense whether this Influence he spoke of was something simple or something more sinister.

The bracelet on my wrist draws my attention. If I want to feel what the author felt, it might be possible to pick up on an echo if I'm able to focus intensely enough on the writing.

I've taken this charm off before and nothing bad has happened—besides the first time when I opened myself up too fully and too many spirits tried to get one last message to loved ones from beyond the grave. Maybe I could try taking the bracelet off now. The house is empty, which limits the amount of interference I might experience.

My fingers tremble against the knot. I don't know why the simple act of removing this piece of jewelry makes me so anxious. I stuff down my nerves and tug the knot loose. When the charm drops to the desk, I brush my fingers over the fading ink of the entry. It's possible some remnants of the thoughts or feelings of the author are still present. I close my eyes and clear my mind. After several seconds, nothing happens. I take stock of my energy and realize the mental wall I used to keep Owen and Fox out of my mind when we were bound is firmly built up in my head. Of course I can't sense anything. I need to drop it if I want to get any read on this page, but doing that is easier said than done. The fear that kept me locked behind this wall for four months swells to a crescendo. What if I drop my defenses and all the things I've been working so hard to keep out rush in? Then again, there's no one around right now. I'm not bound to anyone, so I shouldn't feel emotions or hear thoughts from people far away. With my lack of practice these last months, my range is probably shot anyway.

If I want to learn any information locked away in this page, I need to get over myself.

I take in a deep breath and hold it for a beat before blowing it out, lowering the shield around my consciousness as I do so. After another second, I open my eyes. The world hasn't ended. There's no flood of thoughts or feelings assaulting me. I can do this.

I touch my fingers to the grimoire again and focus on whoever wrote these words. As a psychic, time doesn't restrict me the way it does other people. As I trace my fingers over the curling letters of the words, I allow myself to be taken back to the time when this was written.

The first pinprick of emotion is such a tiny blip that I almost miss it. There's a tiny thrill of wariness, followed by a larger wave of vigilance. My eyebrows draw together. I'm not entirely sure what to make of either of these emotions. I don't know what I was expecting, but this isn't it. I'm not sure whether to be relieved or alarmed. I continue tracing the words, focusing my energy on the page, but nothing else comes to me.

I close the grimoire once more, disappointed. I hoped that after finding the information I sought, my feelings surrounding the Influence spell would clarify. The result has been the opposite. What I found should comfort me to some degree, but it doesn't. Something about Influence still unsettles me. I just can't put my finger on what. Although I know Crystal is on the clock, I can't help wanting more time to research this spell. She seems convinced it's the answer to her desire to have her abilities back, but what if her longing is clouding her judgment? I don't want to agree to do the most complex spell I've ever seen before investigating things fully.

I slide the grimoire into the still-open drawer of my desk and open my laptop. As I type into the search engine, I push the charm bracelet to the back corner of the desk. Maybe I'll try keeping this off for a while.

Chapter Thirty-Nine
Crystal

Krissa's ignoring me. She hasn't responded to my texts since school let out, and I'm doing my best not to hyperventilate.

She still hasn't agreed to do the spell, and the eclipse is tomorrow.

I do my best to convince myself she'll come around, but the fact is there's not much time. Like many spells I've worked before, this one requires the elements to charge for at least a day before they're ready for the casting. That's why even though Krissa hasn't agreed yet, I'm going to get everything set up.

When I push through the door to Hannah's Herbs and am greeted by the familiar tinkling bells, Krissa stands at the register ringing up an order. Hope bubbles in my chest. Maybe she's been extra busy here at work and that's why she hasn't responded to my messages. But when she glances up to greet me, the practiced customer service smile on her face slips incrementally. She's not happy I'm here.

Instead of stalking straight for her to tell her off for not agreeing to do the one thing that could actually help me, I offer a small wave and pick up one of the woven baskets by the door. Ignoring her, I walk purposefully toward the bundles of dried herbs, selecting the ones I need from memory. I have a list written down, of course, but I don't need to consult it—I've been over the spell too many times.

I feel her eyes on me as I walk from one decorative aluminum planter to another, selecting the required elements. I listen as she chats with the customer at the register. The older woman must be a regular. I can tell from Krissa's tone she's distracted. Good. Let her be.

By the time the lady at the register finally leaves, I'm ready with my own order. Besides the two of us, the shop seems empty. I walk straight to the counter and set the basket upon it. Krissa peers into it, her eyebrows high on her forehead.

"What's all this for?" she asks as she begins taking bundle after bundle out and setting them on the counter.

"I think you know. I figure I can do the prep work, and when your shift ends, you can come over—or maybe we could meet at Griffin's place..." I trail off deliberately, giving her the space to respond.

She rubs at her wrist absently, and I can't help noticing she's not wearing her usual bracelet. "You realize I haven't said I'll cast the spell yet, right?"

I cross my arms over my chest. "And you realize that if we don't do something soon, Brody and Kai are going to kill my family? I doubt they'll give me an extension because you want to think it over." Although I keep my voice low, I glance around the shop to be sure Jodi or another employee isn't hidden in an aisle nearby.

"I get that," Krissa says, her voice tight. "But you have to understand...there's something not right about this spell."

I swallow. Does she know I got the information from Sasha? Is that why she's so hesitant? But no, if that were the case, she would just come out and say it. I do my best to keep my face impassive. Maybe this is about something else entirely. "I thought you wanted to help me. You promised you'd do anything."

She sighs. "I did—and I will."

"All evidence to the contrary," I snap. "I've given you a spell that could actually do everything we need it to. I need to contact Bess. You've tried, Lexie's tried—Felix says it has to be me. I need abilities to contact her, and even you said the spell to let me borrow your magic won't work. That leaves us with one choice—this choice. If this spell will give me my magic back, why don't you want to do it?"

"It didn't say that."

I shake my head, sure I heard her incorrectly. "What didn't say what?"

"That information you had me look over. It didn't say anything about returning lost magic. That's not what it's for. I don't know where this Influence magic is coming from. Do you?"

The thought hasn't even occurred to me. She's right—the spell doesn't appear to be designed for someone in my unique situation. Still, it does seem to be capable of fixing my problem. "Magic is all around us—in every breeze, in every raindrop, in the ground beneath our feet. That's got to be where the magic comes from."

"But it doesn't say that. If this spell were just about charging elements with the magic that occurs in nature, I don't see why it would need to be so complex."

"What, so now you're some expert at magic? Aren't you still totally new at this? Six months ago, you didn't even know how to light a candle—now you're some super genius when it comes to every spell ever written?" My tone is bitter, but I don't care. Doesn't she understand what's at stake here? Sure, she says she does, but does she really get it? No, of course not. How can she? Everything always seems to work out for her. Her mom died in our reality, but she's alive in this one. Now her dad's back in her life, and she and her parents live their little fairy tale life at Jodi's house. The perfect family. Why would she care if mine is destroyed? She couldn't care less when my aunt Crystal died because it didn't affect her directly. Why should this be any different?

Krissa runs both hands through her long, pale blonde hair. "If I just had more time..."

I snort. "That's one luxury I don't have. Now, are you going to let me buy these things?"

Her fingers flit over the different herbs, but she doesn't enter any information into the register. "I don't know how to describe it. I just have a bad feeling."

I reach across the counter and grab a brown paper bag. "I have a bad feeling, too," I say as I stuff the bundles of herbs into the sack. "I have a feeling that if we don't do this spell, I'm going to be an orphan. And you know what's worse? I'm pretty certain Brody won't stop there. So maybe it'll all work out and I won't be alone for long."

Krissa's face pinches. "Don't be so dramatic. I'm not saying I won't help, I just—"

I snatch the bag off the counter and pull a bill from my back pocket. The herbs don't cost nearly this much, but I'm too angry to care about correct change. "By not helping now, that's exactly what you're saying. I get that you've got reservations, but if you're really my friend, you need to put them behind you. You say you want to help, you say you won't let anything happen to me or the people I love, but when push comes to shove, you don't really care."

She opens her mouth to say something, but I don't want to hear it. I spin on my heel and stalk toward the door. When her voice follows me, I cover my ears with my hands. Maybe it's childish, but I don't care. She doesn't care about me, so why should I care about anything she has to say?

***

I tap my steering wheel nervously as I drive over the familiar streets on my way to Fox's house. I'm still not sure that I made the right decision, but I have to do something. I don't want to put anyone else in danger, but Lexie is already involved, so bringing the others in on what I'm doing doesn't seem as big a risk.

When I pull up in front of Fox's place, my old usual spot is empty, and it's tempting to believe that nothing has changed—that this is just another circle meeting where my friends and I will practice spells that have little consequence on our lives in general. It's tempting to believe we're meeting just for fun.

Fox's monster truck is in the driveway, so I know he and Dana are already here. Lexie's car is on the street, and I assume she brought Bridget, so that means I'm the last to arrive. I didn't invite Griffin—too big a risk he'll tell Krissa what I'm up to.

Before stepping out of my car, I make sure I have the folder with all the information about the Influence spell. When I cross the front yard, I'm overcome with memories. How many times have I been at this house? How many hours have I shared with these people? A pang of guilt shoots through my stomach. With the exception of Dana, I've shut all of them out of my life. After I lost my abilities, it just got too hard to spend time with them. They tried for so long to make me reconnect, but I shut them down at every turn. Still, they all came when I asked for their help. I don't deserve friends like this, but I'm thankful I have them.

As always, Fox's front door is open. His dad, no doubt, is on one of his cross-country trips. It's the reason we always met at the Holloways' house instead of somewhere else—their father is almost never home. It's served us well in the past, and I'm once again thankful for it tonight.

The quiet cadence of voices meets my ears as soon as I enter. As usual, everyone is in the basement. I make my way to the stairs, avoiding the creaky floorboards out of habit. I know this house nearly as well as I know my own.

The conversation continues as I descend, but there's a drastic drop in volume when I make it to the basement. All eyes flicker toward me. I can't blame them for their curiosity—I was rather vague in my text. The fact that they don't know why they're here adds even more value to their presence.

I've gone over what to say dozens of times in my head since I first decided to contact them, and I still haven't figured out the perfect words. So, instead of something drawn out, I decide it's best for everyone for me to just cut to the chase. "I need your help."

Fox tilts his head to the side. "Yeah, figured."

I press my lips together, fighting back a wave of embarrassment. My friends aren't stupid. I backtrack. "Thank you for coming." A surge of affection rises in me. Why did I ever feel the need to shut them out? We've been together through so much. Why did I think they couldn't help me through this, too? I swallow around the lump in my throat. "I'm so sorry—"

Lexie waves a hand before I can get anything else out. "We know. We're awesome, you love us. We're not here to make you apologize—we're here because you said you need us. Can I assume I know a little about what's up?"

Gratitude toward my cousin swells. I can't let myself forget that time is of the essence. "Yes, you know a little bit." I launch into as brief a description as I can give about Brody's appearance in Clearwater and his demand for information from Bess. I explain what we've tried already and give the shortest explanation of Influence that I can.

"So," Bridget begins slowly, "you want us to help you...charge the elements?"

I nod. "And cast the spell. Krissa promised she'd help, but I don't think she's going to come through. I need you guys. I know I don't deserve the right to ask this of you, but—"

Lexie stands, crossing to me and holding out her hand. "I've just been waiting for you to ask. I want to help you. We all do."

Fox glances around. "If this spell is as crazy as you say, shouldn't the whole circle be here? What about Griffin?"

"No offense to your brother, but I can't be sure he won't just run and tell Krissa. She doesn't like the idea of me doing this, and if she knows I'm doing it behind her back, she might try to do something to stop us." As Lexie and I settle down on our usual spots on the couch, I turn to her. "I have to ask for you not to tell Felix either."

"You can trust Felix," she insists.

I hold my hands up. The last thing I want to do is fight with her. "Look, I know he's a good guy with a good heart—if he weren't, he wouldn't have tried to help already. But he poses the same risk as Griffin—he might go to Krissa. Can I trust you not to tell him?"

Lexie's jaw is set in the maddeningly stubborn way it gets when she wants to get her way, but she nods. "Fine," she grumbles.

"Thank you." I know she's not happy about it, but I don't need her to like it, I just need her to do what I ask. I open the folder and pull out the pages describing the actual spell. I stopped on the way to make copies for everyone. I hand a set to Dana, even though she won't be participating in the casting. I give everyone a few minutes to look over everything. As she reads, a line forms between Bridget's eyebrows. Lexie bites her lip in concentration. Fox is squinting at the text. I can't blame them. Krissa wasn't lying about this being the most complex spell she's ever seen. I feel the same way, and if the looks on everyone else's faces are any indication, they're in the same boat.

Fox runs both of his hands through his hair and whistles. "Yikes."

Bridget lets out a relieved sigh. "Oh, good. I'm not the only one."

"Oh, come on, this spell isn't that hard," Lexie says.

I raise an eyebrow and she offers a small smile.

"Okay, maybe it is pretty hard, but it's nothing we can't handle. I mean, we have to, don't we?"

She's right. I don't have to say it for everyone in the room to know it's true. When I told them about everything that's happening, I didn't leave out the fact that Brody and Kai are threatening my family. While I didn't come out and include Lexie in that, I'm sure she understands the implication. We have to make this work. And for the first time, I'm positive we'll be able to do so without Krissa.

Chapter Forty
Krissa

I still feel guilty for not agreeing to help Crystal when she showed up at the shop. I sent her several texts that night asking if she'd be willing to meet up and talk about my concerns, but they were largely ignored. The one time she did respond, she basically said *don't do me any favors* and left it at that. Her sudden about-face in demeanor confuses me. I want to help her; I'm just not sure this spell is the best idea. She just can't seem to understand that. When she didn't jump at another opportunity to convince me how wrong I am about the Influence spell, I reached out to Griffin to ask if she had called a meeting of the circle to have them cast it for her. He had no idea what I was talking about but promised to tell me if he heard anything.

At school the next day, I do my best to put all worries about Crystal out of my head. We'll figure something out. We still have time before Brody's deadline. I've been toying with the idea of amping up the transference spell in a way that will allow Crystal to hold in the magic longer.

As I stand at my locker before first hour, though, it's not the Amaranthine or Crystal or spell modifications at the forefront of my mind. I'm still not wearing the bracelet. I kept it off all evening yesterday, and nothing bad happened. It's true I didn't spend any time with psychics, but hours around Jodi, my parents, and customers at the shop didn't lead to any catastrophes. I thought about putting it back on before I left for school this morning, but at the last minute I decided to try life completely reconnected.

In first hour, I keep to the same back-row seat I've been in for months, but as soon as West walks in, I know something is different. I'm digging around in my backpack, but I know when he arrives without looking up. While most people register is nothing but a soft glow in my mind, West is a starburst. I've forgotten how different it is to feel another person with psychic abilities. I'm so surprised that my head snaps up and I make eye contact with him for a split second. To my great relief, he doesn't immediately look away.

Throughout the period I'm acutely aware of his presence. Even Lexie's consciousness is brighter than others in the room. I make sure to keep myself in check and not dip into their thoughts, but just being able to feel them, to feel that they're different in the same way I am, is comforting.

In second hour, it's nearly impossible to keep focused on whatever Mrs. Bates is droning about. Owen is in second hour. For some reason, it takes much more concentration to keep from experiencing his emotions. Maybe it's because the binding spell had us connected in such a close way, or maybe it's something else. But there's one point when Owen is handing an assignment to the person behind him that his glance rises to meet mine and I feel a spark, a jolt of electricity, as an emotion radiates from him to me. It's a kind of longing that makes me ache. At first, I'm not sure whether it's coming from him or me, since it's such a perfect reflection of how I've been feeling these last few months. I miss him. I miss him so much. Why, in all this time, has it not occurred to me that he might be missing me, too?

During Spanish, my resolve solidifies. We have a test, so Tucker has decided to grace the school with his presence. As the teacher starts class, he studies me, scrunching his eyebrows. "Something's different about you today."

I give my best nonchalant shrug. "Must be my hair." I flip its length over my shoulder for effect.

He shakes his head. "That's not it." He squints in concentration and stares at me so long I feel heat rising in my cheeks. Finally, a grin cracks his face. "I know what it is. I can read you."

I shush him immediately. His voice was louder than I think was strictly necessary, and my eyes snap toward the front of the room where Felix and West sit. I hold up my bare wrist. "I took it off."

He raises an eyebrow. "And what? It's a secret?" He lifts his chin toward West and Felix.

I shake my head. It's not—really, it isn't. Still, it's not like I want to go announcing it. At least, not yet. "I'm going to sit with them at lunch."

Tucker can't quite hide the expression of concern that flickers across his face. "You sure that's such a good idea? Didn't go so well last time."

It's exactly the reaction I was hoping he wouldn't have. "Things are different. Felix and I... I think we're okay now. Not back to the way we were, but maybe on the road. I won't be showing up out of nowhere this time. He'll accept me. They all will."

He hikes an eyebrow. "You sound pretty sure of yourself."

I can't tell whether he's lying, but either way I'll take it. "Things'll be better this time," I say, as if my words can somehow influence the outcome.

Tucker drops the subject after that, and I'm left combating the butterflies swirling in my stomach for the remainder of the hour. Felix glances back a few times during the period, but he never says anything. I wonder if he, like Tucker, can sense there's something different about me today. I wonder if my feelings are reaching him on the other side of the classroom.

When the bell rings to dismiss us from third hour, Tucker squeezes my shoulder as we stand. "Good luck." He offers a grin before heading up the aisle toward the door.

The urges to dawdle at my locker and to run straight to the lunchroom war inside me as I walked down the hall. I force my body to take a happy medium between the two extremes. I stop at my locker for my bagged lunch, but I don't linger. I do my best to erase the last four months and remember what it was like when walking down to the lunchroom was just another part of my normal routine. Of course, I can't pretend like no time has elapsed. That was the problem the first time I tried this. I have to accept the fact that things are different now, that my place in our circle of friends will have to change. But I refuse to believe I won't be allowed in that circle. I simply won't accept that.

Although the cafeteria is already buzzing and thrumming with bodies in motion and voices gossiping too loudly, all the movement and noise seems to fade away as I walk past the lunch line and zero in on my target. Bria is already there, nibbling on a French fry. Felix is beside her, but there's no food in front of him. West is just ahead of me and sits seconds before I reached the table.

It's Bria who notices me first. Her eyebrows hike up her forehead and she nudges Felix. Her face gives away nothing. Last time I tried this, it was she who told me to give Felix time. Is she happy I'm here again?

When Felix catches my eye, a broad, genuine smile cracks his face. Without having to force my lips to curl, I find I'm also smiling. Bria's expression is more guarded, and when West turns, his brow knits with confusion.

I take in a deep breath and release it slowly before closing the remaining distance to the table. I nod at the spot beside West. "This seat taken?"

I could easily just sit down, pretend like it's just a normal day, but I've been down that road before. I need permission. I can ask for forgiveness later.

West glances across the table at Felix, who shoots him a look that clearly reads, *Dude, what's wrong with you*? Although it was West I asked, Felix is the one who responds. "That seat's been waiting for you for a while now."

The butterflies that have been battling in my stomach threaten to explode through my abdomen. I do my best not to look like I'm about to throw up. Every bit of me tingles, like an exposed nerve. Three sets of eyes prickle my skin, and I'm aware of featherlight brushes against my consciousness. None of my psychic friends presses deep enough to actually read what's going on in my mind, but I can tell from minuscule reactions that flicker across their faces that they're all surprised with what they find.

"I'm not wearing it," I say in response to their unasked question. "The charm I was using to block myself off. I think I'm ready to rejoin the world. I just hope I'm not too late."

Bria's face softens, and one corner of her mouth curls up in a half-smile. "It's never too late for some things."

I tip my lunch bag and allow the contents to spill onto the table. It's a simple act, but it holds so much weight. No one objects because I'm welcome here. The thought sends a thrill of pleasure through my body. I study the lunch my mom assembled. Even when I went through a spell of bringing home everything she sent to school with me, she never stopped packing me food. She never even complained about how I'd wasted her time. I can't believe the kind of hell I've been putting her through. She hasn't deserved it, not any more than my friends have deserved me pulling away from them. My turkey sandwich is cut diagonally—as usual—and I pull half out of the bag and hold it out to Felix, who accepts gratefully.

"No money for lunch today," he explains around a mouthful of turkey and bread.

Bria snorts. "Yeah, because you lost all of it to West betting on something stupid, no doubt."

I can't help smiling. When I first started interacting with these versions of my friends, West and Felix had bets going about the witches. I wonder what they've been betting about this time, but before I can ask, Lexie slides into the seat beside Felix, holding a tray from the lunch line.

"No complaining about what I bought," Lexie admonishes. She seems to have ordered every fruit cup and salad option available today. "It's not my fault you're too lazy to pack your own—" She stops short when her eyes land on me. "Oh, hey."

And that's it. After a beat, typical lunchroom conversation begins. In less than a minute, I'm laughing at a story West is telling. Bria pegs him with French fries intermittently, insisting he's lying or at least embellishing the details.

Why have I stayed away from them so long? Why did I think I needed to shut them out in the first place?

A voice nags at the back of my thoughts. *You're ignoring the mountain-sized elephant in the room. Sure, they're letting you sit here, but it's only because they're ignoring it, too. None of you wants to deal with the truth—with what you are and with what you did. How long before something brings that up? How long before they reject you?*

I stuff the voice back into the depths of my mind. No, that's just my doubts speaking. These are my friends.

Still, I find my smiles don't come quite as easily now.

I'm finished with my half of the sandwich and am polishing off the carrots Mom packed when someone slips onto the empty chair beside me. I know who it is before I even turn. Now that I'm not wearing the charm, his familiar presence shines like a beacon.

"Owen!" Felix calls across the table. His eyes flick to me before he continues. "Nice to have you join us."

Owen's arm brushes mine as he leans forward to swipe one of the remaining fries off Bria's tray. "It's nice to have the gang all back together," he says, but his voice is so low I think I might be the only one who heard it.

West nudges my shoulder and I lean back accommodatingly as he strikes up a conversation with Owen. It's so easy and natural that it's hard to believe things haven't been this way forever. The nagging voice in the back of my mind tries to get my attention, but I ignore it. I don't want anything to ruin this moment. This is the way things are supposed to be. I can't believe I let myself get so far away from it. It doesn't matter what I've done. I've been so afraid of tainting them with the darkness lurking inside me I ignored the fact that their goodness could influence me just as easily.

The bell to end lunch rings far too soon. The only thing that comforts me as I stand is the knowledge that this isn't the last time we'll do this. Maybe I could even try moving my seats in my classes back to where they used to be. And if I play my cards right, perhaps I can even get these guys to accept Tucker—on the occasions he decides to show up. I'm so caught up in this thought as I walk toward the main aisle in the lunchroom that I gasp in surprise when a hand hooks the crook of my arm and spins me around.

"Owen," I breathe. He's standing close to me—closer than he's stood in months. I can feel the heat radiating off his body. It takes all my willpower not to wrap my arms around him. If I did, I'm afraid I'd never let go.

"Hey." It's clear he wants to say more, but I get the impression he can't figure out how to put it into words.

I don't wait for him to say more. "Can we talk?"

He rubs a hand on the back of his neck. "Do you really think this is the time?"

"Not now," I say, shaking my head. "I was a little overwhelmed when you showed up at my house, but if you'll give me the chance, I'd like to talk. Finally. Can we meet tonight?"

Owen nods. "Tonight," he agrees. "I've got track after school, but we can meet after."

Giddiness bubbles inside me and I can't help grinning. "Okay." I take a step back, but before I can turn to start for math class, Owen swoops down and presses a kiss to my lips. It's soft and over almost as quickly as it begins, but heat sears my lips long after he's removed his. His eyes lock on mine for a second as if gauging my reaction, but neither of us says anything.

"Tonight," he repeats before joining the stragglers on their way out of the lunchroom.

It takes a full ten seconds for my body to start working again. When I finally manage to move in the direction of my next class, my body has a distinctly floaty feeling. Owen kissed me. My friends let me sit with them at lunch, and Owen kissed me. Is it possible that things are this easy? Is it possible that this was the step I needed to take to get things back to the way they're supposed to be? If that's the case, why has it taken me so long?

Chapter Forty-One
Sasha

I pace my apartment like a caged animal. The eclipse is tonight and I've never felt less in control of my own destiny.

Crystal's going through with the Influence spell. I followed her yesterday and saw her pick up the herbs she'll need, and later she met with her old circle. I have no doubt when the eclipse happens the Influence spell will be cast.

I just hate that I won't be a part of casting it. What if it's too complex for her circle? What if they get something wrong? I don't want the people I care for hurt because of someone else's ineptitude.

The eclipse doesn't begin for hours. I need to distract myself or I'll go crazy. I alter my course and walk to the kitchen. I grab a box at random from the stack of frozen dinners in my freezer. I don't even care what it's supposed to be. When I bought it, I must've thought it looked good enough to eat—although the jury is really still out on that. These meals all taste so similar that it doesn't matter much anyway.

I pry open the cold cardboard, slice the requisite cuts in the thin plastic covering, and pop the whole tray into the microwave. In just seven short minutes—plus an extra two for cooling—my meal will be served. I'm not hungry, but I need to do something to keep from crawling out of my skin.

Just as I hit the start button, my back pocket vibrates. I grab my phone and check the screen. There's an incoming call, but I don't recognize the number. My instinct is to ignore it, but at the last second my thumb taps the accept button and I bring the phone to my ear. "Hello?"

"Sasha."

My body goes icy. I know that voice. I'd wonder how he got my number, but I'm sure someone like him has no limit of resources. "Brody, hello. What's up?"

He tsks. "You're not a stupid woman, Sasha. I'm sure you can figure out why I'm calling. The eclipse is tonight."

"I know." I try to swallow, but my throat has gone dry. "She's all set to do the spell. You'll have the information by your deadline."

"Forgive me if I'm a bit skeptical of your ability to deliver," he says, his voice silky. "May I ask what spell it is you think will work when apparently nothing so far has done the trick?"

I hesitate. Should I tell him? Holding out might make him angry, and if he knows the lengths I'm willing to go to, maybe he'll put off plans to harm anyone in my family as incentive. "Crystal lost her magic when they exorcised Bess from her. But when she casts the Influence spell, she'll have more than enough power to do what you need."

There's a long pause on the line. "Influence? Interesting."

I hold my breath, waiting for him to go on. It feels like forever before he continues.

"You have forty-eight hours."

Three beeps indicate he's ended the call. I sigh, pressing a hand to my forehead. Forty-eight hours. That should be more than enough time.

Someone clears his throat behind me. I jump and spin around, expecting to see Brody standing in my apartment. When my eyes land on the intruder, I almost wish that's who it was.

"Elliot." How long has he been standing there? I didn't hear him let himself in. We didn't have any plans today, and I silently curse his penchant for popping in on me.

His eyebrows arch in shock. "Are you insane?"

I force a smile, doing my best to play his question off. "Hello to you, too."

He strides across the apartment and grips my upper arm, squeezing until it hurts. "Influence, Sasha? *Influence*? What the hell are you thinking?"

I gulp. So, he did hear that. My mind gropes for a reasonable explanation to dismiss my conversation from moments ago, but I can't come up with anything.

Elliot searches my face as if he's staring at a stranger. "I don't know what you're playing at, but you can't mess with Influence. Did you ever wonder why no one in the Devoted ever went through with that spell? Even the ones who were most desperate not to send their kids away? Influence is serious business, Sasha."

The condescension in his tone spurs me to action. "Don't talk to me like I'm stupid, Elliot. I know the risks. You don't understand."

He releases his grip, but the ghosts of his fingers remain on my flesh. "I think I do. I think I understand better than you. Sasha." He breathes my name out like a gust of wind. "I thought you were getting over this whole revenge thing."

Tears prickle my eyes. I hate that the disappointment in his tone is enough to break me. "It started out that way, but it's more than that now. I screwed up, okay? Is that what you want to hear? When I contacted the Amaranthine, yes, I wanted to hurt Krissa and her circle. But now they're turning on *me* and threatening to come after you and Anya and Misha if they don't get what I promised. It's the only way to keep you safe."

"Safe? That's the last thing we'll be if someone wielding Influence is let loose on the town. It's not magic, Sasha, and it'll consume whoever it touches."

"But it won't be our problem to deal with." It's what I've been convincing myself since I decided on this course of action, but out loud the justification sounds thin. "Krissa will—"

"Dammit, Sasha! Do you really believe the Influence won't affect you? Don't you realize Krissa won't be fighting it alone? There's no way Anya won't do everything she can to help, so saying you're doing this to keep her safe is bullshit." He spins on his heel and stalks toward the door.

"Where are you going?"

He pauses only briefly when his hand touches the knob. "I think you know."

Chapter Forty-Two
Krissa

Owen and I have a date tonight. I still can't believe it. I can't go more than a few minutes without brushing my fingers to my lips, just to remind myself of the feeling of his pressed against mine. But something tells me I won't have to rely on memory for much longer.

We're going to watch tonight's eclipse down by the river. In addition to the location providing us an excellent view, it will also afford a measure of privacy—one I know we'll need for the conversation I plan to have, and that I hope we'll need for making up for lost time afterward.

My heart is lighter than it's been in four months. I'm so excited I can hardly think straight, and I'm very glad I'm not scheduled to work. At first, I try to wile away the time until Owen's done with track at home, but nothing holds my attention for long. I try to shed my nervous energy by going for a walk, but it has the opposite effect. Finally, I make my way downtown and spend some time in the clothing store owned by Lexie's mom. I decide to buy a new outfit for tonight. I know it's silly and Owen probably won't care, but I can't help it. I feel different than I have in ages, and I want my outside to reflect my inside.

The only thing tempering my excitement is knowing Crystal had wanted me to cast the Influence spell tonight. I promised to help her get the information the Amaranthine want, and I know Brody's deadline is approaching. But she sat with Bridget during sixth hour today and she's ignored all my texts. I can't help her if she doesn't want me to.

After trying on a dozen different things, I finally decide on an outfit: simple black leggings and a flowy paisley-print dress in blue—like Owen's eyes. After paying Mrs. Taylor, I leave her store and step out into the bright sunshine bathing Main Street in its glow. Spring. A time for rebirth. I feel that.

I glance down the street, considering stopping in for something at the coffee shop, when a familiar form catches my eye. Elliot. He's coming from the direction of the bookstore, and he looks like he's on the warpath about something. I take a moment to reflect how I'm glad I'm not on the receiving end of that glare, but then his eyes lock on me. What the heck? Is he mad at me for some reason? It doesn't seem possible. What could I have done recently to offend him? I haven't even interacted with him since the night at Anya's apartment.

Elliot stalks straight for me, his eyes never leaving mine. When he's barely an arm's length away, his lip curls in a sneer. "Are you completely insane?"

I stare blankly, not sure what he's talking about. Does he know about my plans with Owen tonight? I reject the idea. Even if he did know, what would make him react like this? It's not like he has a vested interest in my love life. "Care to elaborate?"

A muscle in his jaw jumps as he grinds his teeth. "Are you are or are you not working with Crystal Jamison to cast the Influence spell tonight?"

For a moment, I just stare, too shocked to respond. How does he know anything about this? Did Crystal say something to it about Anya? Even if she did, why would Elliot be coming at me like this? "No, I'm not. She asked me to, but I had a bad feeling about it. I told her we'd find another way to get the information. Why? Why are you suddenly so interested?"

He curses under his breath. "That's quite the instinct you have there."

I have no idea what he's talking about. "Care to clue me in on what's going on here? What do you care? What does it have to do with you?"

He blows out a breath, looking exasperated. "If she goes

through with this, it's going to involve me and everyone else in this town—bare minimum. Do you have any idea what the spell does?"

Although I'm not actively trying to read him, the distinct tinge of fear tickles the back of my throat. "I'm starting to think maybe I don't. I thought it was a spell to give magic to someone without it, but I'm beginning to think that's not the case."

Relief mingled with worry colors his features. "Come with me." He reaches for my arm.

I take a giant step backward. "I'm not going anywhere with you."

He holds up his hands, a tacit promise not to grab for me again. "Will you come with me to your aunt's shop? Anya's working today, and she needs to know what's going on. And it seems like you need to know to, since you don't really have a clue."

I consider his request. There's no danger I can see going to the shop with him. We're not far from there now, so it's not like he would have any opportunity to do something malicious. Not that I think he would—but it's best to be prepared for anything. The shop is a safe place, and as hard as it is to admit it to myself, I trust Anya. In the end, it's the look in his eye that makes me agree. There's something going on—something serious—and I'd like to know what it is.

I nod and the two of us start down the street. His legs are longer than mine, and I have to rush to keep pace with him. When we make it to Hannah's Herbs, Elliot enters first. Anya greets him warmly, but her expression clouds when she catches sight of me coming in behind.

"What's going on?" I'm not sure if it's the fact that Elliot and I are walking in together or that she's a psychic that makes her mood turn so quickly. She is refilling the aluminum planters full of herbs, and as Elliot and I cross to her, I scan the shop for customers. When my eyes don't catch sight of anyone, I stretch out with my mind to confirm the place is empty but for us.

Elliot's lips are pressed in a tight line. His nostrils flare as he breathes in and out. Anya studies him closely, and when he doesn't say anything, she turns to me.

"What's happening?" she asks, her voice heavy with concern.

Unbidden, a face flashes in my mind. It's not someone I've ever seen before, but her features are similar enough to Anya's and Sasha's for me to take a guess at her identity. Anya must have another sister, and it's her she's thinking about. While part of me feels bad for gleaning this information from Anya's mind, another part can't help remembering a time when catching glimpses like this was normal for me—part of daily life as a psychic.

"Misha's fine," Elliot says. He must have also picked up on the flash from Anya's mind. "It's Sasha. I should've told you when I first found out, but I thought I convinced her..."

Anya places soft hands on Elliot's shoulders, ducking so she's in his line of sight. "You can tell me anything. You know that."

He does his best to avoid her eyes. "She's the one. She's the reason the Amaranthine are here."

"What?" I snap. This isn't what he said to me on the street. He was talking about the Influence spell. What do Brody and the Amaranthine have to do with that?

"Why?" Anya's voice is much softer than mine.

"I think you know why." Elliot finally makes eye contact with Anya. "She's been lying to us. She hasn't moved past Seth's death. The only reason she would've contacted a group like the Amaranthine is if she wanted to stir up trouble. She knows how bad they are. When I found out they were here, I went straight to her. She promised she would do everything she could to help Crystal so nothing bad would happen to her family. But I never thought..."

This trailing-off thing he's doing is annoying me. I want some straight answers. "What did you think? What's going on?"

He ignores me, keeping his eyes trained on Anya. "I think she's convinced Crystal to do an Influence spell."

Anya's arms drop to her sides and she takes a step back. "Are you sure?"

"Pretty darn."

I wait for someone to continue, to clue me in on what's going on, but neither of them speaks. "Okay, someone care to fill me in?" I ask, the words coming out sharper than I anticipated.

A few seconds elapse before Anya brings her eyes up to meet

mine. "Do you know what Influence is?"

"It's a way for people who aren't witches to acquire magic," I offer. I know it's not a complete definition, but it's a pretty accurate summary of what I know.

She shakes her head. "It's not magic—not in its real sense. Magic is pure; it comes from nature. Influence is... It's something else—something darker. It's born of a desire to manipulate and control. A person can work spells with Influence, but at a price."

"Then why does Sasha want Crystal to do the spell? If it's so bad, why would she—"

"Don't you see?" Elliot asks. "She hasn't moved on yet. Our whole lives we were told to wait for the day when Seth would return. And then he did. I don't know if you realized it, but that was kind of a big deal for Sasha." He purses his lips just slightly, enough for me to understand it was important for him, too. "And then he was gone. Not only him, but everyone we'd ever known. Anya says it's the way things were supposed to be—that she'd seen visions of his demise. I choose to believe her. But I don't think Sasha's at that point. She's still hurting—still looking for someone to blame."

"I just don't see why she wants to hurt Crystal," Anya says. "It doesn't make any sense."

"Crystal's not the target," Elliot says. "She's just a casualty."

I suck in a breath. "She wants to hurt me. If she knows I'm the one..." I can't bring myself to state my crime, but I know I don't need to. "If Crystal does the spell, Sasha has to know I'll do everything in my power to undo it, to make sure Crystal's safe—to make sure Clearwater is safe. This whole thing—she's doing it to get back at me."

"We have to stop it," Elliot says.

"Thank you, Captain Obvious," I mutter.

Anya shakes her head. "It won't be enough. Even if we can stop Crystal from working the Influence spell, there's still the Amaranthine to deal with. If reputation holds, they're not the kind of people who will simply cut their losses. They'd rather kill Crystal and her family to prove what happens to people who cross them. And if Sasha is the one who brought them to town, that means she's in the cross hairs, too."

"And us," Elliot says. "You, me, and Misha."

My mind is reeling. We have to stop Crystal from doing the Influence spell, but if we do, what's to stop Brody from retaliating? He only gave her until tomorrow to get the information. I doubt he's the kind of person to grant an extension.

"Lexie," I murmur.

Elliot looks at me. "What?"

I shake my head. I didn't even realize I'd spoken the word aloud. "I was just thinking... If I'm not doing the spell, and Crystal can't do it on her own, she must've found someone else to do it. Lexie."

Anya nods. "You're probably right. We need to find them. They probably have no idea what it is they're about to unleash."

I pull my phone from my back pocket and pull up Lexie's number. The line doesn't even ring before dumping me to voicemail. I attempt to call Crystal, Bridget, and Fox but am met with the same results. "Dammit."

Anya brushes my shoulder. "The eclipse is supposed to start around eight. We still have an hour to find them."

Elliot nods. "At least. To harness the full power, they'll have to wait until closer to the full eclipse. Still, better to find them sooner than later."

Anya fixes me with her gaze. "This is your old circle. Where would they meet for a spell like this? They could do it indoors, but it would be better to be outside, in full view of the moon."

I chew my lower lip in concentration. I suppose they could try to cast the spell in Fox's backyard, the same place they cast the one that anchored them to Seth's crystal. But it's spring now, not fall, and they won't have the cloak of darkness to hide them. Where else might they do it? There's the clearing by the river where we did the spell that took Crystal and me to the past. That's one possibility. But if Crystal has even an inkling I might try to stop her, she'll likely choose a different location.

"I think we're going to need to spread out. I've got a few ideas, but Crystal's going to know I know them. If she's trying to hide, I'm not sure where they might be."

The corner of Elliot's mouth turns up in a wry smile. "Good thing we're psychics."

"There are ways to get around being detected," Anya warns.

I sigh. "Well, then, we better get started."

Anya glances around the shop. "I hope Jodi won't be too mad I'm closing up a bit early," she murmurs, striding toward the front door to lock it. "You mind?" she asks, catching my eye.

I nod and start for the back door. Before I reach it, the phone in my hand vibrates. A glance at the screen reveals a text from Owen. *Practice is over. I'm gonna head home to shower and change. I'll let you know when I'm on my way to pick you up.*

I stare down at the screen as I lock the door. Owen. How can it be that less than an hour ago my biggest worry was what to wear for our date? I told him I was finally ready to explain why I've been pulling away from him. Will he give me another opportunity if I cancel now? If I tell him why I need to put our plans on hold, he'll want to come with me. But I can't let him do that—it'll only put him in danger. I don't want to give the Amaranthine any reason to come after him.

I tap out a message: *I have to take care of something. I'll let you know when I'm finished.*

As I turn to head back into the main part of the shop, I add one more thing to the list I'll have to explain to Owen later.

Chapter Forty-Three
Krissa

A reddish-orange smudge encroaches on the white face of the moon. The eclipse has begun and we're no closer to finding Crystal and the witches than when we started. A locater spell turned up nothing, so we've been searching the old-fashioned way. Between the three of us, we've checked every place in Clearwater I can think Crystal might have gone. Just to be safe, I checked Fox's house and the clearing by the river. In fact, Anya and I swept much of the riverbank, but we turned up nothing. Elliot checked the other witches' houses. We checked the library and the school, the forest clearing where we once hoped to harvest Althea root for a spell—in short, everywhere it's even remotely possible they might be. It all turned up nothing.

The three of us have regrouped at Anya's apartment. I run my hands through my hair as I sit on the couch. "It doesn't make any sense. They can't have just disappeared."

"They haven't, but they obviously cast a spell to cloak their energy. I've got nothing." There's an edge of irritation in Elliot's voice.

Despite the fact that it was he who pointed out the true nature of the spell Crystal plans to cast, I can't help being surprised by the fact that he's putting so much effort into finding them. I haven't given Elliot much thought beyond him being one of Seth's followers, someone willing to do anything to help his long-awaited master rise to power. I know Anya believes he changed, but this is the first time I've seen it with my own eyes.

"What happens if we can't stop them?" It's the question that's been rattling around in my mind since we started looking. "Any spell can be undone. Even if they manage to pull this off, can't we just undo it afterward?" I hate to admit it, but that might be the easiest course of action for us. Crystal needs to cast the spell to contact Bess. I wasn't able to provide her with my own magic for long enough, but if she has the power of Influence behind her, she should be able to do it on her own. After she's done so, we can simply undo it. It seems straightforward enough to me.

But Elliot is shaking his head. "It's not that easy. This isn't like borrowing energy from someone else, or even using herbs or stones to enhance an ability. Magic comes from nature—nature chooses who can wield the power. What this spell does is circumvent that. Influence fills an empty vessel with power. The abilities don't come from nature; they come from somewhere else. Somewhere darker. And darkness isn't easy to get rid of."

My body tenses. I know that's the truth. Darkness is always difficult to remove. When the circle was anchored to the crystal containing Seth's magic, the hatred and fear that had festered for generations infected each one of them. Under its influence, each circle member said and did things that were tremendously out of character. And that was just an effect of magic soured by a dark soul. How much different would power pulled from a dark source be? And how much harder would it be to overcome?

Anya paces in front of me. "Is there somewhere outside of town they might go?"

"I can't think of anywhere." It's not as if the group would simply drive outside the town line in search of a likely spot to cast a spell. They'd have to know the place already, know it's safe and they won't be disturbed. Also, it's not as if they had a lot of time to plan this. They won't want to be far because they won't want to draw suspicion from their parents. Everyone was at school today, so it's not like they've been setting up a secret lair somewhere. They haven't had time. No, they'll have to be somewhere they've been before.

Elliot stands. "Well, we're not doing anyone any good just sitting here. I'm going to go back out there—retrace my steps.

There has to be something we missed. I'll go check in with Sasha—maybe she's got a clue."

Anya rolls her shoulders at the sound of her sister's name. "I still can't believe she did this," she murmurs.

The three of us exit the apartment and part ways in the parking lot. As I climb into my car, I can't help snorting at Anya's remark. She can't believe Sasha would do something like this? I can't believe she's so naïve as to think her sister *wouldn't* do this. We both know Sasha is capable of much more—much worse. Yes, this Influence spell sounds bad, but she's not actively doing it. In fact, it doesn't sound like simply enacting the spell will hurt anyone—it's just the aftereffects of being filled with the Influence that are dangerous. On the other hand, Sasha has hurt people before. She tortured me. She tortured Anya. Sometimes I wonder if she doesn't forget that—if she doesn't forget how Griffin, Fox, Tucker, Lexie, and I located her in the middle of the woods in an old, derelict cabin...

The cabin. It's out of the way, so there's no worry of being disturbed. There was a clearing around it that would afford enough space for spell work. Could they have gone there? I put my car in gear and do my best to remember exactly where the place was. There's only one way to find out if my hunch is correct.

As I drive, the moon keeps drawing my eye. The dark red shadow is slowly devouring the entire face of the moon. I did my research and I know the total eclipse won't occur for half an hour. All I can do is hope the circle will wait that long to cast the spell. It's complex and takes a lot of energy, so it would be in their best interest to do so. I know Crystal is eager, but I have to believe common sense will win out and the witches won't attempt to do the spell before they can draw maximum energy from the event.

I remember the general vicinity of the woods we found the cabin in, but I drive past a few places before finding the right spot to enter the forest. All this driving is eating into my time, so when I'm finally on foot I move through the trees and underbrush as quickly as my legs will carry me. When this tactic causes me to trip every few steps, I decide to change strategies and work smarter instead of harder. As the moon falls deeper and deeper into shadow, it becomes more and more difficult to see where I'm going. I pull out my phone and turn on the flashlight app to light my way as I trundle over the underbrush. My pace isn't as fast as before, but I'm covering more ground because I'm not constantly falling and having to pick myself back up.

I hope I'm going the right way. Last time, I had a vision, an image plucked from Elliot's mind, to guide me. Now I'm working from memory alone. I try to call up the certainty with which I walked this path before, but it eludes me. If I'm going the wrong way, there is no chance of me stopping the spell. If I'm going the right way, I still might be too late.

I check the time on my phone at intervals. The full eclipse has begun. There are only fifteen minutes until the start of the total eclipse. Unfortunately, I have no way of telling if I'm in the right area. The last time I was here, it was fall. The trees were a tangle of dead branches and the ground was strewn with crunchy leaves. Now, new life is budding all around. The limbs are supple, and what leaves survived the winter are softer and less frequent. There are no distinguishing marks in the woods at all. I could be anywhere.

I've been walking for too long. I should be there already. Maybe I'm in the wrong place altogether. I curse myself. I should've told Anya and Elliot of my suspicion. Maybe one of them would have a better idea where the cabin is. I don't have Elliot's number. I've opened up the text app, preparing to send a message to Anya, when something in the air changes. A faint crackle of something like electricity thrums through the still night. Someone is doing magic nearby.

I must be close. That's the only way I'd be able to sense them through whatever spell was cast to keep their actions private. I pick up my pace, careful to keep my eyes trained just a few steps ahead, allowing the beam of the flashlight to guide me. After a few more yards, the faint chanting of voices reaches my ears. A few steps more and I can pick out the individuals speaking—Lexie, Bridget, Fox.

Through tree trunks up ahead, I catch the first glimpses of firelight flickering low on the ground. It's not enough to guide my way, but at least I know now the exact direction I need to travel. The spell has begun. I know enough about magic to understand that every spell has a tipping point. Magic often has a buildup component when the elements all need to charge and the energy begins to crescendo. Up until a certain moment, it can be stopped and the energy can be dispersed. As I finally make my way into the clearing, I hope this spell hasn't crested that point yet.

Crystal and Dana stand in the center of the circle on either side of the small bonfire. Lexie, Fox, and Bridget stand like three points of a triangle around them, their eyes closed and their hands uplifted. Even though I read through this spell, I can't tell from the words they're chanting what part they're at.

"Stop!" I yell, running toward the group.

Crystal and Dana, who had been facing each other across the flames, turn to look at me, their eyes wide.

"How'd you find us?" Dana asks.

"It doesn't matter," I say, edging nearer. "What matters is you have to stop. You don't know what this spell will really do."

Fox, Lexie, and Bridget continued to chant as if I'm not there. They're so caught up in the spell they don't notice anything is amiss. Overhead, the moon is almost entirely blood red.

Crystal's face pinches. "I know exactly what the spell will do. It'll give me abilities—it'll give me my magic back. That's what it does—it gives power to those who don't have it."

"Maybe—but the danger is where the Influence comes from. It's not natural, Crystal. The power you're about to fill yourself with comes from darkness. It'll consume you."

Dana's face blanches and she glares at Crystal. "Is that true? That's not what you told me."

Crystal's eyes are wild as they flit from Dana's face to mine. "How do I know you're not lying?"

"When have I ever lied to you?"

Crystal's lower lip trembles, and her eyes go glassy in the firelight. "I just... I just wanted..."

I don't bother waiting for her to finish. She doesn't need to. I know exactly what she wanted and why. "The only thing that's important now is stopping the spell." She and Dana both nod. I take a few steps toward Fox, who's closest to me and still oblivious to my presence. This is strange. I've never seen people so completely taken over when working a spell. Crystal and Dana follow my lead, each of them crossing to one of the other witches. I stretch out my hand to shake Fox's shoulder, but before I can make contact, a blast of energy sends me flailing backward. I do my best to keep my balance, but it's no use and I land flat on my back.

"The hell?" Dana yells, her voice shrill with alarm.

"Don't touch them!" I yell.

"Obviously," Crystal returns. "What's happening?"

I shake my head. "It's like the spell is protecting them from being disturbed." I didn't even know such a thing was possible, but the evidence is right in front of me. I struggle to my feet and return to Fox's side, being careful to not get too close. I yell his name at the top of my lungs, but there's no reaction. I can't touch him, and he can't hear me.

"How are we supposed to stop them?" Dana asks.

"I don't know." But a plan is forming in the back of my mind. There was a time, when the circle was still anchored to the crystal, that the psychics and I practiced ways to disrupt spells in progress. Maybe I can use my psychic abilities to separate them from the magic they're drawing on. My fingers brush my wrist instinctively, preparing to remove my charm, only to find it's still not there. The only piece of jewelry I wear is the smoky quartz ring that's been passed down through the Barnette line for generations. Jodi once told me the stone can provide protection, and I have a feeling I'll need that now.

I take in a breath, focusing my senses on my psychic abilities. Although I never entirely lost touch with them while wearing the charm, reaching out to interact with another person's energy is still a bit of a struggle. And right now, I want to connect with three separate people. I'm not sure that I'm up to the task, but I'm ready to try.

As I brush Fox's conscious mind, I allow the panic and dread I'm trying to keep at bay to flood me. If I can overwhelm him with my emotions, I might be able to shake him enough to break his connection to the spell. I reach further and link with Lexie and Bridget before forcing my way deeper into each mind, taking my swirling fears with me.

But they're still chanting. Whatever I'm doing, it's not enough. I can't stop them. They've hit the spell's tipping point. They're calling forth the Influence, and it will find someone to fill. That darkness will go into Crystal and Dana. What will it make them do? How will it change them? What will it do to Dana, who didn't even know abilities like these existed six months ago? She experienced the power of psychic abilities for only a short amount of time, but it was enough for her to be willing to do anything to have them back. And Crystal. Being a witch is part of her DNA. She's been cut off from her natural ability for months now, and its absence has put her and her loved ones in danger. The only reason she wants to do this spell is to keep her family and friends safe.

"You're too late," calls a voice from just beyond the reach of the firelight. Terror floods from Crystal and I recognize who's arrived before he comes fully into view. Somehow Brody found us. I wonder if he was following me or if he found this location another way.

Crystal's alarm ratchets up another level as Brody strides closer. Beside him is a man with scraggly hair, ill-fitting clothes, and a manic gleam in his eye. I pluck his identity from Crystal's mind: Kai, the assassin.

"What are you doing here?" Crystal asks, her tight voice an octave higher than usual.

Brody cocks his head as he studies her. The curl of his lips makes it clear he finds her wanting. "Sasha seems convinced the only way I'll get my information is if you go through with this spell. I came to make sure that happened. But it seems I've wasted a trip. It's too far along. No matter what you do now, the Influence will come fill any empty vessel it finds." His teeth flash in the firelight.

Crystal and Dana exchange wide-eyed looks. "Oh, no," Crystal breathes. "What have I done?"

Once the Influence is unleashed, nothing will stop it from entering Crystal and Dana, the only two in the clearing without abilities. I can't let it happen. I can't let the darkness overtake them. But I know Brody is right—there's no way I can stop this spell now. Even if I could get through to Fox, Lexie, and Bridget, they've hit the tipping point. They could stop chanting now and the spell would still continue. It's like touching a flame to a newspaper—once you get close enough, there's no stopping it from catching fire.

But there is one thing I can do. I don't have the right elements with me, but, just like my friends, I have the power of the eclipse on my side. I drop to one knee, afraid if I don't the effect of this spell will make me fall over. I touch my fingers to the damp, cool ground, centering myself and calling upon the energy of the earth below. If the Influence is looking for an empty vessel to fill, I'll give it one. I'll give it me.

The air in the clearing thickens, making it harder and harder to breathe. The night cools by ten degrees in a matter of moments. I don't know how, but I'm sure this is a sign that the Influence spell is almost complete. I murmur the words of the transference spell as quickly as I can, fervently hoping I can outrun the tsunami that is about to hit us. My breathing grows ragged as it becomes more and more difficult to gulp down an entire lungful of air.

My insides ripple like boiling water and my vision blurs. As phantom slices assail my skin, I think I hear someone calling my name, but I don't stop chanting. With each syllable, my powers flow out of me.

Crystal and Dana double over as if they've been hit in the stomach. Crystal stares at me, her eyes wide. "No," she mouths.

A wind kicks up in the clearing, circling around our small group. It's icy and bites at every bit of my flesh, cutting through the fabric of my clothes and whipping my hair around my face. With it comes a darkness so complete I can no longer see anything in front of me. A rushing fills my ears, but through it I'm sure I hear high shrieks of terror. It's possible they're coming from me—I can't tell. My being is oddly disconnected from my body. Everything is sound and pressure and darkness—and then it stops. As quickly as it began, the wind dies. The air thins and warms, making it easy to breathe again.

The only thing that's different is me. My body crackles as if there's lightning trapped in my veins. My fingers itch with the desire to release some of the electricity building inside me. It builds and intensifies with each passing moment, a swirling storm intent on taking me over completely.

Blackness clouds my vision. Before I'm thrust into unconsciousness, Crystal's small voice reaches my ears: "What did you do?"

Chapter Forty-Four
Crystal

"Well, that was unexpected," Brody says from the edge of the clearing. His gaze lingers on Krissa for a moment before he turns to face me. "You're a witch again."

I open my mouth, ready to disagree, but I stop short. I lift my hands and stare at my palms. My skin seems foreign in the flickering firelight. Brody's right—I can feel the magic coursing through my veins. I would be relieved, except it doesn't feel like I remember. It feels more like it did when Krissa worked the transference spell. "This... I feel different. It's almost like..."

A smile plays about the corners of Brody's lips. "I imagine it's an odd sensation, having someone else's magic take up residence in you."

My eyes dart to Krissa's still form. Fox is at her side, and since he's not completely freaking out I assume she's alive, just unconscious. My brain spins, trying to make sense of the last few minutes. The Influence spell fills people without abilities with magic. Krissa's magic is swirling inside me. That must mean... "She didn't..."

Brody grins and his teeth flash again. "It appears she did. And now that you have some magic of your own, I assume casting the spell to get the information I want will be no problem." His eyes flick to Kai, who cracks his knuckles.

I gulp. I always intended to contact Bess for Brody—it's the only way to keep my family safe. But now that I can actually do it, I'm hesitant. I can almost guarantee the world will be better off if

Brody and his group don't know whatever it is Bess took to the grave. "I don't have the elements I need."

All mirth disappears from Brody's face. His eyes darken and Kai stands at attention, a malicious sneer curling his lips. "I've been more than patient with you," Brody says, his voice low. "But you're out of time and out of excuses. The eclipse will provide whatever power you need. And if it's incentive you require, I can guarantee Kai will have no trouble providing it."

There's movement behind me and a hand closes gently around my upper arm. "We've got your back," Lexie murmurs.

How I wish that were true, but Brody holds all the cards here. If I don't comply, I'm positive Kai will start dropping bodies, probably starting with Lexie. "I'll do it."

"I knew you'd make the right choice," Brody says. He makes a sweeping motion with his hand. "Please, proceed."

Dana, who is hovering awkwardly behind Fox, catches my eye and gives the tiniest shake of her head. I understand her misgivings, but we don't have a choice.

"I assume you've got Krissa's psychic mojo now," I say.

Her eyes dart to Fox for an instant. "Yeah. But I'm not sure I'll be able—"

"You have to," I say.

Without having to ask them, Lexie and Bridget position themselves around the fire. Fox doesn't leave Krissa's side, a fact that doesn't escape Dana's notice. I snap to get her attention. "Focus."

She flips her middle finger but steps toward the fire. Once I join our ring, excitement thrills through me, followed by a pang of guilt. I shouldn't be happy right now, but I can't help that part of me is. Krissa's magic inside me fills up all the empty spaces that have made me feel incomplete these last four months. Although I fought hard not to accept it, there were times I was convinced I'd never feel this again—the swell of power begging to be directed.

I begin chanting. I've been over the spell so many times I have the incantation committed to memory. Dana joins me quickly, but it takes a few times through before Lexie and Bridget catch on. Brody was right, of course. I don't need the elements typically necessary for this bit of magic—the energy provided by the eclipse is more than enough.

As I wait for the spell to do its work, I try to keep my mind off the consequences of my actions. The only thing I care about is making Brody and his people leave this town forever.

The force of the connection nearly causes me to double over when it happens. The last time Dana and I attempted this spell, we were merely borrowing Krissa's abilities for a brief period, and by the time Dana located Bess, our hold on Krissa's powers was nearing its end. But now an enveloping pressure consumes my mind and I know without a doubt it's Bess. Her presence is familiar, like a perfume worn by a long-lost friend.

I lose sense of my body. It's as if I'm floating, formless, in a void. I can't see anything, but I know Bess is near.

"I know what you seek," murmurs a voice eerily similar to my own. "My people have waited generations for what I have to say. I was beginning to fear you would never reach me, that these words would be lost forever."

I can't feel my mouth, but still my words reverberate out. "What's so important that these people would threaten my family?"

"That's simple: Immortality." Bess's words ring as clearly as a bell. "Tell my followers this—and be sure to use these precise words: The midnight stone must be imbued with the power of deepest night. Afterward, all who desire eternal life will drink it."

Questions chase themselves around in my head. What is midnight stone? How does a person drink a rock? What's the power of deepest night? But before I can ask any of them, our connection weakens. Her presence slips further away with each beat of my heart and I'm aware of my body again. After a few tries I manage to open my eyes. When I do, I jump with surprise. "Gah—Lexie!"

"Are you okay?" she demands.

"Did it work?" Brody's voice drifts from just a few feet away.

I place my hands on Lexie's shoulders. "I'm fine." I'm pleased when my voice doesn't tremble. She looks like she wants to press to be sure, but before she can, Krissa releases a low moan.

"I think she's coming around," Fox says, his relief obvious. Dana's brow knits, and I can't help wondering just what kinds of things she's picking up with her new psychic abilities.

I turn to face Brody as Lexie goes to check on Krissa. "I have your information. I need to know that when I give this to you, you're going to leave town immediately."

It's clear Brody is doing his best to keep his face neutral, but he can't entirely suppress how anxious he is to learn what I found out. His eyes are brighter than usual and he rubs the pads of his thumbs across his fingertips. "I have no interest staying in your hovel of a town. I know the Devoted were obsessed with it because Seth lived here, but the Amaranthine place no particular value on it."

"Okay." Part of me thinks perhaps I should hold on to this information—or at least hold back part of it as a bargaining chip of some kind. But if Brody and his people leave, there will be no need to negotiate. Besides, I don't want to give him any reason to follow through on his threats. "You might want to take this down, because Bess was very particular about the wording. She said the midnight stone must be imbued with the power of deepest night. Afterward, all who desire eternal life will drink it."

Brody's eager expression clouds. "What's the midnight stone?"

I shrug. "I figured you would know."

"Imbued with the power of deepest night," he murmurs, his agitation growing by the second. "There must have been more. What else did she say?"

I hold up my hands. "There wasn't anything else. That's the message. Now I made good on my part of the deal. I expect you to do the same."

Brody sneers, but I turn away. Krissa's making more noise now, and Fox and Lexie are attempting to help her to her feet. A relieved sigh escapes my lips. Once the Amaranthine are gone, we can figure out what's going on with Krissa and what we need to do next.

Kai speaks as I start for her. "What now?"

The answer seems obvious. They have what they came for. All that's left now is for them to leave. I know they have questions about what Bess's words mean, but that's not my problem. I held up my end of the deal.

"I need to report to Jade," Brody murmurs. "She won't be pleased."

A smile tugs at the corners of my mouth. After all his threats and harassment, Brody didn't get what he expected. And it sounds like his boss is going to be upset. Ahead of me, Krissa is finally getting her feet under her. Her head is still down, her pale blonde hair obscuring her face like a curtain. Maybe she was wrong about the Influence. Besides it overwhelming her when it first rushed in, she seems to be handling it fine. For the first time in months, I'm confident things are going to start getting better.

"And me?" Kai asks, his voice husky.

Brody is quiet so long I almost tune out his response. But when he finally speaks, my blood runs cold.

"Kill them."

Chapter Forty-Five
Krissa

The moon looms red and ominous over my head. For a moment, it's all I can see. But then Fox and Lexie come into view, their faces reflections of each other's. Relief laced with trepidation colors their features. I wish I could remember what happened, but my mind is a jumbled mess.

Hands tug my arms. They're trying to help me stand. I do my best to comply, but my body doesn't feel right.

"I need to report to Jade. She won't be pleased."

I know that voice.

Like camera flashes, images erupt in my mind's eye. The eclipse, the fire. Bridget, Lexie, and Fox standing around the fire working a spell. The Influence spell.

"And me?"

That must be Brody's companion, the Amaranthine assassin. Kai.

By degrees, I feel more in control of my body, but I still can't raise my head. My hair swishes around my face, only allowing glimpses of the world beyond. A crackle like electricity builds in my core. I was too late to stop the spell, so I did the only thing I could think. When the Influence manifested itself and sought a host, the only empty vessel it found was me.

"Kill them."

As if they were the words I've been waiting for, my head snaps up and I can manage my own body.

Crystal spins on her heel. "What? You said—"

"I *said* I'd leave this town if you gave me what I wanted," Brody snaps. "Consider this your consequence for making me wait so long for such useless information." He glances at Kai. "Alert me when you've finished."

"What? You're not gonna watch?" Kai asks.

"I don't get quite the thrill out of it that you do." Without another word, Brody spins on his heel and disappears into the forest.

Kai's expression darkens as he turns his attention to Crystal. He cracks his knuckles slowly, one sickening pop sounding through the clearing at a time.

In a flash, I put myself between him and her. "You're not going to lay a finger on her."

Kai grins wolfishly. "Oh, honey, I don't need to touch her. This is going to be fun. I've been itching for the go-ahead to do some real damage."

"What's he talking about?" Bridget asks, her voice high.

There's a shuffling behind me. "Don't worry, I'll protect you." It's Fox who speaks. He must have moved to Bridget's side, because his voice is directly behind me.

Kai tips his head back and laughs. "Adorable. You really think you're a match for me? I've been the Amaranthine assassin since I was thirteen. The man I killed—the last assassin—held his position for forty years. He had killed and tortured more people than you can ever imagine. Some called him unstoppable, invincible. I took him down in less than five minutes. And you think you stand a chance?" His wolfish grin spreads, changing into a leer.

"You won't touch them," I snarl. Red smoke slips in around the edges of my vision, curling and swirling in hypnotizing spirals. A loud rushing fills my ears. My fingers curl like claws as the Influence ripples like electricity through my body. I won't let him hurt them. I won't let him get near them.

Kai tilts his head, studying me like I'm a particularly interesting bug he's considering squishing. "Oh, this is going to be fun."

He raises his arm, his hand pointed toward me. A wave of energy rockets in my direction, and I'm barely fast enough to deflect it. A shock wave ripples through my body. I have no idea what he just did, but I sense if I'd allowed it to hit me, I'd probably be incapacitated now. The red smoke continues to encroach on my vision, threatening to block it out entirely. I do my best to keep it at bay, to keep Kai in my line of sight. With a sweep of my arm, I force Dana and Lexie to join Crystal, Fox, and Bridget behind me. I don't want Kai distracting me by attacking them.

Kai squints, clearly surprised his move didn't take me down. When he lifts his palm again, I'm ready. As easy as breathing, I summon a shield charm in front of me. It deflects whatever spell Kai threw right back at him, and he has to dive to avoid it. By the time he's back on his feet, any trace of enjoyment has disappeared from his eyes. He's angry now.

Good. I'm angry, too.

"You shouldn't have done that," he growls. "I'm going to make you pay."

The corners of my lips curl. "I dare you."

He shoots off several spells in quick succession, and I'm able to deflect each one. He circles, looking for a better vantage point. I keep pace with his movements, being sure to stay between him and the others.

"I'm beginning to think you were exaggerating about the assassin you had to take down for this position." I watch him closely, taking in even the tiniest movement of his body, anticipating his next move.

He glowers. "Oh, I have no need to embellish. I've decided I'm going to save you for last. You're going to have to watch me kill the rest of them first."

Before I can respond, he shoots off another litany of spells. I deflect them as they come, the hot lightning of the Influence surging within me. It's growing stronger. The red fog clouding my vision grows thicker by the moment.

Just as I'm shielding the group from the last of Kai's attack, he dives to the side and shoots a beam of blue energy just behind me. I'm not fast enough to stop it, and Fox bellows in pain. I glance back just long enough to see him on the ground, his arms around his stomach. Dana crouches beside him.

When I turn back, the red finally shadows my entire vision. It takes over, and I lose all sense of what's happening. My body bubbles with a rage unlike anything I've ever felt before. An emotion this intense should frighten me, but it doesn't. I'm exhilarated. The hot lightning snaps and sizzles in my body, building and building until I'm afraid I'll combust with the power of it. But just before I'm sure I'll explode, everything rushes out of me, taking the red smoke with it.

I blink and the world comes into focus again. Kai is nowhere to be seen. I spin on my heel, looking in all directions, but he's not standing anywhere. It's only then that a sound registers to my ears. Whimpering. Crystal, Lexie, and Bridget hold each other, terror streaking their faces. I can't say I'm surprised—Kai was pretty intent on doing them harm. But when I follow their gaze, I realize that's not the thing frightening them. Part of the ground just beyond the bonfire, where Kai had last been standing, is torn up as if something large and heavy impacted it at high speed. I squint in the semi-darkness surrounding it. There are odd shapes that at first glance appear to be pieces of upturned earth, but upon closer inspection reveal themselves to be chunks of Kai's body. It's as if someone put an explosive charge in his abdomen and set it off.

Realization dawns slowly. I did that to him. The crackling energy, the red smoke—when it took over, this was the result. My stomach lurches, but not with disgust—with pleasure.

When I turn to face my friends, Lexie, Crystal, and Bridget cower. Dana puts herself between me and Fox.

I exhale as the sizzling in my veins dials back to a gentle simmer. "You're safe now."

No one moves. I scrutinize their faces. They're...frightened. But why? The danger is gone—Kai's dead. The Amaranthine have what they wanted and are leaving town. Something tugs at the back of my mind. There's something obvious I'm overlooking here.

With effort, Fox manages to stand. Dana grabs for him but he shakes her off. As he approaches, he limps and holds his side. Kai hurt him. Electricity burns through my veins for a moment before I remember Kai won't be hurting anyone else ever again.

When he's an arm's length away, he reaches for me. I stretch out a hand and he doesn't quite hide a flinch when I make contact with his skin. "Thank you for making us safe," he says, his voice quiet. "Let's get you home and see if Jodi can't figure out a way to make you safe, too."

I nod and he leads me to the woods. Shuffling behind us is my only clue that the others are following. No one speaks. I feel something on my face and reach up with my free hand to wipe it. I'm surprised to find it's wet and sticky. When I investigate my fingertips, I know at once what the substance is. Blood.

There's blood on my face because I killed Kai. I made him explode right in front of me and my friends. My heart thuds in my chest. What did I do? I don't remember casting that spell. I don't even know how to go about doing something that destructive.

It was the Influence.

Even now, I feel it humming inside me, itching to be called upon again.

I don't realize I'm hyperventilating until Fox places his hands on my shoulders and urges me to take a deep breath. When did we stop walking? I glance at our surroundings to find we're no longer in the woods. Fox's truck is a few yards away, and Crystal's Spark is behind it.

"I don't know where my car is." My voice is small and quiet.

"It's okay," Fox says. "I'll take you home." Instead of leading me to his truck, he pulls off his sweatshirt and dabs my face. I shudder when I realize he must be trying to wipe away the blood.

I'm in Fox's car before I realize I was walking to it. Time seems to be skipping. Am I in shock, or is this a consequence of the Influence?

The driver's-side door opens and Fox pulls himself into the cab. He starts the engine, but before he puts it in gear, he covers my hand with his. "I never should've agreed to help Crystal and Dana with that spell."

I want to tell him it's not his fault, but the words won't come.

"Those people have what they want now, and I hope that guy does what he said and leaves town. Then we can focus all our energy on helping you."

My eyes prickle and my vision swims. "I don't know what's

happening to me, Fox. I'm scared."

His stormy eyes darken and in the next breath he's wrapped his arms around me. I grip him tightly, afraid if I don't I might lose sense of myself entirely.

"I just wanted to save her," I murmur, tears trickling down my cheeks. "I wanted to save both of them. And now... And now..."

He squeezes me so tight I can barely breathe. "And now we're going to save you."

ABOUT THE AUTHOR

Madeline Freeman lives in the metro-Detroit area with her husband, her daughter and son, and her cats. She loves anything to do with astronomy, outer space, plate tectonics, and dinosaurs, and secretly hopes her kids will become astronomers or paleontologists.

Connect with Madeline online:
http://www.madelinefreeman.net
http://twitter.com/writer_maddie
http://facebook.com/madelinefreemanbooks

Sign up for Madeline's reader's group for updates and exclusive content!

https://laurealinde.leadpages.co/mailing-list-signup/